THE LION OF PESCARA

by the same author

ANNA'S BOOK

George MacBeth

THE LION OF PESCARA

JONATHAN CAPE
THIRTY BEDFORD SQUARE
LONDON

First published 1984
Copyright © George MacBeth 1984
Jonathan Cape Ltd,
30 Bedford Square, London WC1B 3EL
British Library Cataloguing in Publication Data
MacBeth, George
The lion of Pescara.
I. Title
823'.914[F]   PR6063.A13

ISBN 0-224-02249-0

Extracts from works in copyright by
Gabriele D'Annunzio are reproduced in
translation by permission of the
Fondazione del Vittoriale degli Italiani
and Arnoldo Mondadori, Editore.

Photoset by Rowland Phototypesetting Limited
Bury St Edmunds, Suffolk
Printed in Great Britain by
Ebenezer Baylis and Son Limited
The Trinity Press, Worcester and London

Contents

I	The Bittern	7
II	The Goldfish	55
III	The Horses	103
IV	The Greyhound	151
V	The Tortoise	203
	Chronology	253

—I—

The Bittern

I

YOU FILLED YOUR nose with all you could. The must of old books, Petrarch and Angiolieri; the heavy odour of flowers. The room was a hired one, as indeed was the whole house, the property of the Austrian Prince Hohenlohe. And yet, unusually for you, even in the press of war, the plannings of so many military campaigns, you had had no time to do more than alter the furnishings in some minor details. It was otherwise at Fiume, but then that, as we shall see, was another story.

The heating system was yours, and so were the folios and the roses. Renata, with her chin on her palm and her eyes on her Chateaubriand, was yours. But the former gondolier, Dante, who brought your riding-boots to their fine polish, and the admirable Albina, who cooked your simple meals, came with the house.

They came with two bedrooms, and a grand piano in the long drawing-room on the floor below, and a collection of seventeenth-century handbags, and nineteen marble clocks that all chimed at different times. You had kept those. They fascinated your sense of the quirky and the absurd.

They came, too, with a small, high-walled garden that separated your crimson house from the treacly flood of the Grand Canal, and the two rocking vessels that held your means of escape and plunder; your two alternative

The Lion of Pescara

vehicles for the roads to adventure, the ancient sweep of the gondola, with its hooded veranda, and the smart modern rush of the motor-boat, with its wheel and its darting speed. Means there for whatever seductions time and energy might dictate or allow.

But you were prudent with those. Cautious, perhaps. Too busy with whatever preoccupied your attention or fancy on the front, or in the air, to be quite so meticulous in your pursuit of the joys of the flesh as was your custom. An occasional drift across the canal to the famous Marchesa, the one I used to call the Medusa of the great hotels, who had her own palace on the left side. A rush, once, to a tightly packed room where a new flame touched the keys of a clavichord for a few friends, and subsequently yielded to your pleasure on the water.

The ladies had come, of course, and in plenty since the loss of your eye, and with gifts of solicitation and boxes of your favourite perfumes, but under the strict supervisory care of your daughter Renata, the jealous and unforgiving ward of your cure.

'Later, my dear,' she would say, ushering this or that former companion of your stormy pallet to the doorway. 'Father is still very weak. He has to rest. You must come again, when he can see. He so much wants to be alone with you, and to hear your news.'

You would smile, hearing these lies. You were locked now in the arms of a new and more formidable mistress, your love of war. You needed the flesh of women less, and only as a remote accompaniment to your close alliance with the daily work of battle. That, of course, in time. And in the meanwhile, your chronicling of these exploits, and of your dreams and follies, on a set of cards.

'Renata,' you would say, stroking the bandages on your eyes, 'bring me the cards.'

Renata would rise then, obedient to your least whim, as she always was, and walk to a small jewel-box resting on a marble console near to the door. From this she would take a bundle of elongated white papers, blank on one side, but with writing, wayward and restless, in uneven streams,

The Bittern

like the rain blown on the window, straying over the other.

Nothing would disturb the silence of the room as she did this. Her footfalls would be absorbed in the stately pile of the carpet, and again, they would make no sound as she moved to where you lay on the bed, and placed the bundle of cards in your outstretched hands.

You would run your fingers over the block, smoothing them into a consistent oblong, and then fanning a few out, as if they were there to play whist or ombre with.

'Renata,' you would say softly, in moments when inspiration failed. 'Help me count.'

A clock would chime, a deep sonorous sound, and you would count the beats from one up to four, perhaps, knowing that the pierced hands on the delicate face would almost certainly be fastened nearer to eleven. You had learned to tell one chime from another in your darkness, and you guessed, rightly, that one was the little half-hunter with the silvery tinkle in the closet, or that another was the gold Regency clock with the dying gladiator that reclined on the mantelpiece in your dining-room. Not all were as easy to discriminate between as these, but you were rarely wrong.

'You ought to get a man in,' Renata would sometimes remonstrate. 'They could soon be put to rights.'

But you would frown.

'No,' you would say. 'I like the mystery. It amuses me. You know that, Renata.'

Then, very soon, as you smoothed the cool edges of the cards, and a tinge of hunger began to suffuse your absorption, you would ask, with an illogical and yet entirely characteristic contradictoriness, 'What time is it?'

Renata would laugh, twisting your ear gently with her fingers as she rested on the edge of your bed.

'No time,' she would say, coyly. 'Or any time. You like the mystery, father. You know you do.'

Then you would put on one of those outraged little boy looks of yours.

The Lion of Pescara

'Renata,' you would say, mock-sadly. 'I feel hungry. I need food. One must feed the demon of the retina.'

'Albina is cooking lamb,' Renata would say. 'It won't be long.'

Then you would begin to count, laying the cards aside one by one on the coverlet, from where Renata would pick them up, and check your tally. Outside the window, above the hiss of rain, or the sough of the wind, there would rise the call of a gondolier, as he poled his unseen master or mistress towards the Bridge of Sighs. The heat of the room, stifling to others, would please your temper.

'Three thousand, four hundred and twenty,' you would say, at last. 'You agree, Renata?'

'I agree, father.'

You would lie back, wrinkling your nose. These were the sibyl's leaves of your spiritual autumn, the scattered fragments of your temple of destiny, the tablets of card on which you printed your inmost prayers.

Day after day, dipping a fresh quill in the well of black ink your daughter filled and placed before you on marble, you threw into being whatever insight or cast reflection your troubled mind set forth.

There were few some days, hundreds on others. They poured from the fountain-head of your blindness, the seer's visions of a life given over to debauchery, sacredness, and military pride. Renata gathered the sheaves, and they rested in a box, until their time for harvesting should come.

I see them now, as I first saw them there in your claustrophobic bedroom, as I saw them later in your airy office at Fiume. I see those dignified by the elegance of print, hieratic and soluble, in your greatest book. And I see so many left behind, remaindered and illegible, in their perfumed satinwood.

Some have the coldness of a dream, others the sombre fever of a raid by motor-torpedo boat. A few, though only a few, recount some totally quaint, and at the same time some true and amusing, detail of your daily life.

I remember how you would pluck one of these from the

The Bittern

set, or perhaps a series with a common theme, the modulation of an anecdote. Your urge to revise, to perfect and alter, would grip you through your darkness.

'Renata,' you would say. 'Please read me these.'

Then another clock would chime, and then another close on its heels, the first nine times, and the second three, as Renata began to read. You would visualise the high, florid porphyry one in the corridor, and then the square-cut alarm beside your bed, as you listened.

'A large heron-like bird,' Renata would read, lifting the grim weight of her voice as the candles began to gutter,

> in fact a bittern, walks through the open door with the grace of an eighteenth-century footman, and approaches my bed.
>
> 'Evandro,' Dante says, pausing as he folds my shirts. 'Get out, you brute.'
>
> 'I can smell his breath,' I say, turning from the stool at my dressing-table. 'He's been eating fish.'
>
> The bird advances with great seriousness, and dips its long beak to peck thoughtfully several times at the outline of my thigh under the breeches. Then it turns and with a deliberate waddle, moves behind a Chinese screen in a corner, and is suddenly invisible, and soundless. But the odour of cod still seems to linger in the room.
>
> Wrinkling his nose, Dante picks up, from a side table, a small Venetian flute, puts the tube across his lips, and begins to play, with perfect pitch and timing, an aria of Frescobaldi's. And within seconds, the melody is interrupted by a soft slapping sound. Evandro has appeared from behind the screen, and is making, with only a single affronted glance at the instrument of his discomposure, towards the door by which he first entered.
>
> Dante completes the final phrase of his aria, with a fine flourish at the end, and lays the flute aside.
>
> 'I wonder why a sea-bird should so hate music,' I say.
>
> But Dante only shrugs and continues to fold my shirts.

The Lion of Pescara

Renata would finish, laying the little set of cards together, like a trick at cards. Then you would frown, and perhaps begin to sweat a little. Hearing an incident of this kind, really so trivial in itself, and yet so typical of the bizarre conduct of your wartime household, would sometimes dislocate, in your worse moments, your grip on reality.

The interior landscape in the cauldron of your blindness would once more begin to churn into a fertile life of its own. The trolls of your subconscious would lift their heads from the velvety darkness, and the ballet of the dream be again in action.

Figures known from your flights above Trieste and Garda, belted and capped in the insignia of their regiments, would mix in grotesque abandon, in who can say what abominable practices, with the winged and bittern-voiced inhabitants of a Bosch-like menagerie, a garden of infernal delights.

'Renata,' you would say, fighting madness. 'I have a headache. Would you get me an aspirin?'

Renata would rise, frowning down at your contorted face, knowing the symptoms, reaching into the drawer of the swell-front cabinet for what was needed. You would take the pills, knowing but not seeing that these black airships were more formidable than aspirins, waiting for the glass of water from a silver tray that would send them down to do battle with the enemy in your bloodstream.

You would lie back, feeling the two halves of your nightmare separate and disentangle themselves. The beasts first, shrinking and dissolving into their normal, strokable shapes. Friquette, your fox terrier, now the sole survivor and representative of that great string of racing dogs you had had to leave at Arcachon. Miramar, your tabby kitten, whom you told me once you found too suave.

On the other side, the known and fondled shapes of your new career. Across the back of a gold chair, the muddy khaki of your uniform resting against a swagger stick, the pips of an officer on the sleeves, and the first of your many decorations along the breast.

The Bittern

On a chest of drawers, where Renata had laid a new bandage, and a bottle of lotion for your eyes, an unrolled pair of puttees, and the butt of a revolver protruding from a leather holster. Cartridges intermingled with cuff links on your dressing-table, where the ivory hairbrushes, and the bottles of scent, were now forced companions of a pair of military binoculars, and a case of maps.

For over a year you lived there, before the crash on the sandbank, and the collision with the gun-butt of your aeroplane, alone for the most part, with your faithful Dante, and the culinary attractions of the skilful Albina, to illuminate your solitude. Night after night, under the threat of the Austrian bombers, you sat in the alcove, watching the sun go down, or the girls fanning themselves in their gondolas, or doing their hair up by some remote yet perfectly visible window.

Day after day, you walked the narrow alleys, your mind teeming with plans for a new assault, or a modification to a machine-gun, or a repair to an undercarriage. At a café table in the square, feeding pigeons with an abstracted precision, you ran over the weaknesses in each past flight, or plotted the storming of some held position. In a dark bar, bending above the neck of some casually discovered beauty, you stilled your appetite in the contemplation of a leaflet raid, or the blowing up of a secret ammunition dump.

Then you returned. Buckling the clasp of your belt, strapping the holster to your thigh. Stepping into the bow of that fast motor-boat, and heading in a long V of spume for the train station at Mestre, and the journey back to the front.

I see you shudder now, feeling the urge to write come.

'Renata,' you say. 'Bring me the board.'

You feel the turned edges of the writing-plaque as Renata places it across your belly, run your fingers over the bottom ridge where the clean cards will rest as they wait for the brush of the quill.

To your left, as you reach out, you can feel the cold silver of the ink-well, solid on its baize against the marble of the

The Lion of Pescara

side table. Then the sheaf of quills, trimmed and ready along the stone.

You reach, dip, and begin to write. The words dash and spider over the card, a fresh stab of experience wrought into fluid form. Again you reach, dip, write. The words flow faster now, less legible, more rich.

Giuseppe Miraglia, you write. His face rotting between the candles and the bayonets.

2

I CAME TO see you, of course, twice in uniform, and once in civilian clothes, on leave from my regiment, alighting from the vaporetto at your landing-stage, and looking up under the heavy scent of early laburnum to see your hand lifted in gloved recognition from the first-floor window. Yes, you were convalescent then, though still confined to the stringencies of your bedroom, the distance between the couch and the chair in the alcove.

'Tomaso,' you said, half rising from the Louis-Quinze. 'You old lecher. You are just in time. I anticipate the Divine Marquise.'

'You can see,' I said, with an attempt at jocularity. 'I'm a little disappointed, I must confess. They told me that you were flat on your back still, and almost totally blind. I should not, otherwise, have dared to appear in this dandified garb of peaceable times.'

I felt embarrassed in the presence of your uniform, for this, embellished by a travelling-rug around your waist, was what you were wearing.

'My dear Tomaso,' you said, shaking your head. 'We are old soldiers, you and I. I always imagine you here in boots and spurs.'

Then you leaned forward, away from the light, and I saw for the first time the neat bandage draped around your bald skull, set at what seemed even then to be a jaunty angle

The Lion of Pescara

above your right eye. The eye itself, and its left fellow, were dark gulfs, twin cavities of recovered energy, into which my pity, suddenly roused, leapt naked and swam.

'It's good to see you well,' I said.

Renata, later, told me the worst. You were fit thus, two or three hours each day, in the wake of your cocaine injections. Dressed by your gondolier, and seated at ease in the window alcove, with the light behind your ravished eyes, you could still present some air of untroubled gaiety, a façade of calm or joy, to the visiting friends, mostly female, who had poled their way to your sanctum. Today, for example, the Marchesa Casati, borne from her white peacocks and her overgrown garden, in what wigs and with what wax figurines, time would soon tell.

But no, Renata said, as we sat alone later in that long drawing-room, and she fondled a braided bag, and I drank a tiny glass of grappa, you were only partially fit.

Every night the slant bandage was drawn down again over the unextinguished misery in your eyes, and the darkness resumed its conquests. I had seen already your white hands, like the severed fingers from a statue, moving over the virgin cards, driven by the terrible necessities behind your concealed pupils, and I knew what Renata meant.

One earlier afternoon, arriving unexpectedly, and with only a few minutes to spare for my audience, I had stood in the shadows beside a bust of Scriabin in the gilded doorway, watching your restless head move on the pillows, believing itself to be unobserved, and with some precious interval of its own to be free with pain in. I had felt guilty, said nothing, and soon withdrawn, shocked by this evidence of your real suffering.

So that it felt a source of disturbance then, as not often in former days, under the pergolas near Florence, but frequently later on, sweeping the stale cushions aside to find some hard space to rest on, in your final house by Garda, yes, it became an upsetting thought, as I conceived you suddenly human, perishable, and capable of hurt.

It was otherwise, and more oblique, when the subject

The Bittern

rose, flickering its head like a serpent, under the crisp April sun upstairs in the alcove. We were still waiting for the click of heels, the distant swish of Fortuny tulle, and the purring of ocelots, that might herald the dark Luisa.

'Tomaso,' you said suddenly, and this marked a divergence in the fluid current of your conversation, which had ranged for some time over the demerits of a new French observation plane, 'I want you to approach a publisher, and to negotiate some suitable advance against the receipt of my book.'

'Calmann, perhaps,' I suggested, and, of course, in time it was indeed Calmann, in France, who thinned the great brook of its autumn burden, the strewings of Vallombrosa, and left the illegible to their dry casket, unread to this very day.

But your mind had veered, and I saw your eyes narrow, and drop from the light.

'I remember when I was a young journalist,' you said, squinting down at your hands. 'I was introduced once, in a garden, under a spray of poisonous oleanders, to the brother of Vernon Lee, the English essayist, who had rented a villa in Florence. This brother was a retired English diplomat, they told me. He had served in Lisbon, and contracted there some curious impediment of the spine which resulted in paralysis, and a sort of perpetual nightmare.'

You shrank in your chair for a moment, as if under the impact of a surgical needle. The dank breath of the canal drifted in on the wind, and I gagged, and sat back. It was truly a Venetian moment. The foulness of the air matching the gloomy mood of the talk, as in those plangent later verses of Browning's, where we seem to feel the clogged robes of the doges brushing the sea-swept marble.

'He lay on a sort of wheeled bed, or mobile ottoman,' you continued, lifting a manicured hand as if to trace the outline of this *outré* conveyance in the sunbeams. 'His beard was very neat, and cut in the style of a Spanish grandee of the sixteenth century. I remember his fingers, cool and strong, flexing in mine as though to grip me like a

The Lion of Pescara

poniard. The sun shone down, there was the lethal scent, and sometimes the brush of a deadly petal. Tea was taken, and a kind of small cake, which I believe is known in England as a Jap dessert.'

The story was already assuming the grotesque elaboration I knew so well, and I waited to hear this level punctured by some apt, or even devastating, splash of wit. None came, however. You were serious, extracting no irony as you approached the crisis.

'He used to set snails racing,' you said. 'So he told me. He had so much time. Day after day they ran him out from his room on those iron wheels to feel the weight of the light, and he lay under sky so blue it made him ill, and the vicious minutes became solid, and froze, and refused to move. He had to force them to lift their shells. Try, he said. You can move, I know you can. Even snails can run.'

Then you pushed the travelling-rug aside, and rose awkwardly in your immaculate riding-boots. You began, ignoring my outstretched arm, as was natural for you, and inevitable, to pace to and fro in the short room, one elbow in your palm, and the fingers of the same hand knitting your brows as you recited a lugubrious sonnet.

'Lee-Hamilton,' you concluded suddenly, settling again in your chair. 'You ought to read him, Tomaso. He died of a broken heart seven years ago.'

I glanced over my shoulder at the conventional muted rococo of this Austrian *pied-à-terre* which had suddenly, and through that mere accident of the eye, become the shrine of your agonies, less faked, I felt sure now, than usual. Only the swept mahogany of the bed itself, improved with a cataract of flounces and patterned satins, offered some echo of those former apartments in which I had seen you triumph and astound.

'I know, Tomaso,' you said, sensing my thought. 'I need more furniture. These rooms are so bare. But then I am blind, you see. I live in a world of clocks.'

There had been their chimes, of course, and I needed no reminding of time and its passage. A skeleton gold affair under a dome of glass, like a wedding cake, protected from

The Bittern

flies, had been particularly persistent in its regular marking out of the hours. But what these were, and which we were now at, I had no idea.

Renata had stolen in once, maroon in a dusky cascade of heavy silks. A rearrangement of books on a low divan had marked her discreet solicitude for your patience, or your temperature. No word, however, was spoken then, on the subject of time, or the schedules of the vaporetti, or the absence of any spare room, where a guest, even one so valued as a former secretary, might stay the night.

We were easy companions, then as ever. Once, a pronounced wrench at my waist announced the beak of Evandro, reaching towards the pocket of my coat for a possible steak of halibut, or a forgotten head of swordfish. But this avian intrusion was an isolated one. The room was hotter, I suspect, even than usual, and the bird sought the cold of marble for his pestered webs.

'Luisa is late,' you remarked, at one point, frowning as though in a little distress.

But how could you know, I asked, when there seemed to be no one timepiece that offered some accurate view or hint of the real hour.

'I know,' you replied, familiar as ever with your conniving smile, 'because Luisa is always late.'

No doubt you were right. I knew the exquisite Marchesa only slightly at that date, though an elf on a black card had summoned me once, four years earlier, to a black mass at Auteuil I had been too reverent, or too cowardly, to attend. There are tales of such nights, redolent of so many cruel and blasphemous amours, which I shall tell, following the drift and clue of those eccentric clocks, in their due turn.

'Each phrase in that sonnet,' you said, looping back by a well remembered device to an earlier topic, 'was forged in the crucible of a waking dream. I saw them come, as he lay there, as if constipated and in need of some fruitful laxative, below the sway of the dangerous blossoms. A bell would be rung, dependent from a brass hook on his trundleable coffin, and thus the suave acolyte would appear, servant or sister, with pen and paper to hand. A

The Lion of Pescara

bent head, a hushed word. And, lo, Tomaso, the dictated inspirations were alive like tadpoles on the page!'

I listened, no doubt with my usual grin, to these cleverly switchbacked impressions. You were serious, yes, I can only repeat the dull word, serious. But not solemn. The sarcasms were a sugar coating.

'I tried the same, Tomaso,' you said, spreading your hands. 'He came to mind as the obvious model. I lay in the dazzling aftermath of my collision with the gun-butt, and the boiling heresies of the retina demanded some outlet. It was as if a great serpent, or perhaps rather a mean, diminutive serpent, working in the iris, cried for its mouthpiece from the inner altar of my dream. Where is my Pythian priestess, it seemed to say.'

You rose again, leaning on the withered sill, and glancing worriedly to left and right along the canal, as if seeking some Delphic revelation from the slimy water. But, alas, none came.

'And then, Tomaso,' you said, lifting a finger, and swinging on your heel, in an artificially theatrical gesture, 'I thought of Renata. Renata, the child of my peccadilloes. Renata, the given, unwanted nurse of my ailment. What better work for her than to hear and record my demon's words?'

It was a rhetorical question, and I made no answer.

'No, Tomaso,' you said, leaning forward as if to impart some startling and yet revelatory secret. 'There was a difficulty. I discovered its force and power on the very first morning we bent our heads together, father's and daughter's, to accomplish the holy task. It was clear. It was notable, and it was momentous.'

You paused, solemn as a cardinal.

'The breath of Renata,' you pronounced, 'was as the effusions of Vesuvius. Pungent, exacting, and no more to be ignored than the pangs of gripe or the ringing of the dinner-bell. I tell you, Tomaso. All has been tried. The most exotic of peppermints. The least redolent of spices from Albina's kitchen. Comfits, lozenges and cordials. All have been drunk, swallowed or chewed. And to no avail.

The Bittern

Our only recourse has been withdrawal. And this formal resort, which you see, to these decks of cards. This box of satinwood.'

This awful tale preyed on my floating mind as I chugged in the loaded vaporetto away down the serpentine canal, towards my train, and in time, my unit.

It summed up the visit, or rather, perhaps, that portion of it, a wide and important one, concerning your current mode of writing, and the ripe licence with which you now felt free to assault the inmost recesses of your professional psyche. This was a new genius I had been privileged to eavesdrop on, a more ironic, and yet a more autobiographical one. Less honourable, perhaps, but more complicated.

I watched the troops in side alleys, men in uniform with water-bottles and binoculars, an occasional officer, spotless in boot and glove, the protectors of Venice on their several pernicious or lively occasions. This was your world now. These were your people.

As surely as once before, in Rome, you had encapsulated the sultry spirit of the decadence, the drooping flowers and the mauve hangings of a century that grew languid in repose, you were now the clarion, and yet operatic, voice of a new period, one with its hooves in mud and gore, and its delicate muzzle straining after the resonance of dire flags and stars.

I leaned on the slatted seat of the old vessel, under the flapping linen canopy, making room for a peasant woman with a basket of carrots, and a black shawl over her walnut face, and I looked back, as we fanned away across the open water towards Mestre, at what one day would remain only as a memory, a quiver on the dead rhythm of the cold lagoon. Venice, the great mother. Venice, the jewel of history.

Here as a boy you had helped to carry Wagner on your shoulders to his last resting-place, or so the legend ran. Here, as a man, you were planning, even now, the deliberate and exciting campaigns that would lift the shadow of Austria from our threatened borders, and make your name, in the fecund process, more resolute, and no whit less abused and envied and, shall I say, indexable, than ever before.

So I rose in the stern, seeing the first lights come on, and the wind stir in the twilight. Remembering suddenly your many clocks, and the candleflames that Renata had lit, and thinking how easily reality could become illusion. Was this a real twilight? Was I really here on my way back to Mestre?

Or was I still in that sweltering room, in the buttery glitter of all those mirrors, hearing my stiff chair grind back, as I creaked to my feet, and greeted with a bow, as you did, the entrance of the demanding Marchesa between her Afghans?

3

SHE HAD BEEN the mistress of almost everyone. That is, of almost everyone who counted, and, indeed, to be fair to the lady, of a rather extensive range of unknown figures, of either sex, whose charm or skin belied the plebeian turn of their blood. She had left the bed of the Kaiser, some whispered, for a brisk affray with a buxom serving-girl.

That she went, as they say, both ways, there are many to swear. That she went many ways, there are more. But no one, man or woman, for fifteen years had been a match for the flexible delirium of her appetites, or, at least, had been known to form any kind of lasting alliance with her.

You knew her well, and you might have been that match. Might, in another aeon. But in those too perfect, and yet too hectic, days of the early century, neither of you was prepared to make any restriction in the free play of your appetites. You circled each other, like two leopards, playful and affectionate, and with claws to rip and tear, and yet with nothing to fight or love for.

But, love. In the narrow sense of that mischievous word, there was love, yes. No doubt, in plenty. But far beyond the immediate effusion of what have been called the seeds of the pomegranate? That I doubt. You were both experienced campaigners in the amorous trenches, too skilled in self-preservation to be raising your bald or greying heads above the parapet, or wetting your emotional toes, for that

The Lion of Pescara

matter, below the safe dryness of the duckboards. The squalor of passion was not, in those days, for either of you.

It had blown, yes, and had raged and fallen, and might again, for your sins, but in by-ways, and by accident. There was not the time left, for either of you, to court a grand amour.

To my mind, when I thought about it later, this seemed a pity. The Marchesa was the only woman, on her side, who exemplified the whole spectrum of your requirements. She was rich, well born, beautiful, and as bold and imaginative in the transformation of her environment as you were yourself. A prodigious inventor of spectacles, erotic and damaging. A byword throughout Europe for lust and scandal. And finally, one last thing. She was small. As small as you were yourself.

She appeared that afternoon as the sun gave way to a cool mist, and she was everything that Boldini has made her seem in his most exotic canvases. The dogs came first, a few yards ahead of Albina, to whose lot it had fallen, for some reason, to be her John the Baptist. They sleeked in through the open doorway, and were over beside us, in the alcove, their grave muzzles reaching for your eager hands. You were smiling with pleasure, fondling the fawn parted hair at their Athenian brows, before your portly cook, in a breathless hustle, had arrived to announce their mistress.

'Forgive me, sir,' she was saying, 'but they . . .' And then, interrupting herself, with a glance of flustered horror over her shoulder. 'The Marchesa Casati.'

The Marchesa was wearing pantaloons of some transparent gauzy material, with a sash of peacock's feathers, wound very tight, and a long scarf of gauze floated in the air behind her. She moved, in fact, like a sort of gaudy comet. There must have been something crossed like a bandolier above the narrow peaks of her tiny breasts, but I remember only their delicate outline, their sway under drooping festoons of pearls, as she stooped and put her long hands to your face.

A tall helmet surmounted that pretty hatchet, with a great bobbin of black feathers dipping and slithering off it,

The Bittern

and I wondered, more than once, what force of personality or elastic was required to hold it in place.

'Luisa, you know Tomaso,' you must have said, at some point in the flow of compliments and inquiries, because I recall the sudden turn of that axe-face, under its Periclean helmet, and then the sharp, steady flame of those eyes.

I knew then why men would have died for her, why some perhaps had done so, and not all of their own free will. It was the one moment when she looked exactly as in the Vitellini portrait, when she was twenty. The years drained away, and the gravity and desire of a devouring child surged out like a flood of lava, to swallow and petrify my affections.

She put all of herself in that first moment, as she must have done for so many others, and I could have been her slave, but for the memory of a night in Fontainebleau, when she never took off her green mask, and I stood with my fingers over the wet moss under her toga, as she put her lips to the secret parts of a Roman centurion.

'We met once,' I said, setting my own mouth to her chill fingers. 'But the Marchesa would scarcely remember.'

Of course, she was smiling, but then she was always smiling. It was that eternal, archaic smile of the Greek statues from the Acropolis that had first drawn you to her. That Sphinx-like durability. That air of knowing some secret she shared only with Lucifer.

So I wonder if she did remember, or if that second of mixed pleasure, amidst so many, had made any dent in the pristine monument of her sexual detachment. I wonder, I say.

Yes, but the pride of men, even my own, after so many experiences, has few limits. Those eyes for a moment had knocked me off my pedestal, and I wanted the Marchesa to remember.

'Lewdness,' she said, moving her nails under my lips, 'will get you nowhere.'

I sank, then, back into the background from which I had only for a precious second emerged, and the tournament of endeavour between the two champions was allowed to continue, their greeted page retiring into the wall-hangings, as it were, to chart each flourish of pennant, or clatter of lance, as it might be the harbinger of victory, or the black herald of defeat.

We had stood, I say, and bowed when the Marchesa entered, and later there were other moves; about the room for example, to admire the clocks and flowers; and then downstairs to hear Malipiero, who had called to play for you on the grand piano and to shock Evandro into a vivid demonstration of his hatred of music; and once, at some odd interval, between tea and a final conversation, involving both Dante and Renata, a cloistered period of seclusion, wherein there were squeals and creaks from the ancient plumbing of your private bathroom, or from some other abused and yet still active mechanism, as there was a showing, officially, of what you liked to call 'a few etchings by Rops I have had to store, for want of space, in the cabinet that holds my bath salts and sponges.'

You enjoyed these little subterfuges, that fooled no one, and gave a prurient spice, no doubt, to the easy welter of your indecorous explorations. Perhaps, after all, at this date, they allowed a veil to be drawn, too, across the exact extent of your depredations on the female body. To be more blunt, what cannot be seen can never be evaluated.

At any rate, there were squeals and creaks, and at times a sort of condensed gasping, which brought a twitch to my own relaxed member, I must confess, when I passed the door. But for the most part I sat in silence with the icy Renata, lips pursed, her own I mean, and legs crossed. That is, mine.

'The etchings have passed muster,' you said, as you emerged, rubbing your hands on a mauve towel. 'They have gathered some dust there in the press, and I have had to wash myself to remove the grime.'

But the smiling Marchesa, entirely immaculate in her impenetrable pantaloons, and apparently as tightly wound at the waist as ever, and still on the thin stilts of her Russian ballet shoes, flowed out like a strange steam, or perhaps a genie from a bottle, rubbed into who knows

The Bittern

what astounding emissions by the fingers of emir or poet, and her great eyes opened and flashed, and nothing was said, either about the etchings or the plumbing noises.

Later she was able to charm Renata, she had that easy power, by some apt remarks on the wiles of Chateaubriand, and the prices of French lace at Chambord. She was even able to raise a moue, and a flick of her opening fingers, in praise of a rather underdone mousse that Albina had thought to make this Monday her day of experiment with.

But her main interest lay, not altogether astoundingly, in the brawny physique and thin dark sideburns of the entrancing Dante. A phlegmatic fellow this, I had always found, and at odds with the usual talkativeness you found an asset in those you chose to employ.

But his quiet manner, and a certain sullen docility, seem to have been a spur to the lustful interest of the momentarily unsatisfied Marchesa. Dante had first been seen whittling a stick to a fine point in the garden, no doubt for some abstruse purpose about his gondola, and the Marchesa had remarked on his fine air of Renaissance abstraction.

She had leaned over the windowsill, at some risk to her life, and – yes, let it be said – to my own composure as I viewed the exquisite rift in her buttocks, and had noted the whittling and the abstraction from above, as Dante sprawled on a stone bench in the little garden, a dark bulk below a neighbouring cedar.

The helmet spun, the feather whirled, and the scarf fluttered in the air, as you told the story of Dante's flute and the intransigent bittern. The Marchesa would not be satisfied until we attempted a reconstruction of this bizarre episode, and with the original participants in their familiar roles.

The shirts were laid out, the bird, with some difficulty after its experience with Malipiero, brought in, and the gondolier summoned, flute and all, to the bedchamber.

The Marchesa reclined, superb and oriental, as in some scene from a play costumed by Bakst, on the heaped

The Lion of Pescara

coverlets of your bed, from which you were still banished, though quite willingly, it would seem, in the wake of your wrestle with the etchings, to a hard chair by the wall. I myself had a lowly position on a carved footstool, beside the two Afghans.

Enter Dante, flute at the ready.

Of course, it was all an anti-climax. That heavily feathered bird refusing to move. The gondolier under the boring searchlights of those appreciative eyes, having trouble with his fingering. The Marchesa smiling, smiling, as if her smile was held in place with a safety pin.

Alas, it was as if the rehearsal followed the performance. You were never so liable to that error yourself. You were too careful over the preliminaries. But on that day you sat still, as I did, an easy prey to the tongues, and the swishing tails, of those two dogs, as we strove to contain their enthusiasm for a closer inspection of this graceful internal wader, with the long, dipping neck, and the slapping webs, who had evidently so fascinated their wayward mistress.

Evandro yawned. He eyed the Marchesa as one star eyes another, when the white heat of the lights begins to bathe the theatre, and the make-up is under threat of melting, and the soft hiss of the reels turning announces that battle is about to commence. I remembered your suffocating bedroom, and the claustrophobic ticking of the clocks, when I sat on the Paramount lot in the sweltering twenties, watching the sacred monsters of the silent screen tearing each other's guts, or reputations, out under the all-seeing eye of those inexorable cameras.

She was the prototype of so much that happened then, the enigmatic Marchesa. Each vamp who stepped from her white Rolls had a mental photograph of *les grandes horizontales*, Liane de Pougy or Lady Hamilton, and beyond them, and later, the Edwardian elegance and extravagance of Luisa, La Casati.

The slow reels would turn, the smoke from the long cigars rise blue in the air, and the sweating directors run their pudgy fingers round the insides of their once-white

The Bittern

collars. 'Cut,' they would say, reaching for their tonic water. And then there would come the conferences, the relocating of the properties, the attempts to placate or reconcile the two protagonists, male or female prima donnas, as they wept or raged in their neon-lit palanquins.

It was a panorama of repetitions. The life of illusion so often transfixing the life of reality with its baleful or hectoring glare. The solidity of film replacing the mutability of time. Theda Bara fearful of being cast opposite Rin Tin Tin.

I realised her worries that afternoon, as the gauzy Marchesa, a demoiselle above slimy water in the deep haze of the steam heating, fluttered on those damp cushions, and strove to out-eye a lanky bird.

You were never a fan of film. I shall tell in the right place of how the lethal wing of the cinema brushed your arm, in its time, and what you did to offset its honours. No, you were never a fan, nor indeed a star. You preceded the stars. The stars, even the exotic Valentino, with his own Italian vulgarising of your best gestures, or perhaps, there are some would say, his heightening of your crudity, had to own some debt to your mannerism.

You were what film had to strive to be. The dream in action. The nightmare, perhaps, in the service of a good ideal. But it was hardly, then, this ominous undertone, rather perhaps the sense of times interlocking, of moments fed over moments into the conveyor of history, the blur of the thing itself and its echoes, of the thing itself and its heats, its heats, yes, this was what came to me from that awkward re-run.

I saw the Marchesa's time suddenly as more than operatic, the immediate aria to the applause of the gallery, I saw it as opera fading into the scrolls of the librarians, the Roman triumph become the fustian stuff of Livy.

Two Afghan hounds reaching to sniff and kill an oblivious wading-bird. A former gondolier who is nervous of a society lady in the presence of his indulgent and yet somewhat touchy employer. A poet and his secretary. With noises off from a stout cook and a virgin daughter.

The Lion of Pescara

These make banal materials for such grandiose reflections.

'The French troops,' the Marchesa said, much later when bird and gondolier had been dismissed, and the dogs had put their long heads to the floor, and lay asleep, 'are intoxicated with cocaine. They see everything in heightened colours. There is no discrimination. So they perform great feats of heroism and achieve nothing.'

You were seated then in your window chair again, a little bored, I suspect, or tired, and anxious to be on your own, and come to terms with that awful pounding within the ball of your pupil. But you were too polite to be swift in showing your fatigue.

'Your own parties, my dear Luisa,' you said, 'were to blame. So many young officers were your guests. You taught the whole French army your own delicious habits.'

Of course, to her it was quite a compliment, and she laughed, and touched your knee. She liked the idea that she had corrupted a generation, and almost directly, as it were, through her own loins.

Later they bombed her house, a flight of the most intrepid Austrian airmen, and a vase or two crumbled into the water. That was her price for corrupting the lieutenant in the Light Horse of Novara, or at least for being supposed his confederate. I saw the masonry a year later amidst the St John's wort. I even stooped and lifted a fragment of that hounded palace on my fingertip.

They were bad marksmen. The truth of the matter is that they were aiming for your own smaller target across the canal. But your charmed life, even with an Austrian price on it, was still beneath the protection of the beneficent deities. They took your right eye, but left your life.

So you survived those weeks of enforced withdrawal, and struck back. I shall turn to that. You were not, after all, just an ugly face. You did your bit. Your squadron of twenty planes, yourself there in the spearhead machine, the device on your fuselage shot away, but the motto remaining, *iterum leo rugit*, the extrapolated violence of

The Bittern

your inward imagination, yes, that imagination sank more than one enemy cruiser at three hundred miles.

It threw the development of the progressive conscience into reverse. It brought the Middle Ages back with all its panoply and its equivocal horror. It sold the great into shame and gave their chance to the opportunists.

Writing here, in the desolating anus of Italian grandeur, I lay my own small claim against your style and your oratory, your example and your affairs. I have seen the triumphant armies who marched through Abyssinia driven home with their hands on their heads. The dragnets of your glory, and your passion.

Well. But then who was responsible more than I? The little men who lift the tackle on their shoulders raise the tyrants to their eminences. Alas, yes. But then you were never a provincial Thrasymachus. Not you. You were far too busy. Far too lecherous.

4

Turning again those early pages in your book of darkness, yes, *The Book of Darkness*, that would be a fair title for the gathered prayers of your isolation, I feel some rage, and at the same time some fear and guilt. They flower in crannies of your livid prose. The short paragraphs glide over each other, the electric present works its magic, tense upon tense.

In those early days, you had only to lie and think, and feel. As in the etiolating vapours of a Turkish bath, a sort of blind Homer transported into the Roman ciborium, you began to track through your new experience, the awareness of death.

Yes, you had known the brush of this before. When the sabre cut your head open, and the sting of acid that saved your life removed your hair, in that strange, or rather absurd, duel, where your journalist opponent had struck his effective blow in mere error, and had to apologise and lose, though it was you who were wounded. Then, yes. You had surely felt some touch of the dry mortality in the wrinkling of blood and salves.

But later it gripped more closely.

It was Arcachon that brought the first real casualty, your devout landlord, whom you talked through all that he had to say, at the end, an apparent atheist, a potential convert for the old man's soul to quicken to.

The Bittern

But, he was old. He had to be taken, then or soon, without the vials of energy in his crinkled veins appearing to undergo any change. You only knew him as ancient, as already there, shivering in his dark bathing trunks on the icy brink of death.

It was otherwise in the war. Giuseppe Miraglia was the first. The first who took you into the air and over the enemy lines. The first, later and alone, who crashed into the sea, and died.

He was only thirty-two years old, the age of Alexander the Great, the age you were before Florence, before La Duse, before you had done whatever mattered to you most, whatever you will be remembered by.

I leaf the pages over, feeling them rustle and flee, hearing your own voice, like the wind in the pine trees. It takes over their message, it spells the words out as they once were, alive and true.

I lie in darkness. A darkness of labouring flames.

I write like a man who throws down an anchor, and the rope spins on and on, always faster and faster, and the sea seems to have no bottom, and the hook never seems to bite, or the cable to break.

Then more in the same tone, the scene being set as I, in my less inspired style, have set it already. But then the darkness thickens. The real story begins.

I wake at three, after a night of broken slumber. Five hours of dreams.

A clear day, with no wind. Admirable for the great flight.

I lie awake, in the grip of a strange sense of unease.

At lunch I am so quiet and anxious that Renata asks, 'What is the matter?' But I don't know what to say.

She has filled the room with flowers: red roses, jonquils and violets.

I eat mechanically.

The Lion of Pescara

The sky is blue. I look at the plants in the garden. The wind is low. I hear the drone of an aeroplane passing over the canal.

After lunch I go to the studio on the Zattere. Romaine is waiting.

I cannot disguise my dark mood. She is reduced to a pair of eyes and a chin. No more a woman. A will of art. White silk blouse. Delicate brushes in her fingers.

I take up my pose, dreaming. I don't hear the sort of trivialities she murmurs to keep me amused.

Time passes, I don't know how long. Not long.

I hear someone climbing the stairs. A knock on the door. A voice calling me.

It's Renata. I open the door.

'Come at once. There's been an accident.'

'What accident? Miraglia?'

I think of him at once.

'Let's go. Genua is downstairs. He'll tell you.'

I go down. Genua tells me that Miraglia has crashed in the sea. He is badly wounded. Giorgio Fracassini, who was with him, is missing.

I go with Renata to the Marine Hospital. On the way we meet a sailor, on his way to my house. Genua speaks to him. I gather that the body has been taken to the Hospital of St Anne.

The body. Miraglia is dead.

The sailor offers to take us there in a motor-boat.

The basin of St Mark.

Sky, everywhere.

Stupor, despair.

The screen of tears, not moving.

Silence.

The beating of the motor.

The gardens.

We turn into the canal.

In front of us, low in the sky, near to its hangar, the obscene shape of a moored balloon. The colour of silver.

It's three o'clock. More or less.

The Bittern

I jump out, and go to the desk.

'Where is he? Giuseppe Miraglia.' The porter shows me a door. I go in.

His body on a wheeled bed.
The head shaved.
The mouth closed.
The right eye wounded, livid.
The right arm broken. Swelling beginning.
Complexion olive: an unusually calm expression.
Flecks of cotton-wool in his nostrils.
He is wearing his blue shirt with gold buttons. The one he had on yesterday.

I fall to my knees.

The beating of engines, on the canal.
The heavy sound of feet on the bridge.
A sailor comes in with a bundle of candles. He puts four of them at the corners of the bed.
Luigi Bologna enters. Then Carlo della Rocca. I can't move. I can't get up.
A little time goes by. Then another sailor comes in, and opens a door in the wall, opposite me.
It had been closed.
I hear a voice. Two sailors are wheeling in another body, Fracassini's. It was found two hours later. They put him in the other room.
I go in to look at him. He seems to be sleeping. Peaceable, severe. Dressed in his brown leather coat.
I go back to the other room.
Miraglia's face is covered with gauze.
His body is draped in the flag.

Night comes. I think of all the flowers that Renata had arranged in our vases.

I leave, crossing the bridge.
The moon bright in the sky, low, facing me.
I step down into the motor-boat, and we move away down the canal.
Death is with me, the smell of death. Renata is waiting.

The Lion of Pescara

She knows everything. We embrace, weeping. She wants to come to see him.

I go into the dining-room. I collect all the flowers from all the vases.

Once again, the chamber of death.

Candles are burning. Two sailors on guard. The flames flicker, reflected in the blades of their bayonets.

I lay the flowers beside the body. I feel the shape of his buttocks, his legs.

I lay the white jonquils on the red and green of the flag.

The vigil begins.

The lapping of the canal water against the window.

The cry of the gondoliers.

A strange air, like a mass of impenetrable crystal, around the body.

Five o'clock.

The lapping of water continues.

I get up and go to lie down in a bedroom on the first floor.

White furniture, white bed.

An electric light is blazing down.

I cover my head, so as not to see. I am dead tired, but I can't sleep.

Then I do sleep, and Miraglia is alive.

I dream that he comes to the Casetta Rossa, and I say, 'Is it you? Are you back?'

He uncovers his face, takes off his black cape. It isn't him. It's a mask, one of those white plaster masks.

Time passes, then I wake.

I hear the whistling of the sailors cleaning the hospital corridors.

I bathe my eyes in a handkerchief soaked in cold water.

Is it day? Is it true?

I go downstairs.

The suffocating odour of the flowers, the candlewax.

The black cloth, still the same. The shape of the body, still the same.

The Bittern

The two sailors on guard.
Outside, the sounds of the day, the town waking up, everything beginning again, as always.
I feel a terrible headache starting. I can hold on no longer. I go out on the landing-stage, call the motor-boat.
The morning, cold and ashen.
I go home, at the end of my strength. I undress. My uniform carries the smell of death, it seems to me. The same smell as in my underclothes. I strip them off. I step into a hot bath.
Memories come.
His pleasure when he saw my little Watteau. His mandarin smile when I read him a Chinese poem.
I have to go back at midday. I order a wreath.
Renata is coming with me.
We set out.
Venice in cinders. Death everywhere.
Silence.
Twenty-four hours have passed.

I go to his house.
A weak light in the vestibule. I go up the dark staircase, trembling. A woman's voice calls, 'Who is it?'
'A friend.'
At the top of the staircase, I confront his landlady. She tells me the room is locked. Gigi Bologna took the key when he came, for the sword, the helmet and the medals.
I go downstairs. I feel such a weight of sadness I could never bear to climb them again.
Then, the narrow street.
The Casetta Rossa. Renata, white and anxious.
We sit down at the table. We eat almost nothing. Miraglia is with us, everywhere.
I sleep, rise at three. I take a flask of hot coffee, the same one I used to carry on our flights.
I go out.
A full moon, hard as a stone.
Venice is dead, shut up inside an unchanging jewel, a diamond.

The Lion of Pescara

All along the quay of St Anne I see the shadow of a soldier on sentry duty, outlined against the wall of a house in the light.

Not a breath of wind. Not a ripple on the lagoon. The sky clean.

This is the day of the great flight.

In the chamber of death I meet Ange Belloni. Triangular head, eyes like a falcon's.

We shake hands.

I see that someone has moved the black cloth. The flowers I arranged there yesterday are scattered. A doctor, I hear, has given certain injections to preserve the corpse.

There is no news of his parents. No one knows if his brother from Valona will come.

I uncover the dead man's face. The nose is swollen, bloody, with the nostrils stuffed with cotton. A ball of cotton-wool hides the mouth. The colour of the skin is darker now, less golden.

We talk.

The taste of death is in our mouths.

Eight o'clock.

I go to the Arsenal.

I argue that the great flight should go on. It would be the best way of honouring the dead.

The commanding officer agrees. I am advised to recommend the pilot best fitted to take Miraglia's place.

We talk of the interment. He tells me the father is too old and ill to come. Soon forty hours will have passed since the death. The body must be put in the coffin today. At four o'clock.

So the flight is postponed.

The day passes.

Pearl, gold, amber. The horizon is broken like a long range of mountains.

I watch four sailors lift the wreaths off. The coffin is

The Bittern

open, on the ground. The lid is leaning against the wall, upright.

They hoist the coffin on to the catafalque. Lined with lead. On gold feet.

Then they raise the body, guiding each other with words uttered in hushed voices. 'More this way. More that. That's the way. This way. That's the way. That's it. That's just right.'

The measure is just right. The body is in the coffin, it fits exactly.

I kneel. I look at the corpse. I lay my bouquet of roses on his broken ankle.

I find the courage to brush his hands with my lips.

They place the lid of lead on the coffin.

A welder steps forward with his lamp. The long flame, blue with a yellow tip, roars, and fills the silence with its roaring.

The door has been left open. A chill breeze blows in and makes the candles drip with wax. A smoky stench penetrates my nostrils.

He could never rise now, even if Christ himself called him.

He is still there. But not in our air here, the air I breathe. In his own air, in the air of the grave, in the air of eternity.

I hear a voice, a flat voice, without form. 'The glue, please.'

I turn. A doctor from the Marine Hospital is there. He repeats, 'Now, the glue, please.'

A sailor brings the glue, and I see the welder lay it on the lead. 'Why?' I ask.

He says, 'To protect the metal against humidity.'

So he lets it spread through every gap, into the spaces between the wood and the lead, and then he and his colleague begin to slap their open hands on the sides of the box, like masseurs.

I imagine Miraglia waking inside the coffin, beating against the panels with his fists.

Enough, enough, I say, but the word sticks in my throat.

The Lion of Pescara

Seven o'clock.
 The coffin rolls on a wheeled bed, towards the chapel.
 Outside the eyes of a few dirty children.
 The foul smell of the canal.
 Grey sky.
 Someone says, 'The brother is here.' I see him, small as Miraglia was. A pitted, vigorous face. Black beard. He has a constant, sudden twitch around his mouth, as if he was chewing something intolerably bitter.
 This brother has come from Valona, from the naval squadron he commands. He brings with him the breath of the war.

The priest speaks the funeral mass.
 Miraglia is still there. I sense the presence of his skin. I see the white roses I laid on his feet.
 I lay my hands under the coffin. I feel its great weight. The black cloth covers my arms as far as the elbows.

Outside, the motor-boat, the funeral barge of black and silver, is waiting beside the quay. I step on board. The coffin trembles.
 Then the wreaths, the wreaths, the wreaths come down one after the other.
 They fill the funeral barge, they fill two others.
 And still more wreaths.

The engines come to life. The marine cortège passes under the wooden bridge. A crowd of people looking down.
 We travel slowly. Across the lagoon fouled with the pale colour of sewage. Along the channel marked out by a line of stones.
 Towards the walls around the island of the dead.

We reach the bank.
 I walk again behind the coffin. Again I touch it, remembering him.
 We enter the cloister, under the portico. We are shown

The Bittern

the way to the funeral depot, the waiting-room where Miraglia will lie until Monday, before his interment.

I cannot bear the stuffiness. I go out into the air.

I walk towards the shore, where the boats are waiting.

Someone hands me a message from Eleonora. She is here in Venice. She wants to see me.

I have no more strength. I say I will wait for her at the Casetta Rossa, if she can come there. She has to leave at ten. It is already midday.

On the journey back, my boat skirts the walls of San Michele.

I remember one summer's night, a night in August. We had gone to Murano, by gondola. Eleonora was with us. The lagoon was so phosphorescent that each stroke of the oar created long white flames.

We leant over the water to watch them. The chins of the women were lit up as with fire.

We never stopped laughing and joking, all along the walls of the cemetery.

We listened to the measured plunge of the oars. And under the cemetery walls, the phosphorescence made rings and wreaths of light.

A sort of song of light surrounded the island of the dead.

Miraglia heard that song. He saw that light. He had his place at the heart of it.

Someone rings the door-bell.

It is Eleonora, breathless, veiled. She stretches out her hands. I was waiting for her.

The evening dies.

I have to take her back to the station.

I find a gondola.

We enter a coffin in darkness. The whole canal is pitch black. I can see nothing. This is the same blankness, I think, that there must be in the coffin with Miraglia, surrounded by all those fading wreaths.

I take my leave of Eleonora quickly. The shore already thick with the ghosts of the dead.

The Lion of Pescara

Miraglia is down there, locked in lead.
Suddenly, I feel afraid. Someone is with me. I lie still, my eyes fixed on the window.

I pause in my blindness, my train of thought breaking. My hand stopping.
The card I was writing on slips and falls on my fingers. It makes no noise.
I start to shudder. And I lie without moving, my body frozen, not daring to trace another single letter in the darkness.

Magnificent, yes. But even there, not to be too exotic, I trace the enduring background of your everlasting, and not to be avoided, affairs. A minor part, in the first act, for the talented Romaine, found still in white silks, brushes in hand, as she paints your image, against the skyline, in cloak and beard.
Another, too, for the operatic Eleonora, arriving on cue for the part of your comforter, and so brusquely, yes, as on many another night, so rudely and rapidly, disposed of to pave the way for whatever brooding theme, or alternative girl, your fancy had set its sights on.
But then, behind those. For Miraglia, that love that dare not tell its name, perhaps? You touched his buttocks in death, if not in life. I shall tell of this, and of such-like matters, but in my own dear time.

5

A SURGEON TOLD you, perhaps one who had read a little psychology, how the whole force of your spirit was enclosed in the blind orb of your eye, from which you were driven to imagine the twinned forks of your life, creating the future before it came, reliving the dwindled energies of the past.

Of course, you adored this priestly duty, though even your own hectic imagination was unequal to the full delineation of what that imprisoned elf, time to come, was at work on in his oven. The past, yes. Those ten so adroitly accomplished missions, against the bias of the affronted Venetian commander, who saw you as a form of sexual vegetable, and was loath to regard your bon-bon box as a proper suite of rooms for a decent officer, those bizarre missions, none entirely without military value, are well recorded, albeit with some florid accretions.

But then the rest, those forty more, four-fifths of your war career, remained in the dark wallet of futurity, untouched by the guesswork of convalescence, or even the generalship of hope. You had much left to do, far more than those close to you, seeing that rack of medicines, and the reels of bandages, and the fleeting spurts of pain in your face, and reading, too, those occasional suicidal phrasings in letter or telegram, to which I shall return, could ever have anticipated.

The Lion of Pescara

Every afternoon an amateur quintet would appear, to play you Vivaldi. Every evening, the temperature of the steam heating would be raised, and the scarlet wax candles lit in their sconces, and the law of ten o'clock imposed. Under this engaging restriction, any visitors arriving after the allowed hour were deemed available for whatever punishment, so frequently sexual and degrading, that your active inventive faculty might arrange.

The Marchesa, by fiat of her own will, was not unoften one of these, nursing some macabre doll in her arms, and smiling, as one debased wit suggested, like a satisfied panther who has eaten the bars of his cage. But then your convalescence shrivelled, and you were suddenly well again, and had gone, albeit only for the hours of daylight, and were in the air, like a sparrow-hawk, or a flying squirrel.

You fought on land, on sea, and in the air. For three years you were the most widely travelled of the Italian lancers. Your cavalry regiment, if it followed you in your roving commissions, was known to have charged through the clouds above Pola, surmounted frozen peaks in the Carso, and succeeded, like horses of the sea, in galloping into the Bay of Quarnaro.

I saw you once in the front seat of your observation plane, with its black seagull painted on the fuselage, the leathered head of the pilot serious over your shoulder. Of course, I was only privileged to be there alongside the official photographer, on the ground.

Later, you were given a hand, and climbed on to the wing, and then into that iron-looking seat of darkened basketwork, from which your muscular thighs would work like the limbs of an organ-player as you practised for the bomb-release.

It was always thus. Three lethal contrivances would hang in their black tubes under your legs, their fins notched for a hook that held them in place. Then, over the target, whether some Austrian cruiser in Cattaro, or the bulky fortifications of Pola, your feet would tread the

The Bittern

pedals, and the neat harmonium of death would wheeze into action.

There you sat, in a kind of water-closet of the air, evacuating the high explosive pellets of your warrior's bowels on to an unsuspecting, or at any rate not much protected, foe.

One jammed once, and you had to land, with the shark's wing of your own probable death sneering above the undercarriage. But fortune was on your side, and the trigger mechanism proved faulty. Once again, you stepped down, and embraced your shaking pilot, in perfect safety.

You won medals, you did most doughty deeds, and you knew, alas, what you were doing. Scribblings of accurate map-readings, gun bores, projectile velocities, these together with the cruder, if more vital, statistics of serving-wenches, compete for attention, in the eyes of an indulgent posterity, with the preliminary sketches for some of the best prose poems in your secret book.

Such found their way into many places when you could see. The view from your left eye, when it lifted you free of that restrictive cushioned bed, and laid you back in your motor-boat, and on the fast route to your unit, included a range of surfaces for the stubby pencil, or borrowed, eaten pen, with which you elaborated your ideas.

The cards, forgotten for a while, and resting like the army of Xenophon in their key-locked final position, contained their messages, readable and otherwise, and their successors, the more frail and casual means of conveying notions about the war, and your past and future, took over and flourished, in library or on gondola, in the front seat of an aeroplane or the back seat of a rocking MAS.

There were odd sheets of cream-lined writing-paper, from the Daniele or the Gritti, fragments of theatre programmes, military instructions printed on headed posters, or in well-thumbed manuals, *billets doux*, photographs, and even, too often for the permanent savour of the originals, the margins and spare spaces in whatever books

The Lion of Pescara

came to hand from your extensive library. Yes, you were avid, particularly so, in your encroachment on the gaps and opportunities of the past.

In that vitreous, rather battered edition of Verger's *Dictionnaire de la Fable,* for instance: the one you pressed into my hands once at the Vittoriale as a birthday present for my deaf sister, and which I retained, anticipating her boredom, for my own amusement.

On the back of a somewhat immodest Leda, etched by the English artist Etty, at page 19 you wrote: 'S.V.A. velocity 220. Bomb load 250 kilos, deliver at 0020 hrs from 30 metres at distance 4–500 kms. 2 Vickers machine-guns.'

The English support weapons were already there at this date, evidently. But not, alas, any more, all of your aviator friends.

A few inches from the frontispiece, where a steel engraving of Pallas Athene, goddess of wisdom, sets the right mood for the work, you have scrawled, in a quick fit: *Myriomorphis, the witch doctor. Luigi Gori, both legs split, died the following day.*

But there were other surfaces, less gorgeous than these. On the wrong side of a map you would make some impervious note from which the full flood of a burst of oratory would gush.

> Those soldiers of the line whose feet left their imprint on the tawny clay of Oslavia, those who trampled underfoot the clotted mire of Podgora, those who were ensnared by the red slime of the Carso – from the San Michele to the Monte Nero, from the Vodice to the Ermada, from Tolmino to Pecinka, from Sagrado to Plezzo, from Plava to Doberdo, whose victorious names outnumber the record of Brescia – all, from the first ones who hacked away barbed wire with pincers and shears to the last who overran the passes opened up by the crushing bombardment, all are the heroes of the most laborious battle that has been fought for the cause of free man on the united front.

The Bittern

On the fringes of newspapers, in the endpapers of your pocket diary, even, let it be secretly breathed, on those coarse brown sheets provided for the cleansing of non-commissioned rectums, purloined and applied to a higher purpose, you would slurp down in clumsy pencil some of the most inspired and elevating of your future speeches.

> The men seemed to bite into the blue air. The light multiplied the effect of the impact from moment to moment. That impact itself was an ascension into the heavens. Strength seemed to rebound from death. Death was dragged upwards by ardour and clamour, like a peasant woman caught by the contagion of a tumult who should start singing a song of fury. The fallen were not an encumbrance but an impulse. The wounded became the standard-bearers of the scarlet ensign. The summit was only a sublime feeling in the breasts of those who meant to reach it. There was nothing but rocks, shambles, crumbled trunks, iron spikes, things wrenched apart and smoke and corpses. But everywhere, too, there was the light of Italy, the noon day of Italy.
>
> It was round about that hour. Twenty minutes of rapture had done it. At noon the Veliki was ours. The stupefied prisoners stammered, How was it done?
>
> It was like the flight of a wing that leaves no trace. The first cry had won the mountain. The miracle of the Sabotino was being renewed.

Of course, very few of your later hearers knew about the miracle of the Sabotino, or remembered the impact of shrapnel as being like an ascension into the heavens. They saw only your tiny, incandescent figure, hand on hip, the black patch over your right eye, the sweet fountain of incomprehensible rhetoric pouring out and over their heads from the unseen throat of their elderly but in fact quite genuinely much adored nightingale.

Yes, you were loved, and you were admired. You made that intolerable struggle in the mud and snow sound far

The Lion of Pescara

too elegant to be believed in, but at least you had climbed in person beside them, and alongside their dead friends, up those shell-torn hills. Indeed, at the storming of the Faiti, you had a miraculous escape from death. It survives in the best of all your speeches, the one somewhat portentously named, in the little brown book of them, 'The Soldier's Crown'.

> The shell did not hit me. It only showered splinters round me. I was able to shake myself and go on my way unhurt. Then, Giovanni Randaccio said to one of his men, 'Take the ring off that shell-case. We will make it into a crown for our comrade.'
>
> The soldier set to work. With the point of his bayonet he tried to detach the copper from the steel, working carefully and lightly.
>
> 'Why are you so long about it?' his captain asked him. 'Are you afraid of spoiling the crown?'
>
> 'No,' answered the soldier. 'The crown will anyhow be fine. I am afraid of spoiling the point of my bayonet which I shall need before long.'
>
> It was a manly answer worthy of one who had stormed the Faiti. That bayonet was afterwards stuck on the extreme salient that marked our effort towards the East, between Castagnevizza and Vippacco. It was a bayonet of the second battalion.

The following year, on a day in May, they placed the shell-case crown on your brows, as they might have set the iron hilt of a Persian sword round the forehead of the Greek poet Aeschylus after the battle of Marathon. You drew such parallels.

But I prefer to make symbolism from that forceful bayonet, still stiff with virgin blood, in the mother soil of Austria. You fought, as so many did in Flanders, a war of earth as well as a war of air, and the womenfolk you were spending your nights with were perhaps good fuel for your soldier's thrusts.

It was on the sea, however, that element reeking of

The Bittern

bitter salt, like the taste of tears, that you performed your most characteristic, and most perverse, manoeuvre.

On February 10th, 1918, your three motor-torpedo boats, with their thirty volunteers, bored through the darkness into the narrow strip of water at Farnesina, and blew up the wire across the cove of Buccari.

There they discharged their torpedoes, managed to sink a steamer, and, most important of all in your eyes, put forth on the water three rubber bottles with tiny Italian flags, containers for a carefully polished, and yet rather spiteful, harangue to the enemy, the sneer of Buccari.

The polite version has been too often printed for me to include its anodyne phrasing here. Suffice it to say that the true original, surviving no doubt in the files of some long-retired and no longer red-faced Austrian admiral, was a touch more prurient, a trifle coarser than what is known.

'Tell us exactly what you said,' the Marchesa asked one day, as we paced, the three of us, near the end of the war, in her overgrown and, at this date, masonry-scattered garden.

It was when I first saw the bomb-damage, and slid my fingers through the flakes of marble in the oblivious rose of Sharon. We were standing, late in July, under a chipped statue of Cupid, whose curls and bow had had their surface abraded and shorn by the flying darts of war.

The Marchesa was in a creation of Poiret's, all ostrich feathers and frail silk, and she had the air of a rather bedraggled dragonfly in that neglected garden. There was a tray of shortbread and vermouth near by on a rustic bench, but for some reason all of us were standing, and none eating or drinking.

The Marchesa, I remember, was carrying her favourite fetish, that little wax image of Maria Vetsera, which someone had carved for her at the turn of the century when the Crown Prince of Austria and the tragedy of Mayerling were still romantic memories. The Marchesa had continued to flirt with her toy, and no doubt to use its rigid smoothness on her back passage, in a spirit of reverse patriotism, when everything Austrian had become the work of the devil.

The Lion of Pescara

'After Rudolf had shot her, you know,' the Marchesa told me once, when I asked her the real story of what had happened in the hunting-lodge, 'the emperor had her body fully dressed and removed from the lodge in an open carriage, accompanied by the Baron Stockau, so that everyone could see she was leaving still alive.'

'To avert scandal,' I suggested, and was not altogether surprised when she answered, 'yes, perhaps,' and then added, with one of her naughtiest smiles, 'or perhaps for Franz Josef to indulge his enjoyment of dressing up the dead. He had that foible, Tomaso. He was always excited by a certain stillness.'

'Was that true?' I asked you later, and relished your denial.

'No, Tomaso,' you said, although I think that you were entertained by the notion, 'it was rather Luisa who enjoyed that certain stillness. She was the perfect partner for a time of war. For Luisa the associations of sex and death were, how shall I say, a little too close for comfort. She liked at least the simulation of a last battle and an early demise of her lovers. Indeed there are those, although I am not one of them, who claim that, on some nights, she rode with corpses.'

It all helped, I suppose, to buttress the legend. At any rate, the Marchesa was often to be seen fondling the glossy hips of her waxen Maria Vetsera, that sumptuous commoner who was found dead beside the Crown Prince of Austria in the most poignant of nineteenth-century suicide pacts. I wonder sometimes, though, if she ever asked you, perhaps at the height of the war, fresh back from a daring raid over Cattaro, and still in your stinking uniform, if you would indulge with her in some final act of self-immolation, mutual or not, and allow her the luxury of the last few moments to straddle your stiffening limbs in her ultimate orgasm?

But I never dared to ask.

'I met Bassani once,' you added, 'and he told me the true story of the hunting-lodge. He was there with the two of

The Bittern

them at the final supper. But I never dared to tell Luisa the truth.'

You never stooped, or rose, to tell me either. There were secrets between us, even then. But the words that were in the rubber bottles left in the Austrian bay, it seemed, were not to be one.

You smiled, rubbing the nose of the mutilated Cupid with your forefinger.

'I wrote this,' you said, lifting your hand from the statue, as if in recall. '"Austrian sailors! I could just as easily have come to rape your daughters, and to remove your own cherished anal virginity, as I have done to ravage your paltry ships. But I prefer to be entertained by those lovely spies, your female agents in the stews of Venice. Return when you will to free these abused mistresses from the toils of my warlike ardour. I shall be waiting, in blood and fire, to engrave my memory in your darkest and most ulterior passages. I salute you in traditional Italian style, with my hooked elbow and clenched fist. Signed: The victor of Pola, and the coffin-mate of the Marchesa de Casati."'

Well, there was laughter then, a stepping aside, and a scuffle in the bushes, while I, the eternal watch-dog, the discreet look-out, sniffed the blossoms of a tea-rose, and reflected, as often, on the bonuses of genius.

'I am ripe for death,' you wrote to me, after the death of your mother, a year almost to the day from that morning you collided with the gun-butt, and lost your eye. But it was the Marchesa, that day as so many others, who plucked you there, ripe as you were, with Eleonora's two protective emeralds green on your index finger.

The Marchesa's too, was the name on your lips when I spied on you that earlier day as you lay, I now see so clearly, like your own image of Giuseppe Miraglia, too still to be alive between those barley-sugar candles, and yet too mobile amidst the reflections in the stained mirrors, and under the orchestrated susurrus of so many time-pieces, to be other than a rippling zombie, a man ready to knock on a coffin-lid, a sort of pilot, or dolphin, able to lead the way to the land of the underworld, and there perhaps embrace or kiss this chosen one, whose name hinted at the first syllable of light.

Luisa, yes. But then there were two Luisas, the dread Marchesa, and also that other, younger girl, whom I remembered, under the grim brow of Scriabin, and have heard so often since, her lean fingers perfect on the brittle keys, her head high, as it always was, above the piano. To her I shall turn again, later, your last Luisa. But then, as I have said, I tiptoed away, and left you to your secret thoughts.

—II—

The Goldfish

I

THERE HAVE BEEN SO many images. That portrait of Cadorin's, where you posture in the nude, with a monocle in your eye. I see it now, in its marble niche in the hall at the Vittoriale. But the one by Sibellato, painted at Venice, where your eye is bandaged still, and you play with a lizard, where is that in the wake of the war?

The eye takes in, the imagination connects. The eye, yes, roving over a girl's thigh, or the slender foot of a greyhound; or the finger, gloved or naked, reaching under and through, to caress a pouting nipple, or prod a bronze elbow; even the slavering lips, mouthing a human shoulder, or a cold, sculpted face.

You began with sculpture. Began, I mean, your erotic career, if your own legend serves. Thrusting your whole fist, and withdrawing it bleeding and raw, from the bronze mouth of the Chimera, in the museum at Arezzo, and so bleeding, and filled with the transferred violence of that wrought image, forcing your eager lips on the burning innocent lips of your childish partner in art, the gentleman's daughter you had gone there walking with.

I like the tale. It has the ring of truth, the Chimera's ring, symbolic and tractable. You were always a lover of the solid, and the twisted. Sculpture lay all around, in your every house. You collected Buddhas, at one epoch, and I spent many a tiresome hour acquiring new examples, of all scales, for your mounting collection. There was one, I remember, that you carried all through the war, and exhibited, in your palms, when compelled – rare as this chance was – to attend the reprimand of a superior officer. The small figure, portly and calm, had the motto, in a fine Art Nouveau script, *I don't care a fuck for this*, carved in its lap.

At Arcachon, as in Florence, the casts of statues, normally Greek or Roman, and done in a friable plaster, bust or head or full-length figure, were never far from your hand. You moved through a stony world, or a world of miming stone, where your trailing fingers could always alight on a fragment of Athenian grandeur, or a chipped survival of Latin excellence, all done life-size in the best modern reproductive style.

You had Zeus, three-quarters of him, with a very considerable, though battered, organ, dependent, though as if arising, from a lacquered plinth. A somewhat hairy Euripides – or was he Neptune? – surmounted a narrow mahogany bookcase, that was filled with aeronautical magazines. The study, loaded as it was with books and papers – books usually on the walls, or on thrusting buttresses that came out and jogged the arm, like the memory, and at times in whirling or creaking rotundas, or movable susans, that stood on pillars and tipped out or clung on to whatever they contained, or were failing to contain – groaned, as it were, nevertheless, more with the intervening and ghostly figures, white as though from the eternal shades, of the classical heroes, the Greek gods, the Roman emperors.

That was the study. In your bedroom, of course, or rather in your official bedroom – for you always had two, the other to be shown only to the fresh amour, when the first had been proved unoccupied for its doubting and jealous *regulière* – there was always a bronze of the Charioteer from Delphi, his arms out above your bed, the reins and the horses absent, only his eyes, two flaring holes in that rounded skull, staring away towards the infinity beyond the final climax, the end of the great race

The Goldfish

in the black or gold-lined sheets, where there were only two runners – or, and I must be honest, on some occasions, three – when the tape came into view on the last stretch.

You arrived at Arcachon in the summer of 1910, in dramatic circumstances, or rather with a certain spy-story mysteriousness, engendered, and with much skill, by that exotic moth of the decadence, the wilting Comte de Montesquieu, or should I have written – the names blur so much now, in the shreds of history – the Baron de Charlus, or yes, alias, this too in the fictive trickle of the nineteenth century, the so totally etiolated des Esseintes, who commanded, at the age of thirty, a black banquet – everything black, the tears running on net stockings, tar jellies, jet napery, overdone meat – for the loss of his potency. I shall turn, shortly, to this *outré* episode – the flight from Paris, it might be called – and in so doing will elaborate that exquisite, albeit now elderly and a trifle infatuated, I fear, descendant of d'Artagnan, a man of myth, a man of riches, and a man, too, of some power to turn verses.

But shortly, yes. The essential image, first. There is always that, wherever you were, whoever for the present holds your attention in her wavering, or robust, hand. I have drawn your temporary blindness, and reduction to the horizontal level, in the aftermath of your collision with the gun-butt, amidst those glossy mirrors, ticking accurate clocks, albeit all at odds, and meandering candles, in the steamy swamp of Venice.

Beside the bare dunes, where the dry wind swept the waves into long, disconsolate clusters, and under the melancholy pines, redolent of sweet resin, and plastering the floor of their great forest with a bed of soft and yet arrogantly scented needles, my second image of your slow life in pictures must now emerge.

There stood, like a witch's cottage in a fairy-tale wood, the Villa Saint-Dominique, with its pitched, very steeply pitched, slate roof, its almost American wasteland of fretwork eaves, and barge boarding, and rather useless,

The Lion of Pescara

rotten-looking balconies, and its vast spread of high, small-paned and heavily curtained windows.

They came in close, those trees, whispering at nights, and waving their boughs during the day. They tapped the chimneys, and failed to hold off the wind, and were a nuisance to the visiting motor-cars, with the drip of sticky precipitates, that wore into immaculate paintwork, and set chauffeurs polishing and cursing.

Over the lawn, under them, there spread an array, often desolate and rain-sodden, it seemed to me, of curled wickerwork chairs, only suitable for the sort of English lounging that you never did at your afternoon tea. You were always indoors, or on a horse. You preferred to nibble at a cucumber sandwich or biscuit a little further from the reach of wasp or dropping cone.

There were days when you strode, yes, or much more often rode, along beaten pathways down to that exacerbating shore, where your drear barge, the *Astrolabe*, waited to be oared out into the awful current, and show your white-suited form, and your favourite animal of the day, slim-snouted in the bows, to those distant, allured lorgnettes, or even adjusted field-glasses, which watched from the cover of the headland.

An effete young Spaniard, the Marquis of Casa-Fuerte, one Illan Alvarez de Toledo, accompanied you on some chill mornings, your two pretty heads – his, of course, a little better covered with hair, and younger, too – only partly visible below a silk tent erected in the stern, from which the French sailors, got up as gondoliers – anticipations of Dante, alas! – would attempt to pole.

There were outdoor moments, yes. But the crucial one I select, and lay flat for the brush of my glue, involves that so crowded, and so called, study. You are standing beside one of those immense, but somehow enormously gloomy, windows. The sky, overcast, admits very little light. Shadows, like dark rats, appear to scud through the room.

You had stood so far several afternoons, your hand on one or other of those white sculptures, your face depressed and brooding, a cloak slung open over your shoulder, a

The Goldfish

clean white collar on, your beard – a beard, yes – rather neat and tidy. Your conversation flowing, or drying up.

Sometimes, although not often, you had walked through on to the terrace and taken a book, and attempted to beguile your boredom with a manuscript of Plutarch, or perhaps your own life of Cola de Rienzo, and always you had stood, even in the presence of visitors, in the attitude of preternatural stillness, exceptional movelessness, which I must attempt to capture.

You were being painted. Even at that exact moment, one day in July, that I must extract, and quite shortly focus on to, you were being painted, standing then in the middle of your cluttered room, and for a second appearing, when Rocco Pesche, your manservant of many years, announced the lady's arrival, almost astonished.

I like to think that this astonishment, albeit so fleeting, and such a minor strand, for the painter, in the many moods that may have threaded your features, is there, glimmering, in the finished work. I find it, or an echo of it, under the melancholy, and the so many other grander expressions that the literate and the critical have extracted and written down.

I had a room in the house, in those days, when I was not in Paris, or hunting for one of those many obscure or improper publications that you would send me for across the face of Europe, ransacking ancient libraries, or pestering great noblemen, or foraging in the mustiest undershelves of the dirtier bookshops in Naples or Verona. I loathed the seaside flies, and the dead spiders, and the moist sheets, and the amazingly inadequate steam heating, so unexpected a hazard in the life of one used to your care for a high temperature. But the house at Arcachon defeated you there, and was even too much for the kindling skills, perfected over years of practice, of the match-wielding Rocco Pesche, and the large-eyed newcomer in your life, that servant I shall call, as you always did, Aelis.

I shivered, therefore, at Arcachon, and left as soon as I could. So that what I shall say of that special confrontatory moment, when Madame de Goloubeff, your Russian mis-

The Lion of Pescara

tress of two years' standing, and a lady so statuesque and classical as to have formed a model, *en buste,* for the great Rodin himself, alighted from her Mercedes, and was shown in, and then saw you standing, your eyes on the sea, and your hands on the goldfish bowl, where your Chinese pet, Li Tai Pe, was moving at ease in its watery element, and then saw, too, your image on the canvas, half-formed as yet, but already no doubt with the bitter pleat at the lips, and the mouth as they said like a crater, and then saw, her gaze rising, like Venus perhaps come from the waves, to the luminous, huge eyes, and the square-cut head, and the dark American hair, of the painter herself, your Rome-born mistress of two weeks' standing, Miss Romaine, as she then was, Brooks, this I shall certainly have derived, in essence, if not in treatment, from the testimony of that oracle of reticence, but my confidant and occasional tool, Rocco Pesche, who was there and saw, and heard, and indeed remembered, it all.

Perhaps already, the image is clear. Not this time the withdrawn cavalier of that later epoch, wounded and in some genuine agony of body and spirit, the horizontal man, alone with his thoughts and under the nursing attentions of his virgin daughter, but now the upright and vigorous horseman within his own domains, on foot, indeed, but fully dressed, and attended in the striking coincidence of a passionate career, by not one but two of those ever-present acolytes of the Muse, the ladies of the bedchamber, the frail maidservants of his energy, the contrasting inspirations of a spring of poetry too thick and fast in its origins to be satisfied with any lasting or single imbiber, or for that matter, any one source.

So there are three elements in this remarkable picture I strive to paint. The picture itself, to which I return. The earlier mistress, to whom I shall also return. And the new girl in the landscape, the Yankee dauber.

She was thirty-six years old when you first met her, at an exhibition, and later a restaurant, in Paris, and she was as rich, through private means, and people dying, as your heart might require. She had already a hint of that style she

The Goldfish

shows in her own best image of herself, the battered top-hat on her head, at a slightly jaunty angle, like the Baron Samedi after a night's carousing, and a slightly voodoo look in her eyes, too, crossed with that little girl yearning and simplicity, and then, later, the leather gloves, turned back at the cuffs, and some of the butch properties she took over from Nathalie Barney, an occasional cane, and a way of stooping forward, like an osprey after a fish. But in those days she was still a painter, and not a character, and the best artist in black and white, outside Mondrian, the twentieth century has produced, that is, in black and white in oil, as it were, where the black and the white are in dim reality all the other colours muted out.

You sensed the way to her groin at once, of course, when deprecating the over-colourful canvases of Capiello, and remarking how much could be shown without using any colour at all. So you went, the two of you, out to Versailles, and you shot eggshells on a little fountain at a fair, and you won – one of the two of you, there are various accounts – that little orange fish, Li Tai Pe, which was also a mute witness to the arrival of the ponderous Russian on that momentous day.

Later she died, alas poor fish, when you sent her away to live with Romaine again at Versailles, and the tiny body, pining for her Italian poet, all Chinese and committed and lovelorn as she was, was buried in the grounds of the Trianon Palace, and the night before, so you swear to me, you had dreamed that she was in trouble. Not so much, of course, as she would have been had her tenure of the Villa Saint-Dominique intersected with that of the stilted and music-hating Evandro, whose taste for the elimination of fish was equalled only by his dignity in the expression of his dislike for Frescobaldi. But then you were lucky – some benevolent spirit, I think, intervened – in the combinations of your animal friends.

Not so with women. But here I anticipate. Romaine is alive still, no doubt, somewhere in that vast American wilderness that will govern us all in these post-war tragedies, but no longer known, as she then was, for the star of the canvas I think she could be. A clumping, dowdy woman now, I fear, with her heavy paramour, and not much in demand with the men who used to admire her muted tones. In bed as in paint, perhaps. But then who am I to say?

You kept her letters and telegrams, and over a hundred of each, in the Room of the Stump at the Vittoriale, with all your other unopened, or often unanswered, correspondence, and the ones I read there on my filing days, had a fine turn of phrase, now and then, and a power to chart some real depth of feeling for your isolation, and your impossible quirks.

She loved you, yes, and her love comes burning through that malevolent oil, and may still perhaps, where it hangs, or used to do, in Paris. I venerate its tones. I see it shimmer in puce and mustard, vomit-colours, and yet so appetising, like egg and liver, that forgotten tastiness of pre-war times!

2

I SHALL BEGIN with something from your own poem on that remarkable picture, a sonnet of course, done in French, and with a breath of Hérédia perhaps in its closing alexandrines:

> Here in your eyes I see where something burned
> And left its ash, and now your darker gaze
> Bright on the Gorgon's hair, in untouched awe.
>
> This is the famous purple dye of Tyre
> Twice round your neck; and this the wind of hope
> That lifts your hair, and crowns you with its breeze.

One might think from this that you were talking to yourself in these lambent lines. But there, I have been a little deceitful.

No, the obliging sonnet is not, of course, on the subject of your own portrait, livid against the curling waves. You wrote it for that matching canvas Romaine produced of herself, standing in the same attitude, and in front of the same stretch of shore.

Those were days of identification, the lovers waking with each other's image, *à la* John Donne, in each other's eyes. 'Twas but a step, no doubt, to transfer this image, two times over, changing only the length of hair, and the little beard, on to a pair of canvases.

The Lion of Pescara

There was Whistler in both, of course. The American dream, in those days, was always to surpass that electric reticence, to outflank the peachy florescence of Sargent and leap on through even greyer wastes than the most delicate of the nocturnes. I think that Romaine tried to be Debussy to Whistler's Liszt, and with some success.

In the finished picture, you stand with your head turned towards the right, your right arm leaning on some invisible pillar, the rose-grey fingers tucked, as it were, slightly in to your waist. A dark cloak enshrouds your shoulders, muddy black above the slate of your three-piece suit.

Indeed, slate forms the central tone, light slate of the waves, darker slate of your tie. That, and the bruise-purple, shading to leaf-sere of the troubled sky. And there, a little left of centre in the picture, like a dodging target, the leaden yellow egg of your bald skull, the moustache looking painted on, as it were for disguise, as in a French farce.

Romaine's own picture, you must be saying, has hardly such a masculine oddity. But then the heads are less, in their way, the point of these disturbing images than the oily swell of those colours, whirled and muted. Even your white collar, stiff and clean, as one must guess, has the look of a table-cloth where someone has tipped yolk on the linen.

Turning, though, from this quiet, wondering image of the poet in exile, which was on that summer's day still rather far from completion, let me fix my attention once again on the potent intruder to this charmed new circle of love, the dominating and fairly colossal Madame de Goloubeff.

Statuesque as she was, those shapely Juno limbs were apt enough for the melting entwinements of hungry passion. There was nothing stony, it seems, nothing of marble or plaster coldness, about the body of this Russian lady in coition. She had a complaisant, as well as a rich husband, and his almost, shall I say, Tolstoyan reasonableness ensured the good woman a free run in the satisfaction of her baser desires.

The Goldfish

We know a little of these, I mean the world has heard already, through the letters published, I think a trifle indiscreetly, by M. Pierre Pascal. There are more, which go further, and I have sipped on their lusty phrasing in the cool halls of the Vittoriale. But I shall confine my choice of example to those well known:

> I am dying from the desire to bite the nape of your neck and lick your armpits.

> All night, as I worked, I felt on my chest the hard nipples of your infrangible breasts. All day, as I slept, I felt your warm mouth run all over me.

Of course, it was one particular area that you liked the warm mouths of your women to run over, and we have ample evidence that Madame de Goloubeff became an expert in these oral attentions you so much craved.

I can sense those rosy cheeks, as of a Venus disturbed at her washing, and the bow of the lips opening like a sea-anemone to enclose the darling stalk of your eagerness amidst the frowning busts of the senators, and the snail hair of those eyeless boys, endlessly dragging their listless legs upon plinth or column.

Classical scenes, unclassical practices! It was rather the nymphs and satyrs copulating in the foam than the Laocoön strangled by snakes that you admired in those days. You were Zeus to her Leda, the rampant river god to her bending Niobe.

Romaine, one fears, with her dry wit, and her Transatlantic hygiene, can hardly have been so uninhibited in her arousal. But then, who knows? Women are strange creatures, and you taught a number your own disgusting, or satisfactory, tastes.

Imagine, though, this throbbing sculpture of animal sexuality, debarred from her lover, and driven on the back seat of her trembling Hispano-Suiza from Paris to that sinister forest amidst the sand dunes, arriving at the height of passion, and finding you cloistered with another woman, a foreigner in a smeary smock, with enormous

The Lion of Pescara

eyes, and a top-hat, and a cool air of being surprised by nothing.

There was more than one such visit, of course. I coalesce, and I synthesise. At the worst, if not on the first occasion, the outraged lady was turned away at the great iron gates, up which she was seen from the studio windows to climb like a frustrated orang-outang, orange and hairy, in a most unsuitable travelling-coat.

'I shall kill the man,' she was heard to cry, and I know from Rocco Pesche that a revolver was waved, either before or after this ascent of the gates. 'I shall kill the man, and then I shall kill myself.'

On that occasion, I believe a window was at last opened, as the lady collapsed, fatigued and in some distress, on the other side of those wrought-iron gates, and you leaned through the aperture in a red hunting-jacket, the perfect English gentleman, all concern, all good manners.

'My dear Donatella,' you called across the lawn, and through the straggling trees. 'I am so sorry to be unavailable. Please do come again tomorrow. I may then be free. I do apologise. But this painting is taking up so much of my time, and the artist has only a day or two to spare.'

That hint was taken, in time, and Romaine went back alone to Paris, from where she commenced her intensive battery of recriminatory, and somewhat elegantly plangent, letters. You were left *in situ*, to be pestered, and no doubt sucked, and slobbered over, by your jubilant, and never-endingly jealous, Russian.

She took a house near by, in the woods, and was said to languish there, and to solace her loneliness, on those many days when there were other causes than painting for your unavailability, with the crafty muzzles and the slippery limbs of your private string of greyhounds. Since, of all your girls, she was the one who best understood the needs of dogs.

Indeed, it was Madame de Goloubeff, reduced to this final service, who kept that rangy stable fed and exercised through the worst days of the war, and saw to it that all, or almost all, survived with coat and belly more or less intact

The Goldfish

and in fine condition. Let her take her mead of praise for that.

It was often there, amidst your greyhounds, under the pergola strewn with roses, or beside the kennels, embellished as they soon were by a pillared entrance featuring sculptured hares, that I used to walk and discuss your financial plans.

In the wake of that earlier Florentine exuberance, of whose full glory I shall have much to say, there were debts in plenty, creditors in shoals, and a wealth of middle-men, agents, and would-be exploiters and aides whose one object was to get rich quick, and to leave your affairs in much the state they were before.

'There must be an auction,' I had to hint one day, as you sleeked the nose of your favourite, Altair or Helion, and stooped like an old woman selling apples above the basket of her puppies.

'I have written a time-table for their feeding,' you said, ignoring this ill news, and your fingers unfolded a neatly inscribed sheet of your best writing-paper. '7a.m.' you continued, reading as if the words were a new elegy. 'Bowl of milk. 11a.m. Gog, Magog, Undulne, suckling. Afterwards another bowl of milk to all six. 3p.m. Bowl of milk. 7p.m. Timbra, Altair, Pisanella; suckling. Afterwards bowl of milk to all six. 10p.m. Bowl of milk, the mother to suckle all her young.'

After which you folded the paper, kissed the bitch on the nose, fondled the puppies, and stressed your prescription.

'It must be exactly so,' you insisted. 'A greyhound is the most noble, but also the most vulnerable, of dogs. They are free of that vulgar habit of faithfulness, which with the poor in spirit passes for a virtue. But they do need the right spaces between their feedings.'

Like women there, I remember thinking, and if one adds the Marchesa Casati, who had recently been telegramming you from St Moritz, to which alpine retreat she had gone, she said, to die, and perhaps also another two or three whom I shall allow to remain nameless, excepting, I think, the blameless and so operatic Eleonora, who had

The Lion of Pescara

carried, she said, a Grecian bee in her hands, and withstood the sting seven times, until the poor creature died on its last incision, and, alas, had thus had her ravaged skin in bandages for three weeks, with her and the others there were certainly half a dozen, as ravenous for their feeds as those groping puppies there in the basket, and, yes I must say this, too, as carefully loved in your own way, and in compliance with your own written or spoken prescriptions.

But this was not what I said aloud. I had other, more pressing matters in hand. 'The goods at the Capponcina,' I had to say. 'They are up for sale. They must all go.'

You had come to Paris, and later to Arcachon, in a kind of reduced flight, unable in any way to meet what you had to pay to survive in Italy. On the heights above Florence, that lovely villa had stood unoccupied, and withstood for a time the storms of the furious tradesmen crying for cash. But its day at last had come. Your whole world was to go under the hammer.

It preceded the same fate for Europe by a mere four years. There were bills to pay for a century of extravagance, and the Austro-Hungarian Empire was only one of the many casualties in the tail of your own less international, but still very considerable, and dramatic, collapse.

'In my whole life,' you said then, staring down at the blue-grey hide of the panting beast at your feet, 'I have made only one etching. It depicts a greyhound, sinuous and inexorable as this delectable bitch at my shoes, and the creature is nuzzling the foot of a near-naked woman, reclining on a couch, and half-veiled by a gauzy material ornamented with the signs of the zodiac. You would like the etching, Tomaso. It is very much your taste.'

I saw it later, a poor copy, worn and raw, in the museum at Bayonne, to which it was given, before his death, by your French translator, Georges Herelle. But this was another of your dreams, as I already knew. The etching was done by Sartorio, albeit no doubt on your most careful instructions, and therein the body of your early mistress, Barbara Leoni, Jewish in looks, and like a boy in her

The Goldfish

buttocks, reaches to tease the languid animal from an ocean of transparent drapery.

It has the look of a rat. Like a long instep, with ears. Which may be why you chose to remember the girl's foot, and the bitch's tongue licking the toes. As later, claiming you bore the corpse of Wagner to his last resting-place, you substituted the hero of your novel, this time *Il Piacere*, for your own less totally skilful personality.

The engraver there became yourself. Alas, you were never to master that etching skill. But you bore, yes more than one brave man, to his grave. That fantasy, and in Venice, too, came true.

On the day I brought you the catalogue of the sale, against the advice of Rocco Pesche, who said you would hardly stand the shock, you were equally absorbed in other matters, dividing your energies between correcting the manuscript of a poem on the Turkish War, and confiding to Aelis your views on a new variety of furniture polish.

It was a hot morning, and neither Romaine, walking on the beach and searching for different shades of razor shell, nor Madame de Goloubeff, exercising with dumb-bells in the tennis court, was in the house. You were calm, and in the throes of the sort of domestic life you so much enjoyed, and rarely had.

'Aelis,' you said, resting your hand lightly on the serving-girl's shoulder, 'you have to rub as if you were laying saddle-soap on a piece of tack. With a swooning, absorbed motion. Like this.'

'There are twenty pages of detail,' I interpolated as you gently massaged the rather shapely trapezium below the blue apron the girl was wearing. 'All accurate, so far as I can make out. The solicitors are checking.'

'Satsuma cups,' you said, flicking through. 'Did I really have seventeen satsuma cups? I scarcely recall such a well-extended phase of my Japanese interests. You know, Tomaso,' and this was your transference to that third strand in your current thoughts, the correction of the manuscript, 'I have never been keen on the humble comma.'

The Lion of Pescara

'I do know,' I said, and at that time I still wondered why you were always too sparing in your use of this convenient element of punctuation.

'I will tell you why, Tomaso,' you said, and you settled yourself on the floor, cross-legged, facing the girl who sat with her eyes downcast, a little coyly I fancied, and of course this was the period when even I was unsure if she had yet passed from the role of occasionally flattered woman-friend into that much more intimate one of companion of the bedchamber. 'And I will tell you, too, Aelis. It has the same interest as the right method of using furniture polish. Or collecting satsuma cups.'

You drew your fingers along your brows, and then picked up a small lotus cane that lay on a low table.

'The problem is this,' you began. 'In the first place, our word for comma, or virgola, is the, what shall I say, the diminutive of our word for ferrule, or virga.' And you lightly tapped Aelis on the bare shoulder with the cane, causing her to shrink away, and a pink flush to come on the skin. 'My dear,' you continued, all solicitation. 'Forgive me. I must have hurt you. A tincture of ointment is called for, and I shall ensure that this proper salve is laid on, in a few moments, with my own hands.'

This answered, I thought, my unspoken question about the bedchamber, or would soon do so. But I listened, as you continued. 'In the second place, in the Abruzzi, I have to tell you both, we have a particular sort of strong cheese which our gourmets will never eat until it is alive with parasites, and almost crawls, as it were, across the plate. I can never see a comma without remembering those little worms.'

I watched the blushing face of Aelis, and I thought of the larger comma the poet would no doubt shortly exhibit for her subtle annihilation in the customary manner, between her teeth. But you were only this third person, the playful poet, for a second, and then, again, I was close to your darker dreams and fears, as you laid the cane aside and allowed the glossy pages of the catalogue to riffle in your fingers.

The Goldfish

'Enamels, ivories, damascened boxes,' you murmured. 'All these things are no more than the casual accumulation of a life that must be perpetually reincarnated, and lovingly renewed. A worm-eaten carving, a beautiful though cracked glass, a rusty sword, even, may be easily renewed, or replaced. It requires the energy of imagination to accept the destroying as a stimulus to one's voluntary . . .'

But your voice trailed away, and I think that I realised a moment after Aelis did, as she rose, brushed her apron, and went without a sound through the door towards the kitchen, that you needed to be on your own for a while, as you were always too polite to say, but not always too courteous to indicate. So I rose, too, realising now that the girl had a subtle insight into your moods already, but not knowing then how long she would stay in your service or with what complete and obliging acceptance.

Longer than I, even. Closer than I, certainly if the arts of the couch and the harem can bring such closeness as money and books never will. But there was a kind of closeness, too, in what we had, you and I, and it came, tenderly, and with a sort of shy fervour, in moments like that one in February, with a breath of snow in the air, and an untouched plate of herring in front of you, when you opened the *Corriere* and murmured, 'Have you seen the account of the sale, Tomaso? Do you know they sold my desk for five thousand lire, and I only paid a mere fifteen hundred. I had scarcely thought that I had made so good a bargain.'

There was no more said, only the slight stiffening of your lips, and your gaze rising to go through the window and out across the terrace, and towards the sea, as if you had felt, suddenly, that you might have had enough, that the time might be due to say, yes, I will go, take my leave, say goodbye to the whole business, once and for all.

But you never did. The dark lady was always loved, but never taken. And only one or two of us were privileged to see your more immediate encounters with her. One or two, and once or twice.

3

It was Donna Maria, of course, who introduced you to Robert de Montesquieu. The Duchessina Maria di Gallese-Hardouin, to give her a somewhat fuller title, and your wife, to be brief, born to the so-called black Roman aristocracy, and the survivor of this disgraceful, or at least extremely disgracing, early marriage, had lapsed, in this middle of her long career, to the centre of a charmed homosexual circle in Paris, becoming, with her grace, wit and style, what the French often call a *madonne des tantes*, a sort of house-mother for queers.

In a modest apartment, with her magnificent yellow hair done up in a high bun on top of her head, to show her exquisite ears, and her delicate, rather bird-like movements, almost as though she was perched on ankles too brittle to support the folded wings of her buffon sleeves, and with a range of swooping and pecking mannerisms, like some sort of notably elegant heron, or a bittern without its boom, she would issue little cups of tea, fretting with neat hands over the serpentine orifices of her silver kettles, and subtly, at times almost too subtly, introducing her friends to each other in discreet whispers.

There it was, I say, that you met, fleeing with a pair of crocodile suitcases from the machinations of a man desiring you to make a reading tour through the pampas of Argentina, the persistent and, alas, it must be admitted,

The Goldfish

most generous del Guzzo, and avoiding, too, the enclosing ring of those creditors I have mentioned in the hectic arsenals and long-books of Italy, your much to be thanked, and most apt and suitable, mentor, the now fifty-year-old, or more, and rather bored, though still fluttering, butterfly, our Comte.

'There are stories, I hear,' you told me afterwards, 'that he was once in bed with a lady-ventriloquist, and this wicked woman, anxious to play a joke, and knowing his nervous disposition, leaned over her shoulder in the height of simulated passion and threw the voice of a brutal pimp into the doorway, thus causing the jumpy count to ejaculate over his tartan trousers. These bizarre trews,' you added, 'were then a Scotch fashion the old boy was touting. But nevertheless, he has his charm, and his ancestry. I admire his tone, and he does know all the best people, and many of the very worst, as well.'

This was, indeed, very true. The Comte de Montesquieu had walked in Verlaine's funeral procession, and had offered a little West Indian bird in a golden cage to Mallarmé's invalid son. He had been the mate of Gustave Moreau, in more senses than one, some said, and he patronised the more eloquent of Gallé's vases, on one or two of which his gnomic verses were seen to writhe in bilious green, or start forth in a sort of braille shrillness, against an undersea crimsoning.

Montesquieu was everything that the decadence had fought, or ailed, for, and his range of society acquaintances, one can hardly say friends, for his day, as they say, was almost over, was still quite extensive. You battened, you and he, on each other's qualities, his fastidious touch on the muscular arm of your – I think – rather Mediterranean charisma. The ladies were fond of this. You became the rage of Paris, and there were few salons, flashy, vulgar or of the most refined and easy perfection, where you and your ageing borzoi were not to be seen, the cynosure of all eyes, and the lodestone, as it were, of most nipples.

Montesquieu would introduce you, and you, after that, would astonish Montesquieu. The conquests, whether of the various *filles de joie* in whatever sleazy imitation of the Moulin Rouge might have taken your evening fancy, or, more obscurely, I sometimes thought, of the sporty wenches who frequented the racing tracks, of the bluestockings and the dry countesses, the spry daughters and the creaking chaperones, the famous Negress of Bapaume, and the most notorious blonde of Anjou, the capturings of hearts on sleeves and the conquests of forbidden purses locked in cabinets of American or Brazilian dollars, all, from the wine-swept steps of Montmartre to the railings along the spermy Seine, from Coulancourt on the underground to the bandstands in the Bois de Boulogne, all these and more were accomplished with speed, with the maximum publicity, and, I think, to your fairly total satisfaction.

There were six months of debauchery, and little written. Even you, at last, were showing the signs of tiring. I watched you from my little room alongside your vast suite in the Hotel Meurice, and I knew that the hour of departure, once more, could hardly be long delayed. The vixens were already baying at the door.

Of course, the most particular vixen was the lady whose mother, in those days, one heard, had rejoiced in the name of Zoë de Pelican, and had thrown or torn, no doubt, many feathers of her own breast into pillow fillings to make space for the matrimonial or adulterous couches awaiting her sumptuous daughter. Yes, I refer, of course, to Her Jealous Curvaceousness, Madame de Goloubeff.

'She is said', Robert insisted, as he danced on a pair of green patent-leather shoes between alcove and mantelpiece, on the morning we first were privileged to hear of the lady, and I think it must have been in his own rooms at the Hotel de L'Isly, over a thimbleful of cointreau and a madeleine, which formed his usual breakfast in those days, 'to have been the daughter of the celebrated Admiral Makaroff, who blew himself up with his ship, rather than surrender to the Japanese. But others, gossips, have placed her from Riga, the misdemeanour of a former piano-tuner. She has, at any rate, the authentic Russian madness. She

The Goldfish

breathes the mood of a Dostoevsky heroine through the nostrils of a Coan slave-girl shaped in Parian marble, no doubt by the hand of Praxiteles.'

It was much the sort of puff, or preliminary exposition, I had heard a dozen times already, and I knew that the whiff of mystery, and the solid ingredients of a plumpish sensuality, would have caught your attention, and determined your plans, even though you seemed shruggingly indifferent, as you sifted a portfolio of silverpoints, even, indeed, long before I knew that the lady had already surrendered to your demands for a day at the dogs.

You made the wise choice there, she was mad, as Diana the Huntress was mad, they say, about any spectacle, or pursuit, or conversation, or book, or play, or matter of any kind, that included some reference to, or involvement with, any sort of dog. She was like a bitch on heat, I believe you once said, when I showed her a photograph of White Havana.

So there in the satin sheets, on your large hired ottoman at the Hotel Meurice, while you elaborated your spurious plans for a work to be entitled *The Lives of Illustrious Dogs*, the lady yielded her, as it soon turned out, entirely virginal, and remarkably Lysicratean, thighs, from under flounce upon flounce upon Caucasian flounce of the most muskily redolent and most lavishly frilled white underclothes.

'I have rarely seen the like,' you confessed, or boasted, to me, later on, over a glass of reviving Beaujolais while we were waiting for the lickerish Robert, 'they were oceanic, my dear Tomaso, in their scope and variety, like the many waves of the Adriatic sea on a day of storm and lightning. It was as though the layers were being unwound from a bottomless onion, or, no, the elastic from a brand-new golf-ball driven to the very brink of the hole.'

These coarsenesses were in your vein that year, and I hardly like to dwell on their vague salaciousness, and their lack of poise. You grew more than usual the Abruzzi peasant, fresh from a thresh in the barn with a hay woman,

The Lion of Pescara

less the neutral poetic ironist I enjoyed rather more, and wished would return.

She had so much to answer for, that voluminous Aphrodite of the never-ending cami-knickers, idling in your vestibule with a deft aria from *Tristan* often on her parted lips, or swelling like a spent zeppelin on the best window-seat in your sitting-room when I needed some length with a view of the street to rest my wearied legs on, or worst of all, intruding with dogs, greyhounds like cracking whips, all yelp and S-bend, in the more intimate moments of our financial conferences, or our few times of quiet ease.

It had to end, and indeed it soon did. You grew overborne by the lady's engulfing closeness, her bulk of availability, her chance to be with you all the night and all the day, and yes, even, least wanted occasion, when you were free, you hoped, to indulge in a lonely bath, or be valeted, or massaged, or whatever it was, by some expert Andalusian the hotel had found for you.

So Montesquieu was cabled, and a special council of war took place, in his rooms at the Hotel de L'Isly. Montesquieu was thin, so thin, even at this date, I imagine a sideways look would have made him seem two-dimensional, like a wash drawing by Hokusai, as a shrewd admirer once said, or perhaps, even more, an outline done with a scalpel by Daumier.

His thinness quivered, like a reed in a wind, at the very idea of arranging some way out of your troubles in this entranced and spidery Paris that already had most of your genius warped and sticky in its toils.

'You must go,' he murmured, rubbing his lean hands on a tiny ornament of alabaster, a sort of pig, from Benin or New Guinea, I think, which his fortune had recently extracted for next to nothing from a country sale. 'The matter of Paris itself, my dear Gabriele, is at least as overweening as the immoderate substance of the Russian prima donna. Both must be atoned for, and as it were exonerated, or exorcised, in some moody if reasonably accessible retreat, in the Dordogne, maybe, or afar in

The Goldfish

Brittany, near a dim castle or a scarifying promontory. There are many spots to choose.'

'But when?' I inquired, anxious to bring these aesthetic speculations to some practical, or as it were railway train or steamship, specific. 'The lady is being obtuse, direct, and frankly, Robert, rather awful.'

'Paris, too, I know, I know,' he agreed, with a far-away closing of his lidded eyes, as if squeezing out a whole century of misapplied encounters and liaisons, 'and when, Tomaso, as you say, as how, indeed, must form the area of our deliberations.'

I recall that he had his fingertips together then in a sort of unconscious parody, as it seemed to me, of the still popular English detective, Sherlock Holmes, whose taste for cocaine, and ability to play Fauré on the violin, were qualities the Comte might well have been struck by.

'I shall work at this,' he emphasised, lifting his clotted and singular pig again, and stabbing the air near to his eye with it, 'and I shall in only one moment, I think, have the right and inevitable answer. Yes!'

And he rapped the poor hog down sharply on a fragile, wavering table, where a manuscript or two, surmounted with a meerschaum, tottered and slid away to the floor, before elaborating. 'Arcachon! You need, I believe, the dark wood, and the shuddering sands. A space between earth and water to cleanse your hands, and to solace your tangled spirits, in. It is there you must rent, and this very day, a noble villa. I have one in mind.'

'Robert,' you hinted then, and I realised with a slight shock that for several minutes you had sat in silence, and frowning, and obviously with a further vital piece of information to disclose. 'I have something else to tell you.'

So it was that both of us – for I, too, until then had been unaware of the grip that the fashionable Romaine, with her palette knife and her huge eyes, had already gained on the less worldly side of your being – for the first time gathered that there was to be a partner, and a most important one, in your withdrawal from the entanglements of the frivolous capital.

The Lion of Pescara

It was indeed Romaine, able as the Americans all too often are in these worldly affairs, who in the end obtained that Vermontish house in the woods, dealing with skill and aplomb, in her neat way, with the noble villa recommended by Montesquieu, whose cost, as I later gathered, would have nearly bankrupted even her own fairly considerable resources, but staying with his plan for Arcachon, which at that time, I am bound to say, had the right aura, and was widely in vogue for these half-secret retirements from the gay metropolis.

Half-secret, of course, was hardly what your so carefully engineered extraction could be called. Your baggage, one polished leather container after another, golf-clubs, briefcases, hat-boxes, wallets for papers and trunks for books, things bound in straps and things wrapped in ribbons, one by one, like the animals gathering to enter the ark, were sneaked out by pot-boy and porter, across Paris in cab or hansom, and mustered in sombre state under a coarse tarpaulin in the rooms of the Comte de Montesquieu.

Presiding like a male Mata Hari over this clandestine operation, which seemed to combine all the necessary intrigue of a grand amour with much of the surreptitious vivacity of a cheap novel by Dumas, the Comte twirled his moustache like a villain in a farce, put his finger to his lips as if playing a distraught under-servant in a melodrama, and generally behaved as if trying to make Athos, Porthos and Aramis become the laughing-stocks of posterity in his vulgar re-enactment of their most ludicrous adventures.

It was all like one of his jewelled poems, too much, too late, and too cloying. I grew bored as I vetted each one of his cryptic wires, advising a change of time for the arrival of a valise, or the departure of a Gladstone. The business of the luggage was at last a kind of chore.

But the actual removal, in true cloak-and-dagger style – for the Comte insisted on our faces being covered, and arms being borne, albeit these consisted only of a veteran Chinese paper-knife, with a chipped arc, and a loose handle, since nothing more lethal could be found at the

The Goldfish

last moment – the actual removal, both of your person and your name, proved a vivid experience.

'We must keep the initials,' the Comte decided, running through the enwoven monograms on your silk shirts, 'but I think that a change of name is essential. Gregory Dover might suggest a strongly Anglo-Saxon exile. G. D. Dowgrudder, perhaps, a more American type. Georg de Darmstadt was, I do believe, rather improbably a fourteenth-century maestro of the shawm. Guillaume de Aix-la-Fontaine is much too long, and a trifle unconvincing. I fancy that something shorter, like Guy d'Arbes, would supply your needs much better.'

So Guy d'Arbes you became, a somewhat cowled and startling figure, grasping an oriental weapon, and shadowed into a closed brougham, on a pouring wet night under a conspicuous umbrella, by your testy, though much amused, secretary, myself.

Amazingly, the ruse worked. The Russian madam was put off by my bland hand-spreading, and lack of news, over a gruff breakfast of eggs and liver the following day, when I was helpful, solicitous, and the victim, I claimed, of a slow migraine. She parted in doubt, and in dudgeon, and it took her, all in all, a couple of weeks to find your hideout in those resinous, whispering woods.

Well, hardly. It was one of your own sly telegrams, bored as you had become by the heady but rather cerebral delights of Miss Brooks's company, as you paced with her through a wilderness of fallen cones, or cut your feet on the edges of broken shells, that brought, and almost on the same afternoon, that immense weight of eager flesh, post-haste, to your lonely bedside.

It was all very much Montesquieu's affair. Later, when house upon house had run through his dwindling hands, and he had come to rest in that autumnal masterpiece, with its long slew of limestone steps and the flaking urns, the Villa Rose, I saw him once dodder to a chubby spouting Cupid, over a dank lily pond, and place an orchid, stripped from his velvet lapel, between its dumpy buttocks, and smile, shark-thin still, and lean over the Marchesa Casati, turbaned and kohl-eyed then in his wake, and say to her, 'Luisa, this whole house can be yours, and for nothing, not one franc, if you can but lift the drooping spirits in this melancholy garden, I mean these wayward and yet so flaccid statues, the outward marble of my inner lassitude. I need your help, and our Tomaso here, if he chooses, can walk aside, or watch.'

'Gabriele, you know,' she said, linking her arm through his, and solving my embarrassment in a slinking stroll with him over a plaque of well-groomed lawn, but speaking over her shoulder, 'as Tomaso knows, had a special jewel for these occasions.'

Then she was gone with him, through a gap in a yew hedge, and towards what final intimacies of the gross and elderly, what mind of mine can be jogged to guess at, or yield to? They were ancient ones, he more than she in those days, and she did, when the poor man died, and a year or so later on, buy up for a fair price that villa amidst the laurels, and restore a trace of its former grandeur, and hold some of her most atrocious and Levantine parties there.

But on this day, the last one on which I saw Montesquieu alive, although I do remember the brisk frisk of his grey moustache on the olive skin of his corpse, I turned aside, recalling, yes, that remarkable jewel of yours, where a pair of lovers, heads to feet, as it were, joined in that form of union so many experienced ones like best of all, the abominable practice known as soixante-neuf. It was much later on, and the Marchesa had been out of my life for fifteen years by then, when I remembered that this, too, you had said, was the instrument, when worn and caressed at the dinner-table, that had first produced those signs of a quickening appetite, the shifting legs, the lean forward in the chair, the osprey hook of the nose, that had first enabled you to make way with the icy chastity of the coldly deliberate Romaine.

4

THE TEETERING COUNT remained a promise in your life, and so often a fastidious presence, in those translated months below the needling evergreens. It was there, I believe, on some remote lawn, whirling his diamond stick, and imagining an airy drama in the trees, that he first implanted in your fertile mind the idea of a ballet for Ida Rubinstein.

'She has come to Paris,' the count once stated, on an earlier occasion whose object was to encourage your unflagging desire to meet a new friend, in this case one already the apple, or should I say the Russian vine, of the count's own languorous eye, 'for the sole purpose of showing herself completely naked on the stage. Or so they say.'

Undoubtedly, this occurred to you as a good beginning, but then there were many with such ambitions in those tumultuous years, and it needed a little extra to whet your inner appetites more keenly. With Ida, the little extra proved much.

She was Jewish, in the way so many Russians of high birth were Jewish then, with a kind of sinuous thinness unequalled until the pen of Erté began to work for the covers of *Vogue*, that is with a truly unreal, a dream-like, a woman's Christmas present of thinness.

She was married, and had engaged to appear both so and free, and retained her beery husband, so princely a man of stout, the Guinness boss, that later Lord Moyne, very much in the wings of her swift career, emergent as it first was in the stamping role of Salome, where the dry words of Wilde were soon lost in the pounding on board of those insistent, skilful, rather oriental feet.

She was no dancer, or none, I fear in the age of Pavlova, or even that brave Isadora who died strangled by her own scarf on the Promenade des Anglais, or wherever it was, but then with the elongation, and the dark, so very dark and frightening eyes, and the sense of style, the demerits, or shall I say, the absences, in her repertoire of movements were not so noticeable. She was far too tall, yes, and she never so far as I know, was seen to pirouette.

No, but then there was elemental lassitude, and then atavistic energy, in her extraordinary transitions from braided heaps of cushions on to icy banks of lily-ponds, a barefoot Eastern dervish, dressed only in a toppling aigrette, it often seemed, with such modest and lightly tinted nipples, bobbing in remote splendour under amethysts, that even the prudish could hardly discern their outline, or the lewd, and there were many of those, feel satisfied that she was, in fact, a woman.

This faintly androgynous air, combined with her sudden monopoly of the orient, her blue veils and her green feathers, her ability, as it were, to flick one lengthy scarlet nail and slice off the head of a sea-serpent, or an ermine moth, in mid-air, and her no less amazing power to float through the Parisian world of seducers and women-wanters, as if untouchably select, unattainable as an arum lily seen through the steaming glass of a hot-house, whose windows were wet with the tears of a sultan, these two elements, thinness and orientality, I say, were what most scored their mark in your mind.

As it happened, she formed the centre for a curious triangle of requirements. Montesquieu, infatuated with her, and eager to launch some astounding circus on to the blasé stage which would once again establish his own genius as the entrepreneur of the totally new, saw both a goddess and a star. The absent, though still current and

The Goldfish

somewhat involving Romaine, already tilting in the scale of her bias towards what would soon allow her the quiet epithet sapphic, saw what she had always asked for, a boy in girl's flesh, a streak of Botticelli, an already half-painted model, who would form the core of her own best oils.

Thus the two sides of that iron triangle, the influence of Ida, were forged in the deviant interstices of two oddly ill-assorted artists, the extinguished versifier of the yellow nineties, and the rising painter of the post-Whistler era. Alas, that neither should have lasted longer in the blast of Wyndham Lewis, through the raw breath of war.

Alas, but only half-alas. There was time for the slim Jewess to work her will, and stamp in your masterpiece. You listened, while Montesquieu that morning on the lawn spun his cane and his fantasy, in spidery zeugma, and your own thoughts, not only of slender thighs, twisting like the white flowers of bindweed, and eclipsing the heavier volumes of that other, more Trojan Russian, then banned for her extravagance, and sulking beside the greyhounds in a neighbouring chalet, but also, those thoughts, of a fresh poem, a whirlwind in French, a piece to be danced across the page of history, like a flash of explosive dynamite, more world-altering than the Turkish guns too soon to astound the Italian armies, those thoughts gathered, and wisely bore fruit, and were soon, yes, *Le Martyre de Saint Sébastien*.

You wrote in French, rapidly, and Montesquieu, discreet and at ease, corrected such solecisms, or Italian eccentricities, as might outrage your potential audience. I see him now, stooping like a sort of praying mantis over your shoulder in the study, as he guided the movements of your dashing quill. For a month or two, perhaps, he became my surrogate, as it were, though on a much grander plane, as a few would say, the abused Svengali of your recalcitrant genius, whipping the Muse into new fire, or damping down her more Mediterranean excesses.

Meanwhile, abroad and in France, ever on the move, it became my task to assemble the heterogeneous wealth of St Sebastians, past, future and impossible, as it often

The Lion of Pescara

seemed, from which your grasp would extract the quintessence, and through which the brilliance of that thin woman would lance like a rapier, as her tiny feet rapped through the as yet unchoreographed, or even musically fashioned, movements.

I went everywhere, extracting small bronzes, or their etched equivalents, out of rare cupboards in provincial museums, boring curators until they remembered some thirteenth-century treatment in marble by a long-forgotten Moor, now sweating under the weight of cameos, or hoisting foxy quartos where photographs in sepia, or actual original drawings, badly aligned and yet usable, had retained some echo of a differentiated approach. Indeed, I was on the move like a veritable addict, requiring my daily shot of arrows to keep me alive.

But the method was firm, and it had results. I returned one day in a dense fog, alighting from the diseased Railton you had forced me to hire for a long haul to Pisa, and entrusted in my weary arms with a *lignum vitae* altarpiece, or rather its few remaining grains, where a dim bare man gesticulated under a cloud, lifting a mass of flesh filled with sticks of celery like a child's model of a hedgehog.

'They are in the woods,' Rocco Pesche assured me, glancing up from his polishing of the soup spoons, when I asked your whereabouts. 'A mile or so from the dunes.'

In a cleared space near to the sea, where the fog had chosen to thicken into a petrifying mist, and the only sounds were an eerie distant sucking, as the waves choked on the shingle, I found three shadowy and insubstantial figures.

Montesquieu, in his great travelling-coat, lined with plaid, and surmounted by a fez, was reclining on a stone bench, his hands tucked under a grey muff. Some distance from him, and scarcely to be picked out in the murk, there stood the vague circle of a target, resting on a trestle, and so far as I could see at a cursory glance, quite free from blemish of arrow-shaft.

Nevertheless, as I stepped through the swirls of chilling

The Goldfish

mist, and was about to accost the slumped and so obviously frozen count, there was a low whizz, and something darted, in a swift stroke, like a wasp on a mission, past my ear and into the trees.

'Good shot,' I heard you shout, or rather I heard a sepulchral voice utter from the involving fog. 'I do believe that you hit the mark this time. There was what I should call a smart thunk, as of barb in cork.'

'Not so, also,' I replied, in a somewhat loud and fearsome drawl. 'It was only my indrawn breath. A gasp of – dare I say? – something like fear.'

Montesquieu at this, woke up, or at any rate, removed one weary gloved hand from his muff, and waved it in the air.

'From Treviso,' he murmured, surveying one corner of the altarpiece under my arm, 'and I think a very provincial attempt. The master of Bonn has had his macabre hand in the young carver's offing, and not, I fear, to our advantage.'

'Tomaso,' you said, emerging at this point from the wood, in English plus-fours and hacking jacket, like a caricature, it seemed to me, of a ducal golfer. 'Are you all right? The beneficent Ida and I were practising with our bows in this rather peculiar, and much to be copied, as it were, divine light.'

You were holding a form of engraved cross-bow in your hands, the sort of intransigent engine which must have so terrified the Italian soldiers in some early wars of the thirteenth century, and now a superb anachronism, not likely to have been fired in anger or, for that matter, in joy in several hundred years.

'It does fire rather well,' you insisted, seeing my incredulous look and flexing the interlocking strings in a way that renewed my fear. 'There are reasons, Tomaso, for believing that the cross-bow may have several advantages over the more familiar style of weapon here carried, as you see, by the saint in person.'

She drifted now from the fog, as if on a pair of winged shoes, more tall even than I remembered her, a wood-nymph in a diaphanous dress of some trembling kind of

The Lion of Pescara

muslin, partly covered by a dank stole, of superior sable, and with an immensely curvaceous and slender long-bow, like a dancing partner shortly to be strangled in her lissome fingers, for the moment slid easily under her arm.

Turning, as she reached us, and without any form of salutation, she reached into a now visible quiver of tiger-skin, which was attached to her waist with a green thong, plucked forth a long arrow, as if filleting a salmon, or drawing her own heart out, and fitting this instrument of extraneous damnation to the shuddering string, drew the bow back, with an unsuspected strength, until it bent, and shivered, as if at the point of imminent ecstasy, and then, crying suddenly one single syllable in a language I took to be Russian, but which might, equally easily, have been Hottentot or Mesopotamian Arabic, released the arrow in a straight, howling flight, amazingly, straight to the centre of the target.

Of course, it was only three yards away at this point, and such misty proximity diminished the strangeness of her feat, at least in my own jaundiced eyes, but the preliminary gestures had certainly been forthright, and elegant, and I clapped with the same politeness as the gratified Montesquieu, whose delicate slapping hands, in their puce suede, made somewhat less of a noise than mine.

'Bravo,' however, you cried, with a quite extravagant surprise and enjoyment, it seemed to me, and flung down your solid antique woodwork in order to embrace the sultry archer in your outstretched arms.

This conjunction, as others had done before, drew attention to your unsuitable shortness for this kind of linkage with the towering spindle of your accomplished young bow-woman. You gripped her, in fact, rather close to the buttocks, and even that seemed to require a certain height of reach, and some hint of the tip-toe in your stance.

But somehow, nevertheless, there was a conjoined force in your two bodies, the lithe spear of the dancer, driving up like a skyscraper into the mist, the earthy stability of the miniature poet, all fire and enthusiasm, as the words of his imaginative praise showered up like a firework.

The Goldfish

Romaine was in Paris that afternoon, though not on others when there was archery and some flights of wit and passion amidst the dryer firs, and she made her more vicious portrait of the two of you, the naked Ida bound at the stake, humiliated and flat-bellied, like one of those hunger-smitten corpses of whom we have seen the photographs taken by the British at Buchenwald, and you, the squat and obscene dwarf in a kilt, with an iron breastplate, and a mask, standing on a small, round object, a sort of palette, it seems, in order to be high enough to launch your pretty arrow, and beyond you both the grey sea, that sea over which the soldiers were carried into Abyssinia, and over which, later, the survivors of the holocaust of your heirs, the remaining Jews, have been smuggled into Palestine.

Strange that the very thinness of such extreme beauty, that confirmed angularity, like the strokes of a thing of beaten metal, which Romaine captured so well in her many photographs of Ida, and soon, one year, I think, later projected into that masterpiece, *le Trajet*, where the slender body, whiter than the soul of a Nordic winter, penetrating with invisible merit into the skin of a cloud, or a streak of semen, or a lash of oil paint, and flowing out from that in the beak of a bird of prey, or, no, rather a killer whale, or a pure shark, savages over the canvas, a dance of abandoned light, her bared ear so vulnerable, her twisted hair so female, her groin shaved and for ever closed at the core of thinness, yes, very strange that this, precisely, in those terrible images, that fed out a year ago over the front page of the *Corriere*, thinness, emaciation, lack of flesh, should have given the fate of her whole race such poignancy and such power to tap on the springs of guilt.

Yes, she was thin, they were all thin, but for Ida that anorexic attractiveness, that wonderful stripped-willow look, which was far, too far perhaps then, ahead of its time, soon flared like a tortured image of lust, of a sexuality too far extended to live, in those ten or twelve barren nights on the stage. The audience dwindled. First, yes, there were plenty, the riotous friends of the count, and the curious,

The Lion of Pescara

and the critics. But near to the end, there was only, it seemed to me, that fastidious, haughty aristocrat of the senses, alone in his gilded box, dipping over empty stalls to be seen applauding.

Well, you were too resilient to care much then, or indeed later. The life of action was already seething to full peak in your veins, and that early struggle with Turkey, even if largely neglected in your *oeuvre*, still triggered underneath, I think, as you read about Marinetti and his excitement at the bombardment of Pola, the realisation that your time was fast approaching, a new life, a more fearsome and telling involvement in the rapid flow of the world.

So you met your idol, Debussy, had a lunch or two with the maestro, and this made up, I suspect, for much of the subsequent lack of approval. Debussy, the greatest, or some would say the most opportune, of the French composers, had done your score, and it would survive.

You had had such odd relationships with the scions of the musical world. With Strauss, alas, nothing, although there were plans, largely unrealised. With Wagner, yes, that imaginary encounter that I have already touched on. But with, best of all, Puccini, an intimate, and indeed a rather gourmet, dinner.

'I took him,' you told me once, over quail's eggs and caviar in a restaurant in Palermo, 'to a little place in Le Havre that I had had specially recommended by the Marquis of Casa-Fuerte. There was wine, of the best. Rather dusty and warm bottles handled with reverence by ancient waiters. Low voices, and much discussion of fine points. An array of dispassionate courses. Fish after soup. Fowl after fish. The expected savouries. Mousse or soufflé, or even both. I hardly remember. And then,' at which point I recall your pausing, napkin to your lips in infinite recollection, 'the Sauternes. It appeared as if like a sacred vessel, borne as it were in the lap of the most illustrious of all these quite clearly aristocratic waiters. A glowing valve of a bottle. A bowl of glory. An incandescent flower. A glass was dried, warmed, held up to the light. The wine

The Goldfish

poured. In a most memorable, a most delicate and inevitable cataract. Never-ending, as it seemed, into the sparkling crystal. And the hand of Puccini, Tomaso, that hand which had stroked into graceful fortune so many instruments, to the melody of his genius. That hand reached out to hold and sip. And then. Then, Tomaso. That most illustrious of the waiters, frowning, stayed his arm. "If Monsieur pleases," he whispered. "A little cheese first. To cleanse, as it were, to clarify the palate." Why, Tomaso, Puccini was in ecstasies. We spent all the evening in the last refinements of culinary discussion. We never got off the food. So our collaboration, beyond the momentary magic of this one meal, was left unorganised, unspoken, and, alas, it has never taken place.'

But, yes, there was one passing collaboration, in a less aesthetic field, a more prosaic and yet elementary and striking one, that was consummated in 1910 at the Hotel Meurice, one evening while you were dressing for dinner with Eleonora, and the electric lights failed.

'Marconi,' you cried, snapping your fingers. 'How fortunate that the great electrician is occupying the suite upstairs.'

Up to which, in your shirtsleeves, and with diamond cuff-links dangling, these very ones I have in my dressing-table today, you strode with purpose, and there, exercising the whole of your sudden charm, and against all the criteria of those formal times, introduced yourself, and at once your impossible problem.

'Which only you, maestro, if I may make history in this way by asking,' you said, in your best rhetorical style, 'can solve.'

So Marconi came downstairs, and stood on a Louis-Seize chair, and unscrewed the bulb, and made some adjustment to the socket, and restored the illumination, like a common electrical worker brought in from the Bourse.

It helped, although of course, only a little. You were both too short-sighted to derive the full benefits from a bright light that others might. In the war, later, when better friends, there was one occasion when the two of

The Lion of Pescara

you, in the uniforms of officers, were seen to salute, in perfect unison, and without a moment's hesitation, a sergeant-at-arms, outside your barracks.

Marconi now has become that man of light, the most famous Italian, perhaps, of our troubled century, and its one good angel. But you, alas, are become the man of darkness, the opposite pole of his benefaction, and soon, too, to be forgotten, perhaps, even for your great vices.

Your little imitators have gone too far beyond the mark in the misty forest you set for the arrows. The posturing maniac in Germany, whom you called the Charlie Chaplin of the Nibelungen, has upstaged your archery.

5

SOMEHOW, IT ALL came to a head in Genoa. Invited, as you were, to deliver the opening oration at the inauguration of a monument to the expedition of Garibaldi, you took the opportunity to make your entrance, a return to Italy after what was, after all, only six brief years, a triumphal matter, a sort of heroic if somewhat stuffy progress, through a moth-eaten line of greatcoats, and a staid Victorian line of top hats, the carefully preserved insignia of the local burghers, the veterans of *la belle époque*.

I advance too fast, however. As always, the threat of your destiny, as Clotho or Lachesis unravels the cotton, or shall I say the years, hurls me on beyond the right moment, into later estuaries, even deltas, where the great water has broadened, or at last shallowed, if there were to be such a word, into other pastures or sandy beaches than the rich foregrounds I have to fasten my preliminary eye on.

You had let the Turkish conflict by, as I say, too fastidious to be wearied or worried over the intervention of the Futurists, with no more interest, you believed, than to puff the flagging careerists of the *avant-garde*, spending their idle weeks touching things in gloves, to appreciate, as they said, the texture of the world, and even, at war, extolling the shells bursting, through their volatile

The Lion of Pescara

mouthpiece, Marinetti, with a certain detachment of able violence. But you were on the watch. Those shredding antennae of yours, like nail scissors in their meticulous anticipation of what was growing too far, fanning and feeling through, picked up what was real and what would come.

So the big war, the true war, as you knew it was, could hardly be any surprise. It found you, of course, in Paris. Unaffected by the abyss into which *Le Martyre* had plunged, and where it lay, as it were, forgotten, you had languished only a little while in your web of seclusion. The need for the bright lights and the fresh ladies, a diversifying of the bitter triangles into which Romaine or Ida, Madame de Goloubeff or Robert de Montesquieu, no matter who, would mould the easy metal or your springy relationships, even a sort of elemental call of the hunting blood, the twitch of the Abruzzese, had soon pulled you, like a drawn cork, from the rotting piles of the Villa Saint-Dominique, and, so extracting, delivered you, panting, and eager for new fields to conquer, into the fetid swamps of Montmartre.

Actually, it was a furnished apartment, and the Avenue Kleber, where you began your first and most fruitful task of those early war years, I mean the composition of a film script. But then, you were still renting, and returning often to, the so rudely jilted Villa, and the rather specific term 'film script' in fact only covers a somewhat easy and secular involvement in the deeply religious business of the movie world.

You were still, in one way, a denizen of Arcachon, the man of the woods and the shore who had sat with his dying landlord in the little local hospital, and who would still walk or sail or ride for hours along those perilously abandoned and lorgnette-raked vistas, ready to mingle an afternoon on the brink of eternity with an early evening in the squalid looseness of the purlieus of purgatory, if indeed a forgiving deity would have ever allowed you so high or so interim a lodging on your way to perdition.

But write, and sometimes dance or eat, in Paris you did,

The Goldfish

and for weeks on end. There was even a brief if rewarding escalade across the English, as they love to call it, Channel, to some preposterous greyhound affair, much cosseted and attended upon by the British gentry and such more raffish elements of the aristocracy as would still be prepared to be seen at, and not said to be going to, the dogs. There you met lords and even a duke or two, and were at your best, very charming and well remembered, even years later, for your good manners and bearing and vivid wit.

Of this we had a fine example in the wake of that so controversial and much misunderstood affray of the cinema, your captioning, for I swear it was little more than that, of the early masterpiece *Cabiria*, later, of course, much altered after your unfamiliar intervention, which is to this day wrongly seen as your authentic work. No, it was hardly that. As I have said and will say again, you were cinema in embryo, the germ of the star system rather than the predecessor of Scott Fitzgerald.

Still, you accepted a phenomenal sum for your work, negotiated at some trouble by my own humble efforts, and arrived at after doubling the figure I thought fit to mention as the maximum you might extort from the parsimonious money-men. In the ludicrous inflations of these awkward years, what meaning would fifty thousand lire have, though this – then seeming gigantic – amount is the one you were finally given?

You were never easy with money. It meant little to your immediate mind that it might be wise to retain stocks of this dribbling commodity against the ardours of tomorrow. You spent and forgot. In need, you contrived more.

'Tomaso,' you would say, sharpening a quill, or nibbling, what you always loved, a lemon sorbet, 'we must have funds.'

This royal 'we' would always incorporate myself, your household, your mistress of the hour, your property, and, of course, most important of all, your slinking greyhounds.

The Lion of Pescara

'I suggest we consider a lecture tour of Brazil,' you agreed once, when I had inadvertently been the guest of the then president of that emerging country, who had supposed me to be yourself, and had lavished offers upon me for who knows what minuscule or temporary attendance upon his people's whims.

'Of course,' I had said, and the complex monetary battles towards an agreement for such an affair had begun. But alas with no more fortune attending their outcome than the earlier ones, of which I shall recount a miniature version, relative to your travelling for several weeks in the Argentine.

That visitation, too, was indefinitely postponed, and the egregious Giovanni del Guzzo, entrepreneur extraordinaire, who had offered you the world, or at least a million lire, was forced to make do, not with your actual presence, no, indeed, nor even the 'Ode to the Independence of the Argentine' on which he had agreed, albeit reluctantly, to fall back, no, rather only with (lo, when he opened the parcel in which he expected the reverenced ode would lie) a bundle of baby clothes to keep his little girl warm in the icy mountain air.

There were many such affairs, abortive in their outcome, promising untold riches, or at worst a modest and reasonable competence to keep the proverbial wolf from the door. But you had little concern. Less, perhaps, in those heady days of the onrush towards the war than at other times. There were things coming to birth in you, the dawning of a new era, with which money had nothing to do.

You felt the stirring of a fresh initiative, the gathering of your forces for a public, indeed for a military, career, and the lancing of your darts into the receptive leanness of Ida Rubinstein was only the dry run for a more lethal and a more enduring deliverance of warlike materials.

This was not, of course, to be only a matter of the familiar and solid projectiles of battle, the high-flying and the low-speeding attendants of death, injury and the redrawing of political borders, those shells, bullets and

The Goldfish

torpedoes of which you were soon, as I have shown, to manage your due share.

No, there was first, as there was last, to be the winging of words, the transfusion of passion into literature, though not the cold wayward language of the page, the now exhausted and unsatisfying material of the chronicle, the newspaper and even, perhaps, the stage or the silver screen. These were the interim stops, it now seemed, in your transit from action to action, the conceptual fury of intercourse in bedroom or dance-room that had once led you to poem upon poem of lyrical splendour, dauntless and Shelleyan, lifting above cloud and seawave into everlasting magnificence.

That had been yesterday, the abstracted, readable immortalisation of your own life in private sexual freedom. Tomorrow there was to be the freeing of the world, the forging of a new Italy, even a new Europe, in the meditations of a Nietzschean hero fresh with words on the winds, a mouthpiece ready to fire off, like a trench mortar set on a hill, his own death-dealing or death-defying message of pride and originality.

So it was that you turned to what has been called, later, in the slimy bowels of that little rat-footed and thin-skulled emancipator of hatred, I mean their Dr Goebbels, propaganda, but what in your own day you saw as rhetoric, the sacred vessel known to Cicero and Demosthenes, the first art of the Greeks, the most threatening and most life-infused vehicle of the human spirit the world has known, the art of oratory.

You spoke here, you spoke there, you became the first voice of intervention, the spear to prod the sluggish Italian government to the point of throwing aside its last fetters and opposing the foe. You discovered, almost overnight, it seemed, your power to move the masses as you had often, before, in a room at the Capponcina or in Rome, touched the hearts of the few, replacing the poetry of line and rhythm with the grosser, but more satisfying, poetry of the prose slogan, the great surge of name and feeling, spoken out in a crowd, from a balcony or a plinth, twisted by the

The Lion of Pescara

breeze, but caught and held like a flag in the composite will and brain of the multitude.

You had foreseen and in some way foretold your future here, of course, in those clanking alexandrines of *La Nave*, later to be filmed with some success by Ida Rubinstein, and already the only one of your many stale dramas to have held the Italian boards, and indeed the flush of your patriotism was no new venture, you had shown its tinge through the years from the 1880s onwards, even, in those far-off days, predicting the future use of the motor-torpedo boat in an adolescent article for a small newspaper. But the true rush of your rhetoric, its proper blooming, far beyond the wildest dreams of the poet in *Il Fuoco*, who saw the interior stage of the heart, I think, and the outward stage of the new Roman or Venetian theatre, as the only *arenae* for the tremendous revivication of the national energies that his will demanded, the final tissue-culture of Italian spiritual renaissance, the mature blossom of your speech-making, I say, was to come, not indoors, or on an opera platform, but in the open forum of a public square, beside the *mare nostrum*, a few yards from where the ten thousand set sail to enter destiny, at the sea front in the rather sleazy little town of Quarto.

At two-thirty on the afternoon of May 2nd, we crossed the border at Modane, leaning from the window of a plush first-class compartment, not yet paid for, and you turned, with real tears in your eyes, and said as I seem to remember, 'Tomaso, we are back at last.'

The word of your arrival had been fairly effectively stage-managed, I think, in my series of letters to the newspapers, and the local soldiers at the frontier had seen your picture in their magazines. There were even enough Dalmatian exiles to allow your famous remark, on being presented by them with a plaster copy of the lion of St Mark, 'Italians, when you are made one with the mother country, the real beast in the square at Venice will once again be your own,' to be printed fairly widely, and to assist the rapidly rolling snowball of the movement for intervention in the war.

The Goldfish

But you were truly moved, and so, I must own, was I, by those eager crowds outside the train windows, the reaching hands, the faces upturned for a called and cheerful greeting, or on some occasions for a swift and snatched embrace or a kiss, as the slow train, for it seems to have been a slow one that I had in effect managed to get seats reserved on, slowly, and even more slowly than it should have done, made a royal progress towards Genoa.

There we booked in, though never, I think, or not for many a month, receiving a bill from the manager, at the Eden Palace Hotel, from whose crumbling and suitably baroque balcony you had the stroke of genius, yes, it was almost that, I suppose, to deliver a trial run of your speech for the following day's inauguration.

I remember the double windows of our bedroom, the one above the doorway, and your sudden change of expression as you stepped forward and threw the curtains back, seeing the enormous crowd below that had followed our gasping Mercedes from the station, and how you turned suddenly twenty years younger, as though the troubles and the debauchery of Arcachon and Paris had been melted away in a furnace wind from the street, and there was the blaze of decision in your transformed features, and yet you were still joking and enjoying yourself even as you had the idea and felt the words beginning to surge up honest and strong.

'I shall speak now, Tomaso.'

'Surely,' I was almost protesting, leaning our battered leather suitcases on the satin covers of the beds, but you had already thrown the shutters wide, and had stepped through the glass doors, exactly as you would soon do so many more times, for seven years, all through the war and later at Fiume, and there was the first of those many familiar bursts of cheering, the great unbroken swell of the mass voice calling for you, the right man at the right time, as you had learned in a moment's insight how to be.

I remember standing behind you there in the darkness of the bedroom, a solitary unseen watcher, male rather surprisingly, and on subsequent occasions, alas, and to your own immense amusement, an acolyte assumed in the absence of any female attendant as the natural bedfellow of an eccentric genius, not of course to be bound, as the Greeks were never bound, in the bourgeois chains of a purely heterosexual sort of relationship, and yet nevertheless, or perhaps in consequence of this, in such a fundamentally staid city as Genoa, frowned upon and forced to endure a certain amount of coarse nudging and winking.

An unseen watcher, yes; and an unseen hearer, as the melodious cadences of that unpremeditated oration began to flow through your lips, lifting and falling like a benison of leaves on and over the heads, in more senses than one, of the gathered men, thousands in their boaters and cloth caps, ordinary men, very different from the following day's reception committee in their fancy dress, and a few, yes, even a few women out there, laying aside their baskets, or their skinning knives, where they worked on the quay, or were returning from there, and listening, all listening, like the animals in a remote forest, to this bald Orpheus of their outdoors, the tantalising message-bringer of a new era.

The banal porcelain of the handbasin was transformed as I listened, standing amazed of what you were doing, with a shoehorn in my hand, and a need to pause and empty my bladder, but unable to move, even to lay down an ordinary object, even to satisfy this basic requirement of the body, as I drank in, as if in a kind of thirst, what you were pouring over me there, the wine of deliverance, the stimulating alcohol of a promise, the unsuspected hope of a fresh destiny.

Whether it was a miracle or a trick, many, myself included later on, have disputed, and there was always doubt, I know, allowing for the susceptible weather of those drifting pre-war days, when the young English went to battle 'like swimmers into cleanness leaping,' about how far these crudely patriotic and somewhat overblown sentiments were in themselves, even with your astonishing voice, enough to have done what they so evidently did manage to do, bring Italy into the war.

The Goldfish

But, yes, they did exactly that, when repeated at the monument on the following day in Quarto, and then again at a banquet in the town hall, to the serried ranks of the rich, and then again in Rome, on one occasion with the Queen concealed, and known to be, behind a curtain on your balcony, when spoken from so many balconies, and when reported even, with additions or adjustments, in so many newspapers. You became the voice of the people, and this was the first time for many a year that the people had had a voice.

'Blessed are the young, who starved of glory shall be satisfied. Blessed are the merciful, for they shall be called on to staunch a splendid flow of blood, and dress a wonderful wound! Blessed are they who return in Victory, for they shall see the face of a new Rome, its brow crowned again by Dante with the triumphant beauty of Italy.'

As you reached these words, and ended, in a swoop of power, with your celebrated and then instinctive parody, if I dare say it was that, of the Sermon on the Mount, I let my shoehorn fall, and ran for the lavatory, hearing the voices of a thousand Italians break out all together in the words of 'the Marseillaise', a song very few of them, I thought, had even known the name of before.

'To war, to war, to war,' they began to call, and from then on the journey to the brink and over the edge was inevitable.

That day, I remember, I stood above a blue-veined receptacle that had held the wastes of a thousand visitors from the 1880s to the present day, watching my own paltry edition in a spindling stream, and seeing, as in a vision, the end of Europe as we had all known its lovely shape for fifty years, and the harder, more cruel one that was coming to take its place, a new shape forged in the barrels of guns and the fins of torpedoes, and one that would lift your own fate into one indissoluble from that of the twentieth century.

I stood, shaking the precious drops away, the last of the Edwardian age, in some ways, and I felt my mind race back to your cluttered and statue-filled room at the Villa Saint-

The Lion of Pescara

Dominique, with the easel propped in the study, and Romaine dipping her brush into a new trace of grey on the palette, and your own cloak falling away over the three-piece suit, and under its dark wealth the other, more gaudy suit, the uniform of a lancer, with gold buttons and a flash of red at the collar, as in Romaine's later painting, done on the Giudecca, and on the very day you heard of the death of Miraglia, broken in upon and uprooted suddenly, and, as if a living thing, with a full sense of its own vigour, its meaning and its danger, striking through the canvas and taking its rightful place, the heir to your whole earlier career, the soldier's métier that you had always desired, advancing to grasp your arms under its pips and braids, and fling you forward into the seat of your horse, or your aeroplane or your motor-torpedo boat, and to make you blind, and famous.

—III—

The Horses

I

THERE ARE SO many ways your story might have begun, so many titles I might have given your book. In the case of every great man, there is a beginning, a birth, perhaps not always the real birth, but a legend, a kind of myth which encapsulates the true essence, the blur masked by time.

They say that the corpse of Bismarck was laid in an empty grate, the doctor making a slitting sign across his throat, and the child in all eyes that were there dead, when his mother, turning yards away on the bed, was heard murmuring, 'Listen, is that a rat I hear?' and the boy was alive, opening a raw mouth like a small furnace to cry in pain where the fire might have been.

In your case, the legend was one you fostered, I know, by your own invention, supposing the birth to have taken place on a ship at sea, in the Adriatic during a storm, and the name of the ship you claimed, for some alien reason, hard to refine now, was *Peace*. Yes, that might have given me a fine title, *The Child Born on the Barquentine Irene*.

Your death, too. There are nuances there, in the final words that broke through your dying lips. A Glass of Pure Water. But, no. Neither the beginning nor the end seems where the story ought to begin.

The slides go through the magic lantern in whatever sequence the lecturer may dictate, or the groping hand in the darkness require. Perhaps a few fall on the floor, and

The Lion of Pescara

are taken up and replaced in a fresh, and even a more revealing, order.

Overhead, night after night, I hear the English or the American bombers, patrolling still through the early days of their ceasefire, and I turn the handle and lift the grey squares one after another into their slots, reduced from a film-maker to an old man playing over the fixed memories of a life exhausted in banal service and carbon-copy debauchery.

Florence, yes, that comes later. Fiume, later too. But Florence, this was perhaps the heart of it all, the most golden moment, the little house you bought on the hill to the north-east, above the olive trees, looking down over terraces to the famous domes and towers you remembered from visiting as a schoolboy.

Florence! This was the magic name of your beckoning aesthetic and sexual mentor when, at the age of sixteen, pawning your watch for the cab fare, you came over, hair slicked flat and hands in brushed pockets from your draughty school at Prato, to attempt for the first, enervating time the alluring recesses of a woman's bought, and spectacularly available, body. You were lucky then, or virile, or maybe both. She refused, you used to say, any form of remuneration for her deft service, and even, yes, you were proud of the detail, offered to give you an old violin – a Stradivarius perhaps, but you never went so far – as a parting gift.

So that where, so many centuries earlier, Dante, loitering beside the Bridge of Sighs, as I always picture him doing in that elementary picture by the Englishman Henry Holliday, his hand on a fourteenth-century hip, and the usual ascetic grimace distorting those over-fastidious features as he gives the eye to a twisting slinky-velvet-sheathed woman, alongside a more slender straight-limbed miss in a yellow dress with a flower, who stares straight ahead, and may, I suppose, be Beatrice, where Dante, I say, first caught the whiff of passion never-dying, you, too, a mere boy in a rumpled set of tweeds, with a strong thrust in your sappy wand, inaugu-

The Horses

rated, or launched, your own more debased version of the quest for serenity.

There were many models to enliven this quest, or enrich its value with subordinate meanderings, and your days in the ancient seminary were divided between the unexpurgated editions of Juvenal and those moments when, from the early age of nine, you were able to guide the hand of the sewing-mistress, as she tried on your new nightshirt, into an area between the thighs not exactly required for a precise fit of this newly prepared upper garment. The girl protested the first time, you say, in that so often glamourising and yet quaintly honest memoir, the secret book of your last years, but what of the second occasion, the third, one wonders, for you were ever a persistent seeker after the required satisfactions of your appetites.

No, there was early sex there in the creaking school, for sure, and the usual abstract admiration for chosen friends of the classroom, too, not least that so oddly lashless companion, Dario Bondi, who looked like Napoleon, and cultivated, no doubt, the same penguin walk, and the soaring ambition to make some figure in the world, even although, later, and at the Vittoriale, in shame and penance, that same Dario Bondi, now an abandoned and bankrupt outcast, after years of double dealing, returned to pray your forgiveness for passing off dud cheques, to tide him over until better times, in your by then much honoured and famous name. You forgave him, of course, remembering only the smell of chalk dust in the little dormitory, and the stains of ink on childish fingers, and the long nights run through in the mutual elaboration of Corsican dreams, the manipulation of the Grand Army, the avoidance of any retreat from a Russian adventure, and the common support of a certain gentle infatuation, higher no doubt than the actual coarse involvements of man-love, but a source of satisfaction then, and tenderness, and a lasting boon.

So you survived your Dario Bondi, your little Bonaparte, and your sewing-mistress, and your trips to the stews of Florence, cruising the Renaissance of church and alleyway

The Lion of Pescara

with a copy of Ariosto in your overcoat, and your eyes and thoughts on Donatello's pulpit, and the chapel decorated by Filippo Lippi, and the tympanum you entered the church under by Andrea della Robbia. They were names of heroes then, but more than names, the ikons of escape and glory, too, the precision instruments for the young artist-adventurer to grope his way to power through.

Yes, they recur, and so often, in nooks and corners of your best writing, verse or prose, the immense gleaming forbears your genius recognised and was overborne and fed by, the paladins of a festering classicism.

It was this that you battened on, later and often, grappling and rearranging the guilt and the horror around some profound core of a quasi-religious mysticism, a latent awfulness, below an arch or a colonnade, of appalled, even stunned, magnificence of a Christian awe. I see them now, so many times renewed and exhausted of all they were, turned fresh from simple villas or plain hotel bedrooms into the baroque re-enactments of your early fascination with the age of Alberti, those many hired or purchased apartments of passion and dedication, your several homes.

The Capponcina, there on its hill amidst the sheep and the cypresses, in a little village already famous for the brush-swerve of Böcklin, the least Renaissance of your admirations, whose 'Isle of The Dead' had already set its throbbing heart in the glaze of your Venice novel, The Flame of Life, the Capponcina nevertheless, at a stroke of your will, obliterated this recent aura, the symbolism of the present, and was very shortly your most exacting monument to the thirteenth century.

You hired the house for a high rent, and then paid far more to insist on the owner's own furniture being removed. Your first shell it became, your opportunity, with more money than ever before, to indulge those tastes for the echo and resurrection you so much lusted after.

Of course, there had been some hints of your flair before, even, once, in that former saddlery of the Palazzo Borghese, which you transformed into a condensation of your dream, a bedsitting-room, in modern estate-agent

The Horses

parlance, with a grand piano, albeit untuneable, a bench of antique vellum books, a quantity of damask, moth-eaten but resonant of old hues, and a plaster bust, your *chef-d'oeuvre*, of the Belvedere of Michelangelo.

In Francavilla, too, where Maria Gravina had been left for the Duse, nursing your future amanuensis Renata, there had been some experiments, a Japanese room, a little imported timberwork, and a few sepia photographs. But it was left for the Capponcina, on the edge of the city of Art, your noble Florence, to array herself in the finery of refectory tables, lecterns, and gilded wood.

There was gold everywhere, the saturation deepening from room to room, the shades muted or emboldened for study, meditation, music or repose. The windows were a laceration of stained glass, delicate in fragments that admitted only a thread of light, or engorged into thickened spheres, like alabaster, that admitted only weird glows.

Through these dim colours you moved in a rustle of silken pyjamas, or a swish of some oriental kimono, or mandarin's robe, tinkling little bells for service, and sometimes playing a fugue of Palestrina from the gigantic horn of an early phonograph.

In a swirling darkness, accentuated, as it often seemed, by the heavy odours of rare perfumes, or the last expiring scents of familiar blossoms, or sometimes, indeed, the less amusing aromas of lost or forgotten excreta, where one or other of those inept and scandalous greyhounds had left her calling card, there was little space to move. Indeed, any sudden or protracted intention, signified even by something as gradual as a gesture, might be calculated to impair the balance of hour-glass on occasional table, or Indonesian vase over slipping brocade.

Everything, even in those years, had assumed the mark of your future, much remarked-on style, the D'Annunzian topping-up, as it were. On an ottoman there would lie a cushion, on the cushion a lace shawl, on the shawl a portfolio of engravings, on the portfolio a saucer, on the saucer a propelling-pencil. Sometimes the disturbance even of sitting down would arouse a clatter as of precious or indefinably fragile china in final ruin.

The oppressive heat, moreover, on which I have already touched, was at its high pitch of polish, and the reception hall, where unwanted visitors were kept standing amidst dull marble, was allowed to assume the intense radiant atmosphere of a steam-bath. You would enter, late, all cool in your loose clothes, and have little difficulty in curtailing the patience of even the most persistent of bores, choked, as they would all be, in their outdoor coats.

There were servants, of course, in plenty, a total of fifteen, I believe, at one time, though there are those, I see, who have said you employed a full twenty. But the trinity of influence, I like to think, was formed by Rocco Pesche, already your discreet and immaculately dressed *maître de chambre*, I in my riding-habits or motoring-clothes, and a fierce old virago who ruled your several bedrooms, Anastasia, whose peasant law would allow you, as a man of normal red blood, one mistress at a time, but whose conscience baulked at several.

Several, of course, there were, and not all, to suit the convenience of the prudish Anastasia, in sequence. But you would resort to a range of polite expedients to mask each fresh arrival, or at least her destined fate, from your affectionately regarded old servant's gaze.

'I am going to work, Anastasia,' you would say, drawing a worried hand over your glistening eyes, as you waved over your shoulder to some half-dressed young sportive to quiet her giggles, 'please arrange matters in order that I am quite undisturbed.'

So it would be, and the doors in their oaken architraves, grim below carved mottoes, and in particular your favourite, ambiguous *per non dormire*, which you had once had specially carved above the guest bed for the mistress of the King of Spain, those doors would remain quite firmly closed.

Wakefulness, though, by day as by night, might as easily mean hard labour at your writing-desk in the best of those

The Horses

Florentine years, when twenty-five thousand lines of lyric and dramatic verse flowed from your head.

You would breakfast, and ride, and be at your place by nine o'clock in the morning, standing at your sloping reading-desk, with the first of your twenty quills of the day in your nimble fingers. You had a bowl of the best close by, stripped, as you liked to say, from the living bird, and beside the quills there would always be standing a pitcher of water, a gathering of good fruit, some peaches perhaps, and a few grapes or country apples, and, rather surprising to many eyes, a tin of English biscuits.

'Some weak tea, please, Anastasia,' you would often ask for, too, if the good woman was anxious to know if you would require any further sustenance. 'But it has to be iced.'

Then all day long, amidst the breath of fresh aromatic roses cast here and there across the floor, and the remote sounding of monastic bells for the meals of others, and under the fluid solace of oil-lamps, in a dozen artfully concealed niches and apertures, the subtle clepsydras of yellow glass that shed the smooth glow you seemed to need for the loosening of the locked imagination, you would lift and hold straight ahead of you, in the stance you had learned from a Zen painter, the tool of your Muse, the slim crescent feather of your ink-thrower.

Those were your hours of isolation, the real monkish areas of your otherwise quite unsecluded life, when you worked alone against the demon retarding the breaking of the dam, wrestling from his gnarled grasp whatever souvenirs of the struggle to be clear and free your courage and wit could procure.

Then it was evening, time to change, and perhaps the hour for your horses again. More than any others, these were the years when you rode. In the morning naked, as some claimed, along the sands, or at high noon, when not working, spotless in white flannels and jacket, on your white mare, Undulna, so that ribald bystanders had been heard to ask if you were posturing for your statue.

She was a crook horse, that one. I was there with you the

The Lion of Pescara

day she stumbled on the shore at Pietra Santa, and you were thrown from the saddle, with one foot still caught in the stirrup. You were dragged for a hundred yards, your head miraculously not severed as you bumped over seaweed and lilies, a rash of pebbles, a sudden scatter of broken glass.

'Gabriele,' I called, setting my spurs to my own mount, well in the rear, and far too late for my arrival to have been of much assistance, had not the goddess of luck, as often later, been kind, as she now was, to your misfortunes. 'Are you all right?'

I was on my feet then, bending above the muddy suit, and the bloody head, of what I had almost assumed must be a corpse. But you stirred, looking up with a smile, and a wave of your hand.

'Nothing,' you said. Then you took my helping hand, rose up and walked over to a pool of clean water left by the receding tide, where you washed your face. Then suddenly, turning, you flung back your head, and I saw that you were mouthing something, in silence.

'What is it?' I asked, fearing for a second for your reason.

'I moved through a long time as I lay there,' you said, frowning a little. 'I felt the sap oozing from a broken twig. I heard the hoofbeats of Undulna as she ran on. Then I was in another place, in the air. I had sea-gull's wings on my feet. On each ankle there were two, blue and green. I flew above the sea, very high, for ever.'

Then you whistled, and waited for Undulna to come trotting back, the winged Pegasus, as it soon turned out, of one of the greatest odes in *Alcione*, the one that begins with the flight above the Adriatic on the wings of a gull.

Horses, yes, they were the inner symbols of your lust for speed those years, the flickering waves of your need for youth, to be strong and fleet as you once were, to put over your shoulder the sense of age, and the leaves falling, to be spring and vital, all air and light like the English poet Shelley whose grip you were in.

It hardly, in retrospect, seems odd, after all, that you enlisted, in 1915, as a lieutenant in the Light Horse of

The Horses

Novara. The cavalry of the spirit had formed your regiment for more years than I can count.

Yes, there were horses waiting, and grooms with saddle soap and brushes, every night at the Capponcina, too, when we went back there from the coast, and from our forays to Rome or Naples, and, behind the grooms, and the sports hall with its dumb-bells and its fencing masks, women like horses who loved horses, tossing their manes, champing at the trough, wanting to be ridden, and ready, too, like the crook mare Undulna, to throw you into the mud, and drag you more than a hundred yards if they could, when the fuels of jealousy were kindled, and the fires of love burned.

2

PERHAPS THE *fons et origo*, or at any rate the symptom and the emblem, of this extravagant flair for horses, as she was, indeed, for so much of their supporting panache, from burnished stable to wig-encumbered footman and groom, was the most aristocratic, at least in recklessness, the tallest, and in many ways the most savagely passionate of your several mistresses to this date, the Marchesa (your first of the genre) Alessandra di Rudini Carlotti, a stripling girl of twenty-six, but one who already carried the authority of a much older woman, an authority which she was indeed soon to exercise on her dedicated and sombre predecessor, the incumbent, though, alas, shortly to be sent packing, Eleonora.

I saw the Marchesa first, I recall, at the Capponcina, vaulting lightly down from the back of a spirited roan, and switching her polished leather boots with a crocodile sjambok as she strode, in a man's jodhpurs, towards the rose garden. She was often thus. Tall, in the way that only some English women are normally tall, and with just such a high chin, slight trace of freckle, and flare of nostril, as the western shires are still equipped, I have little doubt, for the slow breeding of.

But she had the corn-yellow blonde hair, too, that is less common in England, and more to be found in the mountains of Scandinavia, that fine Nordic colouring that is

The Horses

ultimately so Greek, or perhaps I ought to say, so Greek in the worn marble style of the better statues. Perhaps that was why you named her Victory, when she walked in the wind like the blown headless figure of the Nike from Samothrace, torn like a flame from the vanished bow of her war cruiser.

She had the fire, and the dominance, of a Viking *materfamilias*, for sure, and she brooked no interference with the sudden outbursts of her heady temper. One day, indeed, on that very Undulna who threw you on to the sands, and dragged you a hundred yards over shell and pebble, she plunged, riding astride like a stable boy, fully clothed into a river, incensed, as she claimed later, by some passing indiscretion or insult as you rode at her side. You went in fast, hard after her that time, and were soon wading out with the lissom, slender but very lengthy and surely most exquisitely dripping and clinging body of the still breathing lady held half in your arms. She was just too big, alas, and the other half required some assistance of groom and following retinue.

She read Greek and Latin, with ease, I hear, and spoke in French, German and English with as much facility as in her native Italian. She made her liveried servants click their heels at attention, she ordered horses and riding-clothes, for herself and others, as others order champagne or handkerchiefs. She was totally, and quite casually, luxurious.

It was thus that your servants quadrupled, your stock of suits rose close to one hundred, your consumption of eau de Coty became one pint a day. She became your mistress, your guide, and your incubus, and without reserve.

I shall tell elsewhere, I think, of the battle royal that led to the final withdrawal of Eleonora, tragic and dignified, from the scene of what was rapidly becoming a world heavyweight title fight, with your own bleeding heart as the prize to be dangled at the victor lady's waist, or perhaps, more suitably, like a cringing dildo between her loins. There was little cringing, of course, in sober reality, but, as always, the clever appearance of a willing

The Lion of Pescara

submission on your part, and a wealth of tears and flowers.

I see her as I once did, with her booted feet on a low divan, smoking a thin cheroot like a Spanish grandee, and insisting that Rocco Pesche have someone in at once to sweep up the ash from a Persian carpet. It was on such carpets, laid out end to end in the gilded stables, that rumour had it the favoured mares were sent to sleep after hours of hunting the wild boar through the forests, but this, I know, was but one of many appropriate though exaggerated mere legends.

You loved her, though. Very much as it now seems, or at least in a new way, and with fresh tenderness. There were months of glamour, flights to her own villa on Garda, with a sailing boat motionless on the lake at dawn, and your window open over the oleander blossom, rides over bare heath or through hanging willows, hunting, talking, or simply trotting for the sheer joy of being on horseback, and with a young mistress, or with a poet for lover. There were days of joy and spendthrift madness, nights of delight and initiation. Initiation, yes. For the pale Marchesa was one of the many you corrupted from a lonely married virginity, albeit one blessed, or cursed, with riven issue.

But the idyll came to an end. The Marchesa contracted a tumour. There was an operation. Another. The danger list. Long hours beside her bed. Long weeks of swinging in the narrow pendulum shaft where life and its opposite seem equal.

You fought beside her. Night after night, week after week. Even the doctors admired, they say, your stamina. You gave up everything. Other women, books, writing, your home and your horses. Hour after hour you sat at her bedside, holding her hand, murmuring consolation in your anguish, pressing her dwindling will to live.

But live she did, and recover, too, and resume her daily rides and her thin cigars, leaning her bony weight on your braced arm. Yes, you were a dwarfish supporter for an ailing Aphrodite, but an assiduous and an attentive one, to be sure.

The Horses

Very soon, though, the crisis came. Not one of the illness, no. It was after this was behind her, and she had regrown her strength and waywardness, that the firm Marchesa began to require one further proof of your dedication. The sacrifice of the vaunted Eleonora was not enough. The expenditure of so many thousands of lire, with a kind of record-breaking insouciance, was now too little. She wanted more.

Marriage was what she needed. And, yes, against all the betting, as I would have said, you were willing to lend an ear to her schemes. The long-suffering Donna Maria was cabled, and gave her agreement. You would both, she and you, consult with your lawyers on the details of a settlement. In Italy, of course, this was then unthinkable. But there was one loophole. You could try, the Marchesa suggested, and which of her subtle advisers had found this machinery I scarcely know, to petition for nationality in Switzerland. You could then, by Swiss law, be divorced over there.

So that Gabriele D'Annunzio, even then for many the symbol and symptom of a new Italy, of the most intense and irrational form of that much maligned and yet sweetly sanctioned malady men call patriotism, Gabriele D'Annunzio, poet of the southern decadence and the vineyards of the Abruzzi, as Italian, one would have thought, as an ice-cream salesman, or a mafia boss from Palermo, or a minor tenor understudying the greatest roles in Verdi, was to cast aside this given birthright, as it might have been a casual veneer, and assume, like his own skin, the more rugged, puritanical, cuckoo-clock mentality of a provincial bank manager, or a climber in lederhosen, or a sort of tourist attraction. It was hard to believe.

At the height of this episode, requiring, alas, our mutual exile for some weeks to Zurich, to which still bourgeois and pre-Dada retreat you had summoned me for your entertainment and advising, while you climbed through the numerous hoops erected in the wisdom of a beneficent Swiss government for the careful screening of those anxious to obtain their cherished citizenship, you and I were seated one brisk October morning outside a thinly populated small café, enjoying a croissant and a lemon sorbet.

It was then, knowing the length to which this time your passion had driven your sense of freedom, bent, as you were, on sacrificing both country and long retained wife, the grandiose and 'black' Roman Donna Maria, for the sake of a lasting alliance, and a sanctified one, with your desperate horsewoman, that I heard from your own lips the account of that first, somewhat legendary encounter with the vivid Alessandra, at a hunting-party not far from Rome.

'Imagine the cool of that evening, Tomaso,' you suggested, endeavouring to form the shape of a balmy if a trifle chill zephyr in the Swiss town air. 'It had a sweet, anticipatory softness. There indeed I was, one boot off on the floor, one still on my left leg as I leaned forward from my ottoman. A small fire smoked in the grate. There was the wherewithal to make drinks in a cabinet near to my single bed.'

You paused then, and I broke a little piece from the corner of my second roll. In those days I had already become your publisher, in more than one venture, and a sudden recollection of the past almost eighteen months, empty of effort, at least in the wearing down of quills, and the consumption of hand-made paper, loomed and seemed very nearly tangible at the brink of my glass.

'Coffee, waiter,' I ordered, from a slight, neat figure, precise as a watch, who stood ready, so it seemed, as our perpetual private flunkey, 'and another basket of rolls.'

I saw your eyebrows arch, and your lips purse as you halted the advance of a tiny teaspoonful of what, in my fierce appetite, had seemed an irrelevance of ice cream.

'Fatness, Tomaso,' you murmured, wagging a finger thick with a pair of rings, one, I believe, still marked with the monogram of the Duse, and grasping her emerald. 'After what we ate, in the riotous hours of this dawn, I am quite amazed at your firm and so obviously still unsatisfied capacity. You are all will, all stomach. Me, I can

The Horses

manage only a little chilled and stiffened water, spiced with a trace of citrus.'

You were then forty, and worried, I knew, about the potential onslaught of a tenor's paunchiness, or a politician's jowls, those hallmarks of the ageing and the unfit so much to be avoided by the man deep in amorous liaisons as you were, though neither, in fact, as yet in any evidence. You were trim and spare, hard from riding, muscular from your daily weight-lifting, and spry from archery and from exercise with your foils. Indeed, the extension built on the Capponcina for the Olympian pursuits of the body was a veritable gymnasium, a sort of museum of arms and machinery kept oiled or polished, washed or cleaned, and in place for a regular employment. Few days were missed at the dumb-bells, or on the static bicycle.

'It was quite a night,' I replied to your gentle admonishment. 'Your genius feeds on its own energy, Gabriele. I require a more humble stoking of the sexual boilers.'

Indeed, there had been rather more depreciating of our Mediterranean powers than later proved wise, and our reputation, I fear, seeping or climbing like some formidable ooze, had already tarnished, if not eliminated, the chances of your suit for nationality being well received. The Swiss were proud, alas, and the combination of a louche fornication with one of their widows, and a somewhat unguarded reference to your sole motive in seeking their nationality, that is, for the sake of your divorce, led inevitably to the unhappy conclusion.

Yes, unhappy then, as it seemed, and yet, I wonder. Perhaps the great affair was already in its decline, and your seeming carelessness in Zurich was only the means to achieve its ending, and with an appearance of tender defeat, and not, as it may have been, the more usual boredom.

'Continue, though,' I insisted, as I buttered a second roll. 'I shall try to be unobtrusive in eating as you proceed.'

A girl went by, twirling a parasol – and I saw your eyes follow her hips for a moment, as you licked speculatively, I thought for a second, at your sorbet. There had been, in

The Lion of Pescara

the past, more than one occasion, when I had been left to pay off the restaurateur, as you snatched your hat and cane and moved speedily in the wake of some such deftly proffered adventure. But you let the girl go on, and returned, frowning a little, to your narrative.

'So there I was, Tomaso,' you murmured. 'Naked to the waist. My jacket over the back of a chair. About to ring for my valet and commence my dressing for dinner. Exhausted from the chase. And yet alert. With that subtly expectant alertness of all the senses that sometimes comes with twilight.

'So. Alert as I was, in ear as in eye, I became aware gradually of a deep, fresh, gushing sound, as of a foreign cataract uprising from some natural cavern in the heart of the mountains. A powerful, cleansing, urgent noise, and one close to, though not in, my own room. It took me only a moment to realise what it was.

'The bath was being filled in the adjoining bedroom. Now normally, as you will appreciate, this is not a circumstance that would automatically attract my ear in a strange hotel. Water flows. Baths are filled. Those who step out of their clothes and into the porcelain are not often alluring, or even desirable.

'But here was a different case. I knew who the bath was being filled for. I had already seen, and briefly met, the inhabitant of the adjoining bedroom.'

You lifted your empty spoon in the air, and twisted the stem in your finger so that the little silver cup was for a moment inverted. It caught the glow from a lamp, and glistened.

'You know Alessandra, Tomaso,' you continued. 'Imagine, then, my state of mind when I tell you that there was a connecting door in the wall of my room. Imagine the conscious attempt to frustrate my expectations with which I grasped and moved round the so sure to be locked and bolted handle. But then. Yes. Imagine my mixture of emotions, in which a kind of lubricious joy surmounted a heart-catching sense of shock, when I found that the handle gave to my fingers, the door swung open, and I was

The Horses

admitted, one boot on and one boot off, naked to the waist as I was, to the bathroom of the Marchesa Carlotti.'

You paused, stabbing gently at your sorbet with the tip of your spoon.

'She was there, Tomaso,' you breathed, spreading your hands, 'and ready, as I have to admit, for that full immersion in the brimming porcelain which the anticipatory sounds through the wall of my bedroom had heralded and prepared me for. They had not, however, and here I must rein back memory, prepared me for the sight of Alessandra, magnificent as Diana when she was surprised by Actaeon, as innocent of covering as the vixen who feeds her cubs, facing me startled, and yet, I must surely confess, with a kind of despairing eagerness of reckless demand, with her golden hair down to her lap, as she glanced up from her somewhat compromising position astride the spirting jets of her fully active bidet.'

'The rest,' I suggested, with a touch of tact, 'is history.'

'Not quite,' you said, with a laugh. 'It was much later, when we lay talking on the coverlet of her bed, long after the dinner that neither of us had eaten, that she came to the climax, if I may use the word, of her proposition.

'"Signor D'Annunzio," she said suddenly, with a light swing to her feet, and a swift step to her dressing-table, from which she lifted, and whirled, a pair of pearl-handled pistols. "We have sinned. We have to die. Now is the time."

'Well, Tomaso, you know, I had hardly stepped through that inviting door for a suicide pact, even one with such a seductive death-partner as the one beside me. I had to think. I had to reason.

'"Marchesa," I said, "we have sinned, as you say, together. We have therefore, I think, only two choices. We may either die together, or live together. The first, I submit in all honesty, we have done already. I died, a thousand times I died, as I lay but a moment ago in your sumptuous arms. There is, therefore, I say, but one choice left. We must live, Alessandra. And we must live together."

'Of course, I condense my argument a little. Your imagination may add the flourishes. But the principle was appealing. The Marchesa accepted my bargain, for such, I fear, she saw it as. And the pearl-handled pistols were spun in her fingers and put away. I tell you, Tomaso, I felt I had had a most narrow escape.'

I smiled as I swallowed my last morsel of roll. You told these flamboyant stories well. They were always true in essence, too, if not always in factual detail. And this indication of an early tenacity in affection had a special ring of the ominous, and of the absorbing. It showed a woman who meant to have her man.

'Gabriele,' I said, suddenly, as I recall that hour, very serious, and quite anxious to make my point. 'This marriage, I fear, will never take place. You are not a man to be eaten up by one woman, by any woman. Even by Alessandra. There must be others.'

'Of course,' you agreed, shrugging. 'Last night, as you know, my dear anxious Tomaso, there were others. But we are Italians. Even,' you corrected yourself, 'on the brink of becoming Swiss. We must exercise our members. What else?'

I poured more coffee, watching the sky darken, as if for rain.

'What else?' I repeated. 'Well, with Alessandra, there cannot be others. Or not for long. She needs too much.'

You laughed, and shook your head.

'No, Tomaso,' you said. 'Alessandra will see the way I am. You are wrong.'

But I wasn't wrong. There was no divorce, and no marriage, and the great affair began its decline with a steady inevitability. There were quarrels. Reconciliations. The Marchesa's two children, most appalling of calamities, both died of a strange disease. She was desperate in her grief. She saw their deaths, in her sense of guilt, as her punishment for adultery.

One day Alessandra disappeared. No one knew where she was. For over twenty-three years, at a Carmelite

The Horses

Convent in the Haute-Savoie, her identity was enshrined under the sacred name of Sister Maria.

She is perhaps the only woman whose memory is not celebrated in any of your extant works. Your life with her, one might say, was its own poem. And one published, I am moved to add with some cynicism, in a limited edition, and for an exceptionally high price.

Be that as it may, on a freezing morning in February 1931, the Reverend Mother Maria di Gesu, Superior of the Carmelite nunnery of Le Repousoir, while inspecting the site for a new convent in the mountains, died in a blizzard, six thousand feet above sea level, perhaps remembering – who can tell? – that Mediterranean Sea beside whose teeming waves she had once ridden bareback, wearing only her bloomers, to your sense of bourgeois shock one morning, and later, too, to the stimulation of your eager frenzy on the bewildered sand.

Such was the course of your affair with the swift Marchesa Carlotti, when it still seemed that you might have at last reached one stable image for your twisting career, that of the grand seigneur, the settled rural gentleman, with a wife tamed to the whip. Alas, it was not to be.

3

OF ALL YOUR dogs, and there were many even in those Florentine days, down to the fox-terriers, brief and barking, so much loved by the elegant Alessandra, the most faithful and treasured, at any rate for some months in the wake of the Marchesa's illness, was your sour-cream greyhound, the predecessor of that immense litter, much cosseted and cared for by the flighty Madame de Goloubeff at Arcachon, the harsh of temper and the swift of limb, Timbra.

What a strange white spot the fate of this elemental greyhound forms on the great, still more than half-barren canvas of your long career, the badger's brush of my memory and inclination, dripping with static oil, tinkers and teases with! I see her now, bitch as she was, or no, perhaps bitch only in the reincarnation of the minute, puking successor in the oval basket at Arcachon, for you could never bear to allow a dying animal to cross the line with its own one possession, its name, gripped for ever between its teeth, but no, there had to be a new Pisanella or White Havane, a Gladiator or a Veronese, even as there had, sometimes, with women, too, to be a fresh airing of the same adored alias, and a second, or even third, Lola or Cinerina to strut the boards of your private stage, and, yes, I remember now, dog as he was, Timbra the first, who flashed across the lawn of your mind, in one last magic

The Horses

swoop, the very moment the servant put a shot in his brain, and yes, for me, there he is now, lean as a willow branch in the wind, as he breaks the coverts behind the house after a fast hare.

Odd work, indeed, it often seems this hatching in with my mental 2B pencil, or scratching out with my etching-needle of unrequired excess of detail. No, but it truly seems more close to brush-work, as I reach through the tangled thickets of recollection to pluck forth some further screeching or twisting miniature that will fill a bare inch or support the recession towards a better block of colour in the middle ground. As Timbra, yes.

Once narrative is renounced, and even dialogue, except for the few suave or determined fragments that serve to prop our scenes, only the flat rhythm and colour, were it not for a certain structure, a kind of pattern of tent-pegs, a skeleton in the snow, would remain. So that when I tell what you were, or seek rather to give the inner feel of your destiny, its momentum as well as its relevance, only metaphors for that itchy poeticising can give the sense. I mean the drift, the shape, the Jamesian figure in the carpet, whatever that might mean when so many of the better Axminsters have become a perpetual all-over powder-blue, or wilting egg-yolk yellow, or vile maroon. But no, perhaps the movement of it, the prose that is, would in some circumstances create its own air of a drift, no doubt, though, for the unconvinced, one dense with casualties, and a mere disaster-area of unclear leads and unhelpful pointers.

Here I stand, raw with ersatz coffee in my ageing bowels, and the sounds through the patched window of children playing on rubble, the neo-realismo of defeat, and I try, or do I, at least I think I try, turning a loaded brush in my fingers, to blot in some further trapezium or triangle in the overlapping quincunx shape that forms my plan.

Venice, first. That long rectangle of war and mirrors, clocks ticking to the constant efflorescence of your own tree of blinded leaves, it was easy, drawing from the wells of your own writing, to fill out some sense of the middle ground there, your life's warlike centre. At Arcachon, reaching high to the top left-hand corner of my stretched and treated surface, I traced in one area of the background, a little to the spatial rear, and leading in, by gradual stages, women and speeches at Genoa, to the red hard middle of the Casetta Rossa. But now, with Florence, and nearly half, albeit only the top, and the further, half of my careful diploma-work already in existence, the smooth brush seems to grate some days, the oil to streak and blur, the figures not to come so easy.

Perhaps, it may be, the far rear, or at least so far as I dare strike, not having known the recesses of your early childhood, and the lure of that wonderful mother, of whom you wrote once, performing the rite of the curfew one night with an unknown soldier during the war, 'and when the laurel was consumed, and my people had departed and the roads lay silent, I stole back to the dying fire and tucked a glowing coal under the ash, as my mother would have done,' so that, indeed, the room would be warm again through such fine prudence in the chill of the morning, no, not having been there, or even old enough, to admire your home life in the later sixties, or to carp at your lecher father's neglect and debaucheries, this Florence time, these easy, early middle days now grown to my dimmest distance, the foothills before the blur of the horizons, perhaps these, the far rear, as I say, as I grope up to my right-hand corner to draft them in, prove harder inevitably.

Here in the book's nadir, the very belly of the whale, a certain gloom of Jonah wells up, no doubt of this, and even, I see, those pearl-handled pistols, and the disappearing horsewoman who became a nun, lack lustre against the archery of Ida Rubinstein or the perverse lubriciousness of the Marchesa Casati. The brush moves too far to the back, and the hand has too little skill, to body forth such tiny remote beings as those in Florence with real force and grip.

So at this pivotal point, one fleck of dazzling white, I place the recalcitrant lovely Timbra, whom one day, with a typically generous and reckless exercise of your style,

The Horses

you allowed to be chosen, as your most cherished possession, as a present for her favours, past, I can scarcely suppose, then doubtless I assume to come, by a solitary and alarming English girl, the brief tenant of a nearby villa in the hills, and whom, the dog I mean, though being warned about, for his feverish and uncanny temperament, this lady took to her garden, or possibly, who knows, to the satin couches of her boudoir, and there, through some ineptitude or perhaps gross malpractice in her play, disturbed, so that the brute bit her.

Imagine, then, the chaos! The servants running, blood flowing, the girl in her underclothes or her beach garments in tears and outrage, the dog a bitter, terrified animal able only to growl and snap, and you, its master, loveless and forlorn, missing your favourite in the evening glow, walking towards the Capponcina, from the woods, and seeing the white sudden streak across your lawn, before the immaculate windows, of the veritable Timbra, returned, it seemed, in a flash of restored elegance.

But, no. At that very instant, you learned later, meeting an ambassador from the villa prostrate with a sort of grief or dread, your uneasy temper being known, or suspected in the neighbourhood, and moving his greasy cap in his hands, the unwilling bearer of ill tidings, yes, at that very instant, your English doxy's groom had taken the snarling Timbra by the throat and put the bullet into his elegance for ever.

So that was Timbra, one blot of colour given a slow rhythm across the background of your days, one moment of ecstasy encapsulated in a vision, closer to the cold reality of his passing than, yes, that later premonition you mentioned to me, when the fate of your little fish, Li Tai Pe, soon to expire and be buried at Le Petit Trianon, was foreshadowed in a dream the night before.

You were prone to such visions, casual or sudden, as you were prone, or rather made yourself available, to such unpremeditated, or at any rate, rather swiftly prepared, encounters as those with a dozen, even a hundred or more, starry-eyed or wanton, or simply female and curious vir-

The Lion of Pescara

gins, and, well, yes I must add, some more venerable matrons, or assured mistresses, too. Like Timbra, some were presents, offering themselves, or offered by calculating donors, eager for services in war, or politics, or more frequently, really, in those days, plain poetry or plays.

A few, though, rewarded as many were with some equivalent of Timbra, whatever at the time you found your most cherished belonging, and such things changed, as your moods changed, a few would arrive unsure of their plans, or your attentions, and be seduced, or corrupted, or exhilarated, or even, sometimes, packed off home unsatisfied. Of these, though not, I fear, of the last category, one might rank Madame de Brun, and though this was not, in fact, her real name, it may serve to mask a still very distinguished lady, and one not unknown in the very smartest echelons of a now puritanical society.

However. I anticipate. Madame de Brun. She wrote her own account of that inspiring afternoon, and I still retain, somewhere, the manuscript in another's hand, a prudently acquired amanuensis, wherein she lays bare some exquisite, and I think rather usual and thus revealing aspects of you. I draw, therefore, from what she had to say in describing this familiar enough adventure.

She arrived, or so we are told, in a sort of breathless prose on which I shall make, and I think largely for humorous purposes, only limited withdrawals, on a warm April afternoon, in 1905.

You were courteous, tactful, amusing. The sound of your voice was both a stimulus and an easement. You said little, it seems, in itself of moment, or striking in phrase or expression. But you spoke with a fluid sweetness, like a brook in the mountains. Yes, she employs that simile.

Well. That was often said. I have testified myself to the power and surge of your voice on more public occasions. It had its modulations, too, and here we have our witness, to a more private force.

Indeed, there is only one sense, the sense of hearing, that seems to have worked for the young visitor, an entranced Shelley in the presence of her first meadowlark, or a Keats

The Horses

with a nightingale, as she floated, so it seems, through the double open doors into the room of cushions and sofas.

There, one supposes, her eyes remained, for a while, still closed. Her nose was the second of the five senses to set to work. The room, it seems, was a blend of a trio of perfumes. Roses, first. The heavy, almost suffocating odour of their full blossoms in bowls and vases, tall-necked or wide-bottomed, in single perfect flowers, or huge bunches, dense with buds, even, it seems, in scattered petals forming almost a second rug on the floor.

Roses, then. And below the roses, a deeper, more subtle and yet less appetising scent, or so she felt, the thickness of diffused incense, as in a chapel, or a monastery cell. It took her by the throat, she says, almost like a warning, an ominous injunction, a moral echo below the atmosphere of sensuality. It made her breath, we may suppose, come quicker. You knew the way to salt and spice the conscience of a pretty woman, teasing its glowing tip until it quivered like her, yes I suppose I must say this, her clitoris.

But last, there was another aroma in the air, the more delicate, less familiar one which nevertheless the lady already knew, since she had soaked, this very morning, her clothes and her arms in its fragrance, I mean the piquant essence of your own invented scent, the Acqua Nunzia. It was everywhere in the room, lingering, then withdrawing, vivid in an alcove, then quiet and unobtrusive over a cushion, a presence and yet a by no means inquisitive one, as discreet and yet helpful as a well-trained valet de chambre.

I remember your Acqua Nunzia too well. There was later to be a period when this allegedly monkish recipe, obtained from some ancient friar in the Abruzzi, but in fact regularly manufactured in quantity for you by a firm of chemists in Fiesole, was to be marketed in a specially designed, and supposedly medieval shaped vessel, with a Gothic label, and thus made to form the spearhead, as other scents were to be for Paul Poiret and later Chanel, in the recouping of your financial fortunes.

Alas, it failed, as they say, to 'take'. It seems a pity. I

liked the scent. I recall it now, flexing these blunted nostrils, as a fragrance between, say, Houbigant's Chypre and Rosine's Nuit de Chine. There was, after all, perhaps a period essence to it, a hint of incense, yes, which is possibly why it would always blend so well with the other atmospheres of the Capponcina, as Madame de Brun seemed to find that it did on her visit.

At any rate, thus drenched, and in some way soothed and edified in this bath of odours, her eyes, at last, and with a coy blue sparkle, flashed open. You were small and neat in front of her, hands akimbo on the hips of your blue kimono, cut, as she claimed, in a sort of mandarin style, but in fact, and to my sure knowledge, simply a blue kimono that had happened to be made for a rather larger Japanese, and thus hung lower than it should have done.

But you were at ease in such loose-flowing clothes, and you moved, we may assume, with assurance towards your dispensing of tea and cakes.

The room, as it confronted the open eyes of Madame de Brun, was darkened by a sort of transparence of curtains, half drawn, to be sure, but allowing only a mauve light to filter in through a canopy of wisteria in full bloom along a balustrade on the terrace, and over a pergola that reached to the windows.

The shapes of the furniture were thus made vague, and seemed to shimmer in a purplish mist, as in those *fin de siècle* canvases by Gotch or Waterhouse, the English leaders of the open-air school that gave the woodlands the comfortable fascination of a spring interior.

And there, like a bald version of the god Pan outlined by Hiroshige, you postured above your samovar, dispensing China tea, which she abhorred, she reveals, and handing fondants and *marrons glacés* on brittle Nagasaki plates through which the same mauve light seemed to glow.

She records little about the slight meal, save for some hint of mint in the tea, and a tendency to a weakening at the edges of the *petits fours*, as if, one might have supposed, they had marched forth as the survivors of an earlier combat of the senses above the silver tea-trays.

The Horses

It was hot, though. She began to feel the dripping of moisture under those carefully powdered arm-pits, I have scarcely a doubt, and there will have been small difficulty in persuading her to a release of those cream gloves that climbed in their fine tension as close to her shoulders as, underneath her lengthy dress, those no less intensely fastened stockings, I am very sure, rose towards her lightly sweating groin.

'Really?' she records your saying, and with a mocking smile, almost of disbelief, as she protested that the room was perhaps a little too hot. 'Allow me to take your shawl.'

Then a sinewy arm, very thin at the wrist she remembers, was briefly, but scarcely perhaps quite as briefly as necessary, around her neck, and the shawl as it swung away was brushing as if by accident, albeit with a sensuous tickle, across her face and her lap.

Well. There is more of this kind. The repeat of the soothing quality of your voice. The sleepiness induced by the heat, or the mauve light, or the mint tea. The ease with which one could lie back along the rather abnormally long settee, and rest on the deep, absorbing cushions. The naturalness with which you came over and sat at her side, on the pretext of showing a folder of steel engravings, which were all, or too many for comfort, it seems, of naked figures in the act of demonstrating how enjoyable had been, for example, The Rape of the Sabine Women.

Later, she awoke. Alone, it seems. And under the eye of the Charioteer at Delphi. So dressed. So took her hat and her gloves and her parasol. So found you seated in the library, in evening dress, and turning over the pages of a novel. So let you kiss her hand and say that a carriage was waiting for her at the door. So let you escort her there, and open the door, and bow, and give your orders to the driver, and send her home, never to see or hear from you again.

She closed her eyes in the carriage, faint and weary, and in a strange mixture of emotions. And then, she writes, she realised, through her nose once more, that she had been given a parting memento of the afternoon. The carriage was filled with roses. The seat, like the bier of

Albine in Zola's novel, where she suffocated to death in the odour of flowers, was a mass of crushed petals, bunches of flowers, single blossoms.

Then she writes, and I believe her, she felt like a toy, discarded and never to be played with again. And she opened the window, as the horses trotted down the hill into Florence and towards her hotel, and, one by one, and flower by flower, she shredded the blossoms with a vicious, bitter intensity into the road, so that her course home left behind a trail of red, as clear and as unambiguous as the maidenly blood she felt now threading through the packed materials of her layer upon layer of cambric knickers below her dress.

I asked you once about her, giving the real name, and you paused a long time, and then smiled, and said, 'I remember, yes. She was pretty.'

'Very pretty?' I asked.

'Of course,' you said. 'Why not?'

4

ONE DAY I drove with you to Brescia. Blériot was there with his monoplane after that epoch-making flight across the Channel, and you were suddenly, as you remembered how Leonardo had made those drawings of flying machines, an aficionado, a willing acolyte at the new shrine of speed, the fragile butterfly world of the air.

I remember that long drive in your Napier Sixty, the long bonnet olive-green decked with incised lines in black and yellow, the brass upright cylinder of the fire extinguisher near to the running-board, the mahogany box for tools, the great iron rack at the rear for our trunks, and you and I tall and vibrating on the dusty bucket-seats behind the double-up windscreen, bemused in our goggles, two swathed exponents of the motoring craze in our leather gloves and English greatcoats.

It was a battering act of homage to the God of motion. Cranking the engine up with an arm-breaking handle, while you sat motionless and impatient at the wheel, I would look back round the polished drums of the headlamps, like aligned cannon in some new warship of the roads, wondering if the sunk barrel of petrol behind the driving-seat would explode in the kick of the motor firing. Alas, I knew little of motor-cars. They were mere vehicles of combustible agony to my amateur mind, still horse-loving, and accepting the dirt of straw and dung more easily than the rub of oil.

But you were an expert. Already, at the beck and call of a new flame, the Countess Mancini, a mad woman with a taste for bright colours, a rich wine-grower for a husband, and a groin like a stoked furnace, you had sacrificed your string of Arab mares for a chugging series of ever more powerful automobiles. It was no longer the race tracks and the stables you frequented, smacking your cavalry twilled thighs with a riding crop. It became the garage I would seek you in, a converted sequence of derelict barns where an overalled mechanic would brood in solemn fury over the peccadilloes of your Renault, or your new Mercedes, or now, yes, this formidable six-cylinder monster from England.

'One last swing, Tomaso,' you would call, leaning over the carriage-lamp on our fateful trip to Brescia. Then, 'Wonderful! Yes. Listen to that amazing power rattle,' as the motor juddered into its famous shaking, and I would run for the step, seizing hold of the wooden grip on the instrument panel as you put the car into gear and launched us forward on what was later to become known through the cinema as a gangster start, your gunman in his motoring-cap, in this case me, clinging for dear life, as it seemed, with one foot on the running-board and one drifting in the air.

'Not so fast,' I would shout, hauling myself in. 'You nearly killed me that time.'

But you would always look over with a huge grin, lift one hand in a sort of salute, and ram the car into a higher gear, forcing it up as fast as you could along those barren Tuscan roads towards what the manufacturers claimed as its 'normal' seventy miles per hour cruising speed. Indeed, on the newly opened English circuit at Brooklands, that already notorious maniac S. F. Edge had averaged something over sixty-five miles per hour for a whole day only two years earlier.

The engine overheated. We stopped several times at wayside inns for wine and fruit, or to look for assistance to

The Horses

pull us out of a ditch, or provide fresh flagons of petrol for the thirsty horses. We lost our way. We were drenched in night rain, choked in morning dust, burned by the midday sun. It was a marathon of endurance, wit and mechanised fantasy.

I still possess a snapshot of the outcome, a boring afternoon in the company of a pompous Frenchman whose only small talk was of ailerons and wind gauges. He stands there under the shadow of his brittle machine, all struts and braced material, with a couple of enormous mistresses, either his or yours, in Edwardian hats and with parasols, and with you to the left, as often in photographs, at a slight angle to the situation, a bearded gnome in white ducks, with what seem to be patent-leather shoes and a flaired velveteen jacket, and a boater with a ribbon. I must have been, I suppose, the unseen man behind the camera.

You were not, of course, in any way bored yourself. It became the moment when I realised that your voracious curiosity, already extended from the minutiae of fifteenth-century art, and women's corsages, to the no less intricate and ingeniously cantilevered machinery of the internal combustion engine, was now in hot pursuit of a fresh conquest, the lore and the gaudy vocabulary of the aeronautical process.

Hour after hour you stood with Blériot, or with his mechanics, keen and virile young fellows, discussing the reason for the slant of a flap, or the options in steering at eleven thousand feet. You were entirely engrossed in this new science of aviation. It seemed, as you later expressed it for me, to go far beyond the simpler excitements of ground propulsion at high speeds. It flung the body, and thus the imagination, far up and out into regions never before examined except in the flights of fancy propounded by Romantic poets.

'Of whom you are one,' I said, resisting the banal allure of these new toys.

'Of course,' you agreed, fingering a small meticulous valve you had borrowed, a silvery hard thing which you treated with the respect you might once have accorded to

The Lion of Pescara

the ear of a favoured hound. 'You see, Tomaso, the twentieth century has become the era of speed. The freedom of speed. The ecstasy of speed. The mechanical orgasm of speed. Why, Tomaso, that ought to appeal to your jaded old appetites, if nothing else does!'

I think, though, that you were already perhaps beginning to sublimate, as that Austrian psychoanalyst has named it, your instinctual desire for a sexual release, an expansion of your consciousness through women. You were subtly transforming the business into something more abstract and more mechanical, and yet also, I see this now, in the wake of all your later achievements, more deeply and widely political than before, I mean into what seemed essentially modern, and thus with appeal to the young, the changers of the world.

Of course, there was also, in this, what the narrowly cynical have called its own sexual element, the uprooting and replanting of a kind of latent homosexuality, a Greek admiration for boys. I see you there with your hand through the arm of a blond aviator in a boiler-suit, his chest bare to the navel and livid with sweat, a broad smile on his clean features, and I wonder, listening to the chat of undercarriages and joy-sticks, if either of you are entirely aware of the undertones, not only in vocabulary and nuance, but in the whole ambience of these airfield encounters.

Later, with Giuseppe Miraglia, as with so many more, it became a reiterated thought, though one with a clearer answer in the comradely matter of total war. We were all, men that we were, a little possessed by each other in that.

So that now, after six years of your heirs in the cult of youth and elegance, the elite corps of the Waffen S.S., and the fighter pilots in Russia, I begin to confirm, old as I am, the more public elements in your new choices then, in the cauldron of 1909. The century was itself young, and you reached for its hand. Those turning airscrews, those jumping cylinders in the engines of all your cars, those muscular and intelligent young servicers of these novelties, these were in most respects, and certainly in their grip on

The Horses

your will to write, the ikons and symbols of what was to come.

It was Icarus, after all, who had held the centre of your inspiration since the great odes in *Alcione*. The Daedalus who makes, and the Icarus who flies and burns, these were your twin heroes, and you were intent on a synthesis of the two. You were not alone, of course, in your love for the naked youth on the promontory, whose wax wings were to melt in the heat of the sun. There were many young dandies in flopping ties and long hair who stood in front of those vast canvases, in the Grosvenor Gallery, or the Ecole des Beaux Arts, or the little dusky rooms behind the Uffizi, feeling the pull of that fallen athlete, with his huge feathers draped round his thighs, and his back on a tall plateau, perhaps, as in Herbert Draper's masterpiece, and a bevy, O yes, most important of all, a pride or a fine seraglio of attendant and mournful nymphs to lament his tragedy, and perhaps to caress his parts.

Indeed. I was one myself. But it took a shift of genius, which is what you found, somehow, in that encounter with Blériot, and in the madness of the Countess Mancini, your last mistress of the Capponcina, to uncover the heart of the myth, and to make it real, and no longer decadent, as it was, but the harbinger of the Sopwith Camel, and the triplane of the Baron Richthofen, and the legendary Amy Johnson, who flew to Australia, and the ambiguously remembered General Umberto Nobile, who abandoned his crew, and even his dog, when his airship crashed in the snow.

You took the fallen aviator, and you made him a god. One after another, your young pilots above the Carso, dark and slender below their flying-helmets, chiselled in the bronze of your prose became like statues on some invisible cathedral of the spirit, or, better perhaps, the pediment of a winged parthenon of the Isonzo.

Speed, youth and masculinity, there were all these elements in the world of racing-cars, and of aeroplanes. There were wings, and there was Icarus. But there was the sun, too, with its burning and its danger. The same sun that you had courted along the beaches at Marina de Pisa or Versilia, naked on horseback, or at ease alongside the unbared favours of Eleonora, or Alessandra, endlessly warmed and solicited outdoors in dazzling rays, as indoors by the steam warmth of your heating systems, that very same sun, symbolic and energising, burned out of the cylinders that fired those machines, in dust and exhaust fumes along lonely country roads, or above herringbone clouds in azure openness high up in the Italian empyrean.

Yes, an Italian empyrean. For there was, finally, the budding of a new patriotism, too, a kind of love of country that sought for some great occasion to express itself in, perhaps a race, or an adventure, certainly a cause with a noble, if doubtless tragic, outcome. The twentieth century was to make your country a place of fresh mark in the world, a leader and an emblem, and you, of course, were to be, in some way as yet unforeseen, the pivotal figure in this enterprise, the child of the sun, the naked statuette with a bald head and a rather bad set of teeth who could charm women, and handsome boys, and would often be thought of abroad, even in England, the country you so much admired, as a mere *flâneur*, an operatic Italian tenor, with a poor libretto, and no music.

You did write, though, in this latter area of Florentine time, that solitary masterpiece first named *Il Delirio*, and perhaps, after all, most accurately so-called, remembering its genesis in the hectic last hours of your crazy relationship with your lustful countess. There were many novels, of course, and often they lie like tombstones over the corpse of a lost or abandoned love. This latest one alone blends many elements, not only the motor-cars, and the flying machines, and the final tragedy of the lady you liked to call your Amaranta, but a handful of elegances, the veils and the Persian trousers, the dash of Fortuny and international scandal, that you were already imbibing in real life through the lips, upper and nether, of your second Marchesa, the malign Luisa Casati.

Yes, she was already there, La Casati, met at Monte

The Horses

Carlo, I think, or Cannes maybe, over the roulette wheel or the backgammon board, and so was Madame de Goloubeff, immense in her Wagnerian sonorities, and luring your eye as well as your ear at those intimate and match-forming concerts occasional forays to France were preparing you for. So that Isabella, your heroine of this book, in some newly conglomerate way, serves to mingle strains or characteristics of quite a range of your mistresses, and hence, perhaps, creates an ensemble more genuinely a piece of art than those earlier, more commemorative volumes.

It may be so, it may be not. Those were the words in the ceiling of the ducal palace at Mantua, and they took your fancy from the first time you tilted up your head and read them as a callow boy. Mottoes. Those were so often later the tools and slogans of your persuasive enterprises, either with women or in war. *But who takes care?* That was one. As in some heraldic pantheon, each line had its own place, and its own usage.

Women, too, had that, some say. And a time will arrive, no doubt of this, and in time, when the sort of man you were, an exploiter of women, a practiser of deceits, a philanderer of the flesh and the mind, will seem a mere historical anachronism, a fragment from a past long outgrown and little understood or admired, as damaging and sinister as a set of manacles, or an iron ring rusting in the walls of a dungeon become an attraction for tourists, a thing to shudder and smile at, with relief, perhaps, and in small comprehension.

I wonder. The inner subtleties of your life with people you favoured highly are hard to fathom, even for those, as I was, your closest servant. So that what might be said about the Countess Mancini, beyond her tawny hair and her white skin, and the final forgetful insanity when she retired to her hospital, or her madhouse, and was held a prisoner against her will, and for her good, must after all perhaps be said in your own words.

Every day you wrote her two letters, when you were apart. One was for her to show to her friends, even her husband. The other was written for her own eyes only. They tell us much, published as they have been, these private effusions, but then there were many such for the eyes of your loved ones. The truth, the fleeting, barren, casual essence of what you felt, or of what was going on, is often more to be sought in your diaries, or your notebooks, those little enshrinings of passing trivia which were later to be written up, and sometimes altered into some more acceptable form, in one or other of your novels.

I quote only one entry, from the end of July 1907, only five short months after the cautious Contessa had first yielded the treasure of her loins at the Capponcina. Few words. But a suave cameo.

> Arrived at Borgo San Dannino, stormy sky. I find Amaranta at the station, trembling all over and afraid.
>
> I was not expecting her. She is wearing her black silk costume and the hat with a feather.
>
> Agitated conversation on the square. In terror, flashes of love.
>
> We climb into the carriage. I speak in that low, rather rough voice which upsets her. So as not to hear it, she covers her ears with a crazy gesture.
>
> We stop at a little inn called 'The Roman Eagle'. We are given a room with an enormous bed.
>
> Feverish caresses interrupted by her childish agitation. Slight taste of iodine on her white skin. The body is still marvellous and my desire still frantic.
>
> A meal is brought which we do not touch. She wants to return to Salsa. After long kisses we go down the wooden staircase.
>
> On the square, a concert of guitars and mandolins. A cold wind has made a stormy sky.
>
> The carriage is drawn by a white horse. The wind blows her veil, through which I seek her mouth. Under the street-lamps I see her terrified face.
>
> It is raining. Sadness. Sadness. Why did I let her leave?
>
> She goes back into her hotel and takes the two boxes of orchids.

The Horses

I find my bed impregnated with her odour; impossible to sleep . . .

How exquisite and yet trivial life is. I keep the inn bill. So much intoxication and so much anguish has cost only twenty-one lire.

So much left in, so much left out. I cut from two images. First. A woman with tawny hair, arms pinned hard behind her back, screaming, screaming, in a small room with padded walls. Impassive men in white coats watch while she spits bloods. The atrocious colour is all I see against the white. The film is a silent one, the sort of costume drama we made so frequently in the late 1920s, a madhouse episode from the eighteenth century, the wife of some aristocrat, who lost his head in the revolution maybe, driven out of her mind by his brutal decapitation.

Yes, but the colour you say. There was no colour, surely? Then why do I remember the colour? Only the second image helps. A man, quite young, is on the deck of a small craft in the Mediterranean. Wearing bathing-shorts. Laughing with two friends. The sky darkens. A storm is coming up. The boat begins to pitch and roll.

Green. The face of the young man is green. He rushes to the side of the boat, vomits into the water. Once. Twice. A convulsive vomiting.

But now the sound has come. The sound of the masses cheering. Cheering for what? Who knows. The film has been playing over two simulated episodes from the far past, allowing a semblance of 'silent' film technique, and some touches of later colour.

Yes, that was you and Scarfoglio, on your first voyage in Greece, I say, turning the handle of the little projector, flinging the film of your life on to a blank screen at the Vittoriale, seeing the lizard eyes of the old roué blink and close, and yes, that woman was the Countess Mancini, you remember, surely you do, Gabriele, the one who went out of her mind.

O yes, of course. Of course. But it was all such a long time ago. Such a very long time ago.

5

So TIME WORE on. Money grew scarcer and scarcer. The depredations of the Russian Madame, succeeding those of the winegrower's countess, were an increasing strain on the patience of your many creditors. Indulgence varied. There were those, admirers of *Alcione*, or of one or other of your magazine articles, recallers, perhaps, a few, of those gossipy scandal columns your several aliases had supplied to the Roman papers, and thus made popular some remote pastry-shop, or sleazy milliner, as the rendezvous for some aristocratic paramour and his tardy consort, those, I say, in these hopeful categories, or wishing to become therein, who were willing, even – a very few indeed these – positively delighted, to extend your line of credit in soapy waves towards an azure and never to be attained horizon.

But most were not so. The tradesmen of Florence were a hard-headed set of men. They had seen extravagance before. Failure in payment, and high promises, walked hand in hand in their brittle minds, and there were some who retained stories, retailed over long generations, that wrenched some moral from the imprudence of great-great-grandparents in the business, who had steered their course on the edge of bankruptcy through a false reliance on the word or the whim of countess this or the marquis of that as far back as the Kingdom of Naples.

The Horses

Bills began to come in. Day after day, the postman in his pointed hat would arrive at the servants' door under the motto, carved in English and later to be immortalised by Baden-Powell, *Be Prepared*, and would send, in a slow cascade, the inelegant envelopes, with their dim windows and angry scrawlings in red ink, on to a scrubbed space on a table, or into the deep, forgetful mouth of one or other of your several mail baskets.

Rocco Pesche would shake his head. Anastasia would cluck her tongue. Lesser figures would fall upon the piles like carrion crows, black in their mourning or funeral livery, and a salver or two of the worst-looking pickings would shortly find their way to my inner sanctum behind the library, where I sat over a late and often lonely breakfast with the *Corriere della Sera*.

'Signor Antongini,' the more polite would say, frowning, or even sometimes wringing their fingers, 'the more immediate of the letters are here. Forgive this interruption.'

I would smile, or wave my hand, or simply groan and put my head in my hands. There was very little to be done. Slitting the envelopes open with an ebony glove-stretcher, or a watch-key, or a metal ruler, or any other instrument, indeed, that might lie in wait, I would scatter the ruined envelope over egg or fish, on the remains of omelet or kedgeree, and would idly extract the neatly folded single sheet.

It made no difference. In the early months of 1910, your credit, and your resources, were alike exhausted. I opened the bills for fun, and to pass the time only. Ten thousand lire here, another five hundred there. Handkerchiefs, socks, a half a dozen silk shirts. Dog biscuits. Gramophone needles. The invoice for a hired sewing-machine. The final demand note from an unpaid lighting engineer.

The paper mounted, the sums of money grew astronomical. I would simply ring the little hand-bell, say, 'Thank you, clear this all up, would you? I shall tell Signor D'Annunzio to do what is necessary,' and

The Lion of Pescara

stroll out on to the terrace for a walk in the snow, or round to the gymnasium for some exercise with the foils.

Later in the day, and more and more often as the year wore on, the creditors would arrive in person, or by intermediary, clanging those monastery bells, and rapping their sticks or their umbrella points against the long-suffering marble of your front steps. A few would be left to grow more and more impatient, in the expectation that no one was at home. But this method soon gave way, of necessity, to some receipt of their claims and their complaints.

At first, it would be an under-footman, greasy in slicked-back hair, with a boot-brush in his dirty fingers, who was sent to accept their message. Later, a more senior fellow, dapper perhaps in a blue uniform with gilded buttons, would run his jaundiced eye over the wilting, or, alas too often, still arrogant and insistent visitor. Finally, the heavy cavalry, either Rocco Pesche or Anastasia in person, would be summoned, as from some enormously important and remote conference, and would thunder along the hall and confront their enemy, sabre in hand, as it were, and determined on overcoming this uncalled-for arrival with the greatest expedition.

At last, however, and by February, it was more and more into my own sanctum, and to my own wiles and devices, that the importunate callers, often with legal support in the form of document or even advocate in spectacles and frock-coat, were delivered. I did my best. I reasoned. I spread my hands. I was convivial, conniving.

'We are men of the world,' I would say. 'You and I, Signor Fratelli, have seen much of the great affairs of our day. My master is not, we are both agreed, as other men. He exists on his own plane. He has access to wealth inconceivable to the more mundane of your clients here in the provinces. But, of course, the manipulation and supply of these vast resources is hardly such a banal matter as the removal of a few copper coins from a leather purse. But forgive me, sir. I am neglecting the manners of a good host, as Signor

The Horses

D'Annunzio would scarcely be doing. A glass of wine perhaps?'

And a bottle of our best burgundy would be drawn from the cabinet at my side, and a generous measure dispensed in one of the finer sixteenth-century goblets.

'Your bill,' I would say, as we drank together, 'will, of course, be met in the shortest possible time. And, most naturally, with some proper addition to cover your inconvenience at what I agree must seem a not quite anticipated delay.'

These methods had had their day. In earlier years, the extension of your credit had so often been wrought in the wizardry of wine, and the delicate stroking of snobbish noses with promises and flattery. There had even been moments when a totally impossible milliner, or an inconceivably irate butcher, had been charmed into full submission at the sudden intervention of one of your greyhounds, taught to lick and fawn with a convincing affability on the gullible knee or the hairy drumming fingers.

Once I recall, but indeed only once, I was grappling with the arm-long invoice of a pair of confectioners, immaculate in velvet-collared overcoats, when you appeared at the door of my study in person, naked to the waist, and with a Malayan kris in your hand.

'My dear friends,' you were quick to say, tossing the jagged knife on to a side table, as the two elderly gentlemen recoiled in a violent shock, 'I am delighted that you have so rightly taken me at my word and come out to see over our little cottage in which so many of your finest masterpieces have been consumed. Why, I still savour the heady marzipan of those *têtes de nègres* on which I was glutting the appetites of a certain lady of our mutual acquaintance only fifteen minutes ago. Forgive me for not being better dressed to receive your visit. I had been at my morning practice. I always castrate a sucking-pig or two before swimming in donkey's milk. It improves the complexion. Will you join me before our stroll round the principal rooms?'

But by this time the two horrified confectioners were

The Lion of Pescara

already bowing themselves backwards into a bust of Niobe on a plinth of porphyry. It rocked, but it stood, and they were all confusion, and soon gone.

'Quite mad,' I heard them murmuring as they fled. 'Entirely mad.'

You were hardly mad, though. Merely reckless. Money meant nothing to you. There had always been something to buy things with. Why should there not always be more in the future? It was simply a matter of organisation, and waiting. That was your secretary's affair.

I tried many ways. But your source of income had always been your pen. You were writing little now and that little was what you chose, and not the remunerative pieces for the popular press that were, at this date, your only possible source of the gigantic sums you required.

In despair, I arranged a lecture tour. Through a miniature impresario of the circuits, one Pilade Frattini, I negotiated a series of talks on flying, which you were to deliver to mixed audiences in selected venues all over the northern part of Italy. At the brink of the flying craze it seemed just possible that these romantic and yet also partly technical chats would excite the interest of the public, and thus form the basis for a continuing series of lectures on other themes of the day. Motoring, perhaps. Or even, poetry.

Alas, they were not a success. Blériot himself could scarcely, I think, have filled an Italian hall with his first-hand accounts of life in the clouds, and your own imaginative flights were inevitably at this date less firmly grounded in reality. The project was a good one, but it had come too soon. The hearty burghers of Mantua and Vicenza yawned through your magnificent rhetoric, and then rustled their chocolate boxes. They wanted sterner, or possibly, more weepy, stuff.

You were angry, then. That inspired mixture of poetry and political acumen that would shortly focus your speeches in Genoa to the power of a political lever that could move the world had scarcely yet found the right form of access. You were either too dreamy still for the

The Horses

masses, or else too practical. The age of Colonel Lindbergh, whose progenitor you were, had still to come. For the moment, and it was to take you another three years to realise this, it was patriotism, and that only, that would raise the people in hordes to the music of your voice. You were a great orator, but you were still singing to the wrong score.

So you broke short your tour, walking off the platform in a half-empty hall at Villaregia. Your contract was broken, too, and the money, every last lira of it, failed to materialise. There was nothing left, no final resource to stem the tide of the creditors.

One bleak Monday, with a storm of hail battering the evergreens, and a shrill wind in the corridors, when you were mercifully in Rome, pursuing the Marchesa Casati dressed as a swine in a masque from the *Odyssey*, the bailiffs appeared with a due warrant, and removed your horses from the stables.

I can see the poor beasts now, rearing and whinnying in the falling flakes, as the unfamiliar hands lift their reins and herd them into the wagons. It was a cruel scene. Your remaining seven servants gathered in the cold, impassive as I was, tight-lipped and near to tears, as Aquilino and Murgiona, Silvano and Ellinor, the puckish roan Tristano, and the tall grey stallion El Nar, the beautiful chestnut Vai-Vai and the dangerous Undulna, yes finally even her, rearing and wild-eyed, not understanding this rape of her comfortable domain in the straw, were dragged out and made to totter up a wooden ramp and on to a cart.

'Nineteen horses,' a man in a bowler hat said with a curt nod, as he handed me a receipt, 'seized in lieu of the Signor D'Annunzio's debts to the tradesmen of Florence.'

Then the horses were gone, neighing their futile protests through the blizzard, as the carts moved away down the forest road, and we were left in the shadow of those great yawning stables, unlikely, as I perhaps alone knew, to be ever repopulated.

So what could be done?

'Flight is the only thing, Gabriele,' I said, when you

The Lion of Pescara

came back from Rome, a swine well satisfied, I think, in the stews of the Hassler, but one without any more a string of thoroughbreds to command at the Capponcina.

We discussed the options. You were already in debt all over Italy. There were bills in Rome as there were bills in Florence. Bills in Venice and bills in Genoa.

'It means exile,' I said. 'The one alternative is to go abroad. Not far, perhaps. But over the border, and into some other country where the writ of Italian law no longer runs. Who knows? Matters may improve. You may soon be able to return.'

I hardly believed this last little crumb of comfort, and neither, I am sure, did you. But you took my point. I meant what I said. Alas, you were never one to enjoy making decisions. But this one, perhaps by a better fortune than you realised, had been made already on your behalf.

'Tomaso,' you said with a smile, 'there are very few letters of difference between Florence and France. To France, therefore, I will go. It will seem perhaps like a minimum shift of scene.'

So to France you did go, as I have related elsewhere, and to France meant only one possible city at this point in time, that welcoming centre of intrigue and culture that had already published *Il Delirio* in a French translation under the name of Donatella Cross, a pseudonym for the Russian Madame. Indeed, she may have had some small hand in part of the work, though scarcely all, I fear, busy as she was kept between other sheets. To Paris, then, we came, and towards that long sequence of adventures and affairs that would shortly lead to Arcachon, and the secretive pines.

It was not, of course, the first time that you had been short of money. It was simply the climax. Indeed, I entered your life in the wake of financial troubles. We had met at a party given by your early publisher, Scarfoglio, when I was apprenticed, as it were, to the lazy trade of books in Milan. You took to my looks, or to my idleness, or to my conversation, or possibly, by some dash of that unerring instinct which was often to serve you with women,

The Horses

through a sudden realisation that I could relieve you of much of the world's pressure.

'Come and see me tomorrow,' you said, and offered a little slip of pasteboard with the neat legend – 'D'Annunzio, Café Greco, at home, five o'clock.' It was your usual hour for business, and there, on a dark banquette over a tiny cup of chocolate, and a frail éclair, you expounded to me your plan.

'My dear Antongini,' you said. 'You are a young man of twenty-four years of age. Life lies ahead of you, boring, predictable, and remunerative. The world of publishing will provide its familiar, everyday rewards. You need fear for nothing.'

I drank my lemon juice.

'Antongini,' you went on, leaning forward with an early sketch of your later irresistible charm. 'You deserve far better things. We are fellow spirits. I require your genius for organisation, you require the stimulus of my admittedly somewhat chaotic imagination. The imagination I give you for nothing. In return for your organising ability, I will pay you a weekly salary, together with full board, and a room of your own, in time, of . . .'

The figure hovered in the air. When it settled it was larger than I might have expected, although smaller than I could have desired. But the die was already cast. I was fascinated by your style, and your wit, and perhaps even more than these by the hint of some exotic destiny that already shimmered in your aura, as if some good fairy or some malignant demon, more likely, with a sense of humour, had marked you out for special treatment.

I was anxious to be part of that special treatment, and to make myself, as I very soon came to be, your closest friend, your confidant, your advisor, your pimp, your colleague, your fellow-conspirator, your comrade-in-arms, your agent, your publisher, your financial guide, your pawnbroker, your research assistant, your companion in many a night on the tiles or in the ditches, your secretary, your philosopher and your scribe.

'Agreed,' I said, and we shook hands over the table.

The Lion of Pescara

It was 1898, and you were already in the fringes, or shall I say the outerworks, of your long and to my mind overoperatic relationship with the demanding Eleonora. It was she, very shortly, who became the banker of our mutual enterprise, and without her funds, and her fame, very few of your gaudy dramas would ever have reached, and far less held, the stage of the day.

True, but you gave her back what she needed even more than you her money, I mean your passion, your understanding of her talent, and, after all, a fine series of vehicles for those O so expressive eyes and that wilting, oppressed stoop of the shoulders, as the wife, perhaps, in *La Gioconda*, whom I see triumphing even now, the crowds wild with cheering, at Palermo in April 1899. It was hardly so in Naples, alas, a few days later with *La Gloria*. Nor with *Francesca da Rimini*, where your hero Malatesta so prophetically suffered the gouging out of his eye.

No, even in the cauldron of your own suffering, you lay at the Red House and remembered that long line of plays, living over again the success and the failures, trying to read out the fickle message of the theatre-going public's acclaim or disapprobation.

'Venice,' you murmured, amidst the ticking of the many clocks. 'Here perhaps, Tomaso, we could found a Latin Bayreuth, where the great Wagner lies at peace. A theatre of the open air. A sanctuary beside the lake. A place amongst the olive-trees whose twisted branches imitate the convulsions of the maenads. The convolutions of our own protracted lives.'

It was built, finally, your dream-stage, but in your final days at the Vittoriale, when the Duse was no longer alive to play in its confines, and the hollow circle echoed only to the wind, and to your own cracking, though still melodious, cadences as you recited to Luisa Baccara, and the clock-watching Mussolini.

But of this more, and in its own place, and time.

—IV—

The Greyhound

I

THE HEATING SYSTEM had broken. This is what I remember best about your last meeting with the men of Ronchi at the Red House before your march on Fiume. All day, and it was a freezing wintry one in the early part of September of 1918, the sort of day that would surely convince the most sceptical that Venetian autumns are more severe than those elsewhere, all day, I say, the flute-loving Dante had sprung from tiny room to tiny room, futile with torchère and lantern in a prolonged attempt to coax one last surge of power from the steam heating.

It was not to be. Some quirk in the manufacture, never, fortunately, to be repeated in your future installations, which were wisely entrusted to another firm, had occasioned a blockage in some remote section of piping, or a flaw in a loosened valve, or a leakage from the main boiler, above whose torpid hugeness, bent like a plumpened Valkyrie, the docile Albina was pressed into service to raise a wax-dripping candelabra, while the frowning gondolier made his final, and unsatisfactory, inspection.

You stood, shivering in a large blanket wrapped round your aviator's uniform, with a glass of Scotch and honey and lemon in your fingers, enduring the early ravages of a bout of influenza, while Dante made his gloomy report.

Impossibile, he murmured, spreading his hands. No power.

The Lion of Pescara

So that you, of all men the most susceptible to a low temperature, were forced to go through one of the most crucial debates of your career, snivelling and on the brink of a fever, while your fellow conspirators clapped their hands for warmth, and shivered from chair to chair amidst those flawed mirrors, and those wildly inaccurate machines for keeping time.

We had arrived the day before, by train from Rome, since you had been invited to make a speech to a battalion of veterans at the ceremony of the password, the kind of ritual occasion of which you had grown increasingly fond, and a wire had gone ahead instructing Albina and Dante to make everything ready for our arrival. Alas, the house had been closed for repairs to the roof, and the Prince Hohenlohe, who was responsible for these, under the terms of your lease, had been worse than tardy.

The cold winds of the canal, and the damp airs of the lagoon, had had months to impregnate the plaster of the walls, and the silks of the tapestries and the chair-covers, and even, I fear, the mechanisms of some of the clocks, with a deep-seated and inextractable dankness. It was not simply, therefore, a temporary lack of warmth we were suffering from. It was a sense of breathing perpetual water.

Only Evandro, stretching his great wings like a feather umbrella suddenly endowed with life, seemed to be in his element, squawking with delight at the discovery of some fertile puddle in the recesses of a little corridor, or piercing an unwary toad with a sudden jab of his vicious beak. I myself had walked round in a pair of English wellingtons, not taking off my overcoat, and solacing an inner iciness with a furtive nip or two from my own hip flask of cognac.

Luisa Baccara, of course, was the first to arrive. You were not yet in that stage of this last affair when the two of you were spending all your time together, although that was to start very soon in the baroque Magyar palace at Fiume. Luisa was following her career as a concert pianist, and had received your wire in Padua, and motored over with a friend to Mestre, from whence her slender darkness, shrouded already in its dedicated mystery, had been

The Greyhound

ferried across the water by gondola, and had alighted, like the lady of the lake, at your friable jetty beside the garden.

She had sat, through most of our heating troubles, alternately entranced and shocked by the survival genius or the false notes of your grand piano, from which she began to extract the most favourable versions of Debussy that she could, anxious, as indeed we all were, to soothe your grated nerves and your gathering illness.

Luisa Baccara was at this date twenty-three years of age, and none of us knew, except she herself perhaps, in the pouting sincerity of her withdrawn affections, that she would outlive all other amours, and be at your side, through sweet times and ill, for what was to be a period of not far short of twenty years. She was a tough one, la Baccara. She had none of the macabre fascination of the other Luisa, that pocket Messalina, nor the sinuous beauty of Ida Rubinstein, perhaps her keenest rivals of those early years, but she had something neither possessed, a complete and absolute devotion of the sort only the now dying Eleonora had offered you before.

So we waited, this freezing, dripping, autumnal, gloomy, Venetian day, Luisa at her openmouthed black instrument, like some great whale of sonority and a kind of water-logged, impaired blowing, I with my snaps of brandy, irritable and worried, Albina preparing lasagne verde for an indefinite number of hungry visitors in the kitchen, Dante brushing shoes that were soiled with mud, and laying newspapers to soak up water along the main corridor, Evandro spearing frogs and booming in delight, and you, the master of our bizarre household, slipping deeper and deeper into melancholy and frantic nose-blowing.

The conspirators began to arrive in the early evening, some by motor-boat and more by gondola. By the time darkness had fallen, a little after seven, there must have been nearly twenty men, and three or four women, gathered in the long drawing-room. First of all the industrialist, Oscar Sinigaglia, whose interests in Trieste were

The Lion of Pescara

to supply much of the finance for what was now planned as a fairly immediate armed march on Fiume.

'Enchanté,' I remember him saying, in bad French, as he was introduced to Luisa, and bowed over her limp fingers, drawing off his kid gloves, and then noticing the incisive temperature of the room, and rapidly deciding to retain the heavy vicuna overcoat he was wearing. He hunched near to the unburning fire – for, of course, no one had thought to buy any coal – and made small talk with a wealth of gestures and a series of dully Verdiesque tilts of his bald head. I never liked the man. He and his money were necessary, but his caution and his dully reactionary politics were outgrown rather quickly in the cauldron of experiment and progressive change that Fiume under your control was soon to become.

'Explain Fiume to me,' Luisa once asked you, before the guests arrived, as you and I were deep in some abstruse discussion about the supply of rifles, or the drafting of a constitution, and she was adjusting the fox-fur around her neck at the piano.

'Fiume,' you answered, laughing through your phlegm. 'Fiume, my darling, is the jewel of the future and the chancre of the past. Let me put it another way. In the Vatican there is a baptismal font made by Carlo Fontana in 1698. It represents in bas-relief Italy between her two seas, with the outline of the Dalmatian coastline, and the port of Fiume beyond. The figure of Christ is depicted on the Italian shore, stretching out his hand to cover the whole area contested by the Slavs. Thus God, my dear, has marked out the confines of Italy. His messengers, myself and my grenadiers, whose representatives will be joining us here for dinner, have the sacred duty of reuniting the Italy of the West with the Italy of the East.'

Luisa pouted, I remember, and then shrugged and played a scale. In another moment, her fingers were tracing out what was later to become the March of Ronchi and to be sung by hoarse and excited male voices in every tavern along the waterfront when our columns entered the Fiuman gates.

The Greyhound

'Bravo,' you cried, reaching over to put your hand on her shoulder. 'That says it all more vividly than any words of mine. Music, you know, Tomaso, is the key to truth.'

Perhaps it was. In this eighteenth-century bon-bon box, with the great shadow of Wagner mistily outlined as it often seemed along the canal, I could feel more vividly the tension of romance and structure, the heady mixings of art and life, music and its resonance in politics, poetry and action, with every hour that seemed to pass.

We had moved through violent, and then through frustrating, times. The streets of Rome and Naples were full of unemployed Arditi, drinking their sorrows away in the quest for women and adventure that has always been the Italian disease. They were young men who had been through fire and slaughter for what they had seen as a better world, a more progressive and honourable Italy than the one their fathers had sent them out to fight for.

Thousands of private soldiers, and hundreds of officers, were lying idle and in search of a cause. They had skills to use, military and technical, and time to brood on what to use them for. An empire across the seas, and a city of revolution to crown its capture, these were the twin, apparently conflicting but so often interlocking goals that the more intelligent ex-soldiers, and of these there were surprisingly many, were beginning to fix their eyes on.

Fiume was the obvious target. The Italian population, well in the majority, had suffered for many decades at the hands of the Croats, and, from farther away, the rule of Hungary. There was insurrection, strife and unrest, in the air. After the war, occupying troops from all the allied armies – French and British as well as Italian – had held an uneasy peace in the town.

But there had been many plots, many schemes, wild or practical, an advance on the town to be led by the Duke of Aosta, a man so fascinated by your own achievements that he even imitated your handwriting, an armed assault by a mercenary army organised by a terrible poet, Sam Benelli, and, of course, more than one vision of an exploit involving your own spectacular imagination and feats of daring.

The Lion of Pescara

Four days before our meeting, the Italian garrison had been withdrawn to the small town of Ronchi, marching out through streets lined with women showering flowers, and chanting Italian patriotic songs, and the situation had entered a new phase. A group of seven young officers had evolved a crisis, and a final, plan. Within the city of Fiume, Captain Horst-Venturi was organised to lead an armed rising, provided that an army of legionnaires, led by yourself, would march from Ronchi and join him at the gates.

It was Horst-Venturi who arrived himself with his colleague Lieutenant Grandjacquet, and clicked his heels stiffly in the hiss of chimes, and tinkle of wine glasses, as Dante tottered in with a tray heaped with bottles. I remember their polish, the high gloss on those boots, the glittering belts, the buttons gleaming, the gripped swagger sticks, the sense of a pair of chocolate-box toy soldiers, the parade ground relish for doing everything in traditional style.

'Tomorrow at latest,' Horst-Venturi said, with a decisive precision, 'I must return to Fiume. I have to know what you will do tonight.'

You were never one to enjoy being forced to make a decision, and this was hardly to your taste, which still ran more at this stage to a period of glamorous discussion, interspersed with breaks for music, and perhaps a little flirting and coquetry. Attilio Prodam, in certain ways the wierdest and most implausible of the conspirators, had long known this. He had brought his teenage, and luxurious, daughter, to whet your appetite, and to twist your arm.

Prodam was a dumpy, broken-nosed adventurer, who would one day end up as a fairground proprietor, and who already enjoyed the operatic side of the plotting, the merry-go-round and the big dipper of politics, more than the banal details of unit strengths and gun positionings. He had arranged for his pliant wench to present a petition the day before to General Diaz, at a public ceremony in Venice, and to do so wearing a ribbon with the colours of Fiume around her throat.

The Greyhound

The pair arrived now, he in a florid Scots tweed cape, she in a dazzling sable cape, with the flare of the ribbon still there at her naked neck, like a flag on a promontory beleaguered by the enemy, and the story, combined with the girl's most evident sexual charms, won over your wavering thoughts, bemused as they still were by your fever, more trenchantly than any of the ultimata from Horst-Venturi and his lacquered little sidekick.

I sipped my claret, on a quiet stool in a corner, and watched the magic work. Under the fiercely chaperoning eye of the slender Luisa, darkly svelte at her piano, there was little hope of any immediate conquest of the fruitful young loins, but I saw your eyes travel down her navel and mark out those shapely contours for a future exploration. If the Prodam girl was to be found in Fiume, then most assuredly Fiume was where you meant to go.

It was certainly where that red-bearded Hercules, your familiar and action model, the philosopher-rebel Guido Keller, meant to go. He had come hard on the heels of Attilio Prodam, and bare-headed, looming like a falling tree through the gilded architraves of that freezing room, his broad irreverent grin very much to your fancy as he drew a bayonet out of his belt and speared a live goldfish from a bowl to offer to the flapping Evandro.

'Guido,' you remonstrated, 'you go too far.'

'As far as Fiume, dear boy,' I remember he answered, and bayoneted another.

There was never any way of stopping Guido Keller. He had flown more missions than you had yourself, been decorated for bravery by the King, lived like a hermit for four months once in a barrel in Papua, so rumour said, and been known to eat live sparrows and drink the blood of dead Maoris. He had a legend around his shoulders like a tattered cloak. He lived for the fun of action. But he created a poetry of ideas through the fun of action. He drove nearer than any of your other colleagues to the total recreation of life as a kind of macabre or violent art.

'The next theatre,' he said once, later on that evening.

The Lion of Pescara

'Fiume is where we must write our new drama. Soon, Gabriele. But cure your cold first.'

So the conversation continued, each man, and some of the women, putting in a contribution that either strengthened or weakened your resolution to accept the Horst-Venturi plan. I sat there to one side, watching the little circles form and break, half hearing the arguments of an ageing general, so laden with medals that his back seemed to bow under the weight, the insistence of a wiry tweeded little lady with the hint of a moustache, who was secretary to some absent anarchist, and, of course, yes, I had almost forgotten that he was there, the interventions of that subtle, forceful, deferential young journalist in the wing collar and three-piece suit who had come in a bowler hat and a pair of grey spats, and who saw everything, and only spoke when he saw which way the drift of the meeting was going, and who was the editor of a left-wing magazine and leader of the socialists in those years, Benito Mussolini.

You had met before, of course, on a number of occasions during the last three years, and you were to meet often again, both before and after the days of Mussolini's rise to power, fuelled and inspired, as it surely was, by all that you had done, as I shall show, in my due time. But at this date Mussolini was in the wings. He was present, and he had his say, but his views were of little significance in what you chose to do.

'The problem is,' you said in a corner to Sinigaglia, as you blew your nose on a blue silk handkerchief, 'that I am committed, for the moment, to so many other projects. An enterprise in the early spring of next year would be very much easier to be involved in.'

I overheard, as I overheard so much, rising to fill a glass, or to refresh a plate with Albina's profiteroles, and I knew already what most of all was deterring your immediate agreement.

'Your flight to the orient,' murmured Sinigaglia, who was well informed, and who knew that the sinister Nitti, our scheming Prime Minister, had secretly offered to back

The Greyhound

your proposed aerial endeavour with the maximum of publicity and funding, in return for your hands-off attitude in the matter of the Dalmatian coast. 'I know, Colonel.'

He did know, too, or guessed, that your pride was always flattered by the use of your military rank, and that herein might lie the way to your seduction.

'Imagine now,' he continued, looking swiftly round for allies, and finding one with his huge hand under Evandro's wing. 'Imagine, Mr Keller, the effect of a flight to Tokyo from Fiume. The impact on the world press of the news that the victor of the Carnaro was taking off from the most easterly aerodrome on Italian soil, the landing strip at Fiume, for his most remarkable exploit to date, his flight with the message of Italian resurgence borne on wings of glory to the yellow races of the Pacific seaboard.'

This was indeed a classic speech in the style copying your own best efforts that so many of your associates were now beginning to adopt, the Dannunzioisation of the language. A matter of flowers and energy that brought many a smile, when it was ill done, to my cynical lips. But you, alas, were an easy prey to the reversion of your own rhetoric.

'Indeed, yes,' you murmured, there might be some fun in that. 'Eh, Guido?'

'Luisa,' said Guido Keller at this, lifting Evandro into the air, with a great squawking and flapping of wings. 'Play some music for the bird of the orient. Make music for the man who flies to convert the samurai.'

There was laughter, then silence and shivering. Then Luisa, always quick to pick up the musical mood of an occasion, let her fingers flow over the keys and into a mélange of Monteverdi and Puccini, hot opera and cool song, and finally a rousing finale with one of the most popular melodies from the days of 1860, when the soldiers of Garibaldi marched into their kingdom.

Suddenly, the freezing room with its wet walls, its breath of mist on all the mirrors, its wrong, dampened clocks, and its wreckage of plates of lasagne and cake, of dirty or full glasses, its plethora of conspirators, military

The Lion of Pescara

men and rogues, its total coldness and lack of cohesion, sprang to a single salute, a circle of upright singers, a crown of power, nineteen mouths around the piano, for those were all that were then left, roaring out the patriotic words, and looking to you at Luisa's side, a tiny frail-seeming spirit, all blanket still and snivelling, but with a blaze of responding joy in your eyes, and the dawn of resolution in your setting jaw.

The last note was struck, held and dwindled away. There was a crackle of applause, and a hint of a cheer. Then you lifted your hand.

'My friends,' you said. 'I will lead the march on Fiume. It remains only to choose the date. Let it be, I say, on the 11th of September, the magic eleventh day on which I always prosper, the day on which I sailed into the bay of Buccari and left my poems in bottles to twist the tail of the Austrian fleet. On the 11th of September, one week from today, I shall lead the march on Fiume.'

So the crown dissolved, the meeting broke up, men reached for their hats or their coats, women shuddered in the cold, some took a last glass of wine, some finished off their profiteroles, one or two drained down their cups of black coffee, and within half an hour the gilded room was empty, only Luisa at her piano playing Bach, and I in my corner turning over the pages of an aeronautical magazine, and you on a long sofa, closing your eyes over your glass of Scotch and honey, remained to echo what had taken place.

2

IT WAS RAINING. I remember waiting there in my lieutenant's uniform, with my swagger stick under my arm, and the wind blowing freezing drops into my face as I stood to attention while you stepped awkwardly down into the rocking motor-boat at the landing-stage.

There had been an ardent farewell with Luisa in the drawing-room, she smothering you with a mixture of tears, remonstrations and kisses, from under an immense fox-fur, you nodding and preoccupied, but as gallant as your cold would allow, as you punctuated your last embraces with long-drawn pulls at a nostril inhaler to stop your snuffling.

It made an odd scene. The dazzling colonel's uniform with your full complement of medals, the trunks and suitcases bound up in leather straps, the diffident hovering of Albina, clutching a package of mint sweets for the journey, the sense of time both static and slipping by, as if two opposing forces were at work in the glimmering room.

Then we were out on the jetty in the wind, with Dante leaning up from the tiller to offer you his knotty hand, and the first stage of that amazing advance to Fiume already in motion. It was a short, fast rush across the lagoon, the stern leaving a long V in the murky water, the bow wave rising on either side into a lofty curl as if broken open by iron.

The Lion of Pescara

We spoke little, huddling up for warmth under thick travelling rugs. Once you looked round at me and grinned. I was moved by the drawn look in your face. You showed all of your fifty years for a moment, and then that boyish excitement seemed to wipe them away like the wrong words written on a slate.

At Mestre the Mercedes was waiting, decked out in the colours of an Italian general, with a pennant flying from the radiator cap and all the brass polished up to a gleaming flow of stars in the flare of the gas-lights. The rain beat on the green bonnet, and the chauffeur stood fiddling with the mechanism of the hood.

You addressed yourself to the gondolier, as he finished stacking the trunks in the boot.

'Goodbye, Dante,' you said. 'I shall see you again, if at all, as the master of a new destiny. Wait for me, and take care.'

Then you shook his hand in both of yours, bowing for a moment, as if under stress of grief, before stepping into the back seat of the car. The rain continued to beat down as Dante stood a little uneasily by the running-board, unsure whether to wave or to withdraw. I was in the front seat alongside the driving wheel, watching through the streaming glass as the chauffeur cranked the zig-zag shape of the starting-handle.

It seemed a long time before he could get it going. Then, with a thumbs up sign, he turned and took his position to the accompaniment of a huge throaty roaring. The music had started to play.

The comic-opera side of the Fiume campaign was already in progress, but none of us was quite sure yet of what parts we had to play. It was as if invisible cameras were turning in the sodden clouds, and we poor singers had to do our best in this first, rather unprepared rehearsal.

The wheels ground in the gravel, Dante did after all wave, and then we were rolling forward into the darkness, rain pattering like little thrown stones, or perhaps almonds for a wedding, along the taut stretched leather of the raised hood.

The Greyhound

It was an easy enough journey to Ronchi, and I slept through some of it, letting my head sink on to my chest, and feeling the vibration of the machine like a distant humming of bees. The chauffeur drove well, and I was unworried by any sudden shocks or tremor. Once I looked back over my shoulder through the partition glass and saw that you had stretched out full length on the seat and seemed to be fast asleep. And there at your feet on the fawn carpet, sinuous and quiet, lay the elegant mottled contours of your favourite greyhound, Delrosa.

I suppose we had always known that your lovely Delrosa would come on the march, and she had maintained a singular unobtrusiveness during our final preparation, unlike the endlessy fluttering and obstructive Evandro.

So that now I saw the dog for the first time, a bizarre accompaniment for a military operation of the danger that ours was to be, but no doubt an apt mascot and a suitable enough emblem for speed and economy.

At Ronchi you were wide awake, leaning forward with maps on your knee, as the headlamps bored their double lanes of bright light along the puddled streets towards the barracks. There Major Carlo Reina, immaculate in a trenchcoat and riding-boots, and with not a hint of concern about the adverse weather in his precision salute, was already waiting in the rain. He had the clipped fair moustache and florid, reddish face that always, I thought, seemed to give him a rather English air.

'Colonel,' he said, and held open the car door.

Delrosa, to his apparent surprise, loped out first, and you were hard on her slippery heels, landing with a splash in a massive pool of muddy water. Poor Carlo Reina's boots were given the first of several shower-baths.

'Alas, we have one problem,' he disclosed, and we walked with him into a guard-room lit by a candle, where a sergeant was waiting behind a typewriter, and a bottle of Scotch stood open on a wicker table. 'Would you pour drinks, Lieutenant?'

I gave us all a generous measure as he outlined the

The Lion of Pescara

situation. It appeared that the camions we were expecting to convey our small army of one hundred and eighty-six volunteers had not materialised. The only way to Fiume at present was on foot.

You had left your Scotch untasted – you were never much of a drinker – and you watched the rain making wavering lines down the guard-room window as Delrosa nuzzled your calf with her slender muzzle.

'Then we must march,' you said. 'Who knows? God may provide what we require on the way.'

I glanced at my wrist-watch. It was just after ten o'clock. You still looked very tired to me.

'Gabriele,' I said, 'may I suggest that we leave it until midnight? I confess to needing a little time to gather my energies.'

Reina glanced at me, and then at your bent figure by the window, shivering still with fever, and intermittently wracked by cough or snivel. You had hardly the air of a great commander about to undertake a forced march for a dawn assault on a remote objective.

'That might be best,' Reina agreed. 'In the meanwhile I shall move heaven and earth to get the trucks here on time.'

So a makeshift arrangement for sleeping was rigged up over four small tables in another room, and you lay down to rest again, with the patient hound, like a Crusader's last companion, sculptured in blue and white, as it seemed, at your feet on the floor.

At midnight, the march began. The rain was heavier by then, and the wind had risen, so that long swoops of water were flung in our faces as we turned along the road towards the sea. The men were cheerful, keyed up by waiting, and ready to break out into patriotic songs whenever anyone gave the lead.

The Mercedes, of course, went with us, and although you insisted on marching in front with Reina, I managed to persuade you into reasonably frequent rests, on the pretext of conferences about the route, in the back seat of the vehicle, where Delrosa, with all the sensibleness of an

The Greyhound

animal that sees no point in getting colder and wetter than she needs, was quietly curled up under the cocktail cabinet.

We should never, I fear, have arrived in Fiume on time, or even at all, but for the ingenuity, later to be so frequently repeated, of the crazy, and yet so oddly practical, Guido Keller. At the first village on our march, a tiny hamlet by the name of Palanova, he vanished into the night with a handful of picked comrades, and returned only half an hour later with twenty-six transport vehicles, and several hundred enthusiastic recruits for the cause.

It appeared that these men had been rather discontentedly guarding a military supply depot, and had soon responded to the rhetoric and the arguments propounded by Keller for allowing their trucks, and indeed their own allegiance, to be commandeered in the name of the greater Italy, or rather, perhaps, what was shortly to become known as the Regency of the Carnaro.

These were the first of many defections throughout the night. Their arrival had a massive effect on the confidence of all. You yourself congratulated Keller in a brief speech in your most flamboyant vein, and after a few choruses of the national anthem, the men piled into the trucks and our advance continued at full speed, and in dryer conditions, and with much more drama and spectacle.

Timing, of course, was the essence of the affair. Inside the city, Horst-Venturi and his men were ready to seize the command-post and insist that the Allied Forces leave, if necessary under threat of arms. But they would make their move exactly at dawn, when your own army was to be knocking at the city gates and prepared to enter.

In fact, for various reasons, there were considerable delays, and Horst-Venturi, so it was later rumoured, actually gave orders to abandon the plan to seize the command-post, and was disobeyed by his subordinates. At any rate, in a muddle very typical of the grandiose and yet seemingly accidental development of matters that fateful morning, nothing very much happened inside the city except for a widespread enthusiasm for your own advance,

The Lion of Pescara

an enormous, almost amorous anticipation, and a parade with knives, clubs and fine clothes, on the part of all the womenfolk of the city, including a good deal of issuing forth to see whether or not your troops were on the way.

We breakfasted on coffee and rolls some distance from Fiume at eight o'clock in the morning, squatting beside camp fires and eating together in the early flush of that intense comradeship that was to be the most exciting feature of the Fiuman adventure. The skies had cleared by then, and the sun was struggling, symbolically it seemed, to make way through a belt of low-lying cloud. It was a dank morning, but at last a fairly dry one.

Your own spirits, and indeed your appearance, had taken on a much brighter tinge, and I was delighted to suppose that your bout of fever might be nearing its end. You fed Delrosa with strips of sausage, and spent a few minutes walking round and chatting with the men, before we re-embarked in our trucks and motored on.

The most striking encounter of the journey, and indeed the only one that ever seemed to presage a conflict of forces, occurred about three hours later, at eleven o'clock. You were leading the column by then in your Mercedes, with only a pair of armoured cars out in front in case of mine-fields, and behind you the trucks rolled in a massive and coiling crocodile. I estimate that we had several thousand men under arms at our disposal by this time. It made a formidable, and a threatening, body.

At any rate, so it seemed to the Italian in command of all forces in Fiume, the General Pittaluga. Earlier in the day, he had instructed the officer in charge of a large band of Arditi, Colonel Raffaele Repetto, to advance and order you to halt, and in the event of your refusing, to shoot you. Repetto had simply saluted, clicked his heels, and made no move.

So that it was the General himself, leaving the matter of Repetto's mutiny to be settled later, who put on his full dress uniform and drove out in his staff car to meet the advancing forces head on. The encounter a few miles beyond the gates of Fiume became a satirical repetition of

The Greyhound

the notorious meeting at the Lake of Laffrey, over a century earlier, when Napoleon confronted the French troops who had been sent to arrest him.

The General's Fiat rolled to a halt in a cloud of dust, and the armoured cars pulled up a few yards away. Your own Mercedes came to a stop. Reina was in the back seat with you, and I was still beside the chauffeur.

'Come with us, Tomaso,' you said to me, as you climbed down into the road. 'This may be history.'

So the three of us, you and I and Reina, like the villains at the end of a Western, walked slowly through the dust in the direction of the General and his staff. We all stopped. It was the General, a very fat and solemn-looking man, who gathered his pomp around him and spoke out first.

'Colonel D'Annunzio,' he began. 'I order you to withdraw your men to their barracks at Ronchi.'

'General,' you replied, with surprising brevity, 'I am afraid that will not be possible.'

The General slapped his gloves in his hands.

'Then you must accept the consequences,' he said.

It was still an overcast morning, and there were drifts of water lying where the occasional sun had failed yet to penetrate. I felt very aware of the dry smell of pomade in the air, the hint of sweat, and the creaking of leather. A long time seemed to go by. I could imagine a remote director in a nearby ash tree about to call out, hold it, hold it, and then, cut.

Then I heard your voice at my elbow.

'General,' you said, very quietly, but loud enough, as it seemed, to be heard some distance back along the column. 'You have only to instruct the soldiers to shoot me.'

Then you slowly unbuttoned your great-coat, and laid bare your chest, along which glittered your rows of medals for valour, with the gold medal the King himself had presented to you at their head.

It was a tremendous moment. There seemed to be a burst of far-away cheering, but in fact there was dead silence. I watched the fat, fleshy face of the General

The Lion of Pescara

working, puzzled, outraged, and then finally, dumbstruck with a kind of awe.

There wasn't, of course, very much that he could have done. I doubt if there was a single soldier in the Italian army who would have been prepared to go down in history as the man who shot our greatest war hero, the Colonel Gabriele D'Annunzio. Certainly, General Pittaluga was not ready to assume that responsibility in person, although the means to carry out the order were there, loaded and unbuttoned, in his holster.

Instead, he went with the tide. He followed the wave of history. With a quick step, he came forward and shook you warmly by the hand.

After that, the remainder of our advance was a triumphal progress. I gave up my seat in the Mercedes, Reina came into the front, and you rode through the gates of Fiume with Pittaluga, her commanding general, there at your side. The streets were lined with cheering crowds, rosettes and flowers were everywhere, women ran forward to press their hands to the windows of the car, soldiers fired volleys of shots into the air, and not a single man had been wounded or killed.

Fiume was yours.

That afternoon, you went to bed, sequestrating a room at the Hotel Europa as your temporary headquarters. You slept the sleep of the just, or at least the audacious, for sure, and were awakened a little after five, as I was awakened myself in the next room, by an eager and elated Guido Keller.

'Colonel,' were his first words to you, 'or should I say rather, Governor?'

He had spent the afternoon in shrewd negotiation, appreciating, quicker than many of the other conspirators, that some decisive action might be needed to confirm your power in a more ritual form. So he had interviewed Antonio Grossich, of the Fiuman National Council, and rapidly persuaded him, some claimed later with the help of a bayonet, that it was vital to calm down the situation by the rapid appointment of yourself as commandante.

The Greyhound

'Governor,' you murmured, he told me later, in some wonder. 'But I only came to conquer, Guido. Not to rule.'

Perhaps the burden of office was, indeed, one you had been loath to assume, and were in some measure surprised, though undoubtedly delighted, to be offered. You had had your plans, after all, for that flight to Tokyo. You had other plans, too, more nebulous but further reaching, for an immediate advance through Dalmatia.

It may have irked you a little to become Augustus Caesar before you had had ample time to savour your new role as Alexander the Great. At any rate, the moment soon passed. I was by your side as you walked through the cheering streets with Keller and Reina to the Governor's Palace, that enormous baroque extravaganza like a railway station, or perhaps a provincial town hall, which had been built in the 1880s, at colossal expense, and by Italian craftsmen, doubtless with their tongues in their cheeks, to house the plenipotentiary of the remote empire that had ruled Fiume until the outbreak of war.

There was still a sort of Magyar swagger about the eleven-bay façade, and the rusticated ground floor, and the lofty series of Corinthian capitals roofing a balustraded veranda, above which the crest of Hungary, and a massive stone crown, and what always seemed to me to be a star of David, were still presiding in exiled magnificence.

Very soon the flag of the Regency would fly up there. But today was the time for rejoicing rather than for consolidation. I stood behind you in a window niche as you stepped through on to that veranda, as you had stepped out before on to the balcony of that hotel in Genoa, and once more I heard the surge of cheering voices, many more this time, and then the fluid music of your own voice, the articulator and the channel of these people's destiny.

'Italians of Fiume,' you began.

And it was several minutes before you could be heard again above the cheering. Then you went on with your simple message, honouring your comrades, unit by unit and name by name, praising the victory of the day and promising a better world tomorrow.

The Lion of Pescara

But it was your action rather than your words that confirmed and symbolised the new mood of the Regency more vividly than any legislation or promise. With Guido Keller and Reina to help you, you unfurled the red, white and green flag that had covered the body of your friend Giovanni Randaccio when he fell on the battlefield of the Timavo.

In a multicoloured cascade it opened out like a tablecloth of patriotic brocade over the dull stonework and the fancy columns. There was a moment's hush, then a deep, solemn murmur, and finally a silence as you raised your hand and proclaimed:

'I, a soldier, a volunteer, a wounded veteran of the war, believe that I interpret the will of all the people of Italy, when I hereby announce the annexation of Fiume.'

Heady stuff. And the square exploded in cheering, dancing, fireworks, cries of Yes, and Fiume, and the celebration, the great party that was to continue for eighteen months, was at last fully under way, though its instigator and innermost spirit, alas, crept away soon after it began to a lonely bed, or rather to a bed shared only for once by a greyhound, and there slept in peace and security until the morning.

It had been quite a day.

3

AMAZINGLY ENOUGH, WITHIN four weeks of this explosion of cathartic enjoyment, I was no longer in Fiume. The organisation of the city's affairs, both internal and at large, rapidly demanded a series of instant, and not always, alas, quite fully considered, appointments. For months there was in effect a tripartite control within the city boundaries, a mingling of responsibility between the National Council, a moribund if not entirely unbenevolent sequence of elderly gentlemen, the Military Command, which more and more came to mean the brighter spirits amongst the more active junior officers, the Praetorian guard whose innermost will, so it often seemed, was the erratic and delightful demon wit of Guido Keller, and finally an only faintly more sober power epitomised by your own direct rule, mediated, as it occasionally was, through a whole gamut of temporary liaison figures.

News of the coup at Fiume, soon to become known, and aptly, through the black flames on the arm insignia of the Arditi, as the city of the holocaust, leapt round the world in the hectic words of journalist, worker of telegraph key or ship's waiter. A motley assembly of incredible visitors, a few truly anxious to assist the new governor in his task, more, no doubt, to profit from his opening of so many doors that had long remained closed, arrived in their dozens, then their hundreds. By train, by ship, and some-

The Lion of Pescara

times even by motor-car or flying machine, these adventurers would land on our doorstep.

The immense marble hall of the Governor's Palace became a sort of oriental bazaar where uniformed secretaries would attempt to sort some order into the constant stream of callers. At makeshift folding tables, arranged as if for some colossal church bridge match, groups of candidates for this or that interesting commission, or secret and profitable plot, would outline their business to sceptical or bored or sometimes even genuinely excited young officers. Under the florid puce scagliola of the Hungarian columns, lights blazed all day in the converted chandeliers, boots clicked on the intricate interlocking patterns of the tiled floor, gloved fingers tapped on the rails of the grotesque balustrade, and pouting cupids held out their gushing cornucopiae in the central fountain.

The great staircase, breaking and rising at a wide landing rich with rococo mirrors, provided the final sorting mesh for the handful who got past the lower screening. There one or other of your more trusted sifters might seize the arm of a Persian diplomat in exile, or a Greek dancer, or a peasant girl with a nice figure from the mountains, anyone, in fact, who seemed likely to diversify your, or their own, day with a scheme, a tale, or some love-making. The last barrier would be passed, and the lofty double walnut doors into the ballroom – which had now become your office, right in the centre of the building, and behind the balcony from which you regularly spoke to the crowds – would be thrown open to reveal the final bizarre splendour of the Governor at work.

Luisa Baccara, who had soon arrived with a dozen Saratoga trunks, largely packed with furs and sheet music, and several boxes of a rare Sicilian sweetmeat that she particularly doted on, would very often be seated at the black Steinway she had commandeered in your name from a local dealer, and had had installed in an alcove with a view of the sea, and the room would thus be filled with the strains of whatever patriotic or melancholy tune might at that moment be appropriate to the wayward lady's mood.

The Greyhound

If sad, the music might well be drawing a mournful, growling response from the desolate Delrosa, couched with her lean head on her paws a few yards from the solid whirl of empire brass and a kind of Coromandel wood which formed your private writing-table. This, of course, would be loaded with files, manuscripts of little-known fifteenth-century poets, magazines about ballistics, an occasional bottle of Perrier or a tray of grapes and apples.

Grapes had acquired a symbolic force for you. At Ronchi on the night of the march, an old woman had offered you a bunch from her garden, but your cold had been too severe to give you any appetite, and you had only, so you told me later, in a letter, counted the number of grapes in the bunch over and over until you fell fast asleep.

'Perhaps when I am on my deathbed, Tomaso,' you wrote, 'an angel will descend from Heaven to offer me that bunch of grapes.'

In the meanwhile, there was always a secular bowl, of Waterford cut-glass from England, and there the purple rounds gleamed on their little stalks, plucked, savoured, and emptied of their seeds into a low spittoon in the form of a tortoise, which was a present from Attilio Prodam. This *outré* figure, alas, had been arrested for some tax evasion a few days before the march, and was languishing in an Italian jail. He was never, in fact, able to join us, or to bring, even sadder loss, his nubile daughter to the city of the holocaust. The tortoise was a quaint apology for his tardiness.

Of the other conspirators, Sinigaglia was a constant source of funds, and a brake on progress, the voice of caution and of diplomacy. The official head of your government was Major-General Givrati, a lawyer from Venice who had had a distinguished career in the battles for the Timavo. As time went on, however, and the more reactionary wing of your support was upstaged in the increasingly transforming and revolutionary adventures of the anarchist elements, a new series of power figures were to emerge, not least the rather sinister Belgian poet, Leon Koschnitsky, who dressed always in black leather, and

The Lion of Pescara

wore dark glasses, and cultivated his hair down to his shoulders.

Later, of course, there was Alceste de Ambris, the slender professor from Naples, with his pince-nez and his wing collars, who drafted that most amazing of modern political documents, the Carta del Carnaro. But of this I shall tell more in my time. The early days of the Regency, when so much was men in open-necked uniforms with bottles of champagne, and their heads in Japanese or Indian bandanas, and women admiring whatever they did, with their skirts up to their waists for dancing, and their hair full of flowers, these I saw and took part in at first hand, always a welcome visitor in the great vaulted ballroom, and the acolyte of your frequent intimacies and confessions. The later days, when the characteristic Fiuman style, so much commented on by those more tourist elements who came to admire, was at last in rich blossom, those, too, I lived through. But the middle days were my own time of exile.

'Tomaso,' you said to me one day, as you pared an orange with a kozuka, and signed letters with a desultory abandon, 'I have a commission I wish you to undertake.'

We were alone, as rarely, in the great office, and your voice echoed around the ceiling, seeming almost to disturb the floating titans, provincial, though Tiepoloesque, amidst their draperies in the centre panel of the stuccowork.

'We need a delegate to the Peace Conference in Paris,' you went on, a little nervously I believe, knowing as you did, that the acceptance of any such mission on my part meant a lengthy exile from the nub of excitement that Fiume had become. 'And there is no one, Tomaso, believe me, I have thought with much care, no one but you whom I trust to do the job. It will require the finesse, and the resource, of a great criminal.'

You had, of course, inevitably struck on the right note to ensure my agreement. After a few moments in which you had painted my role as something between a male Matahari and a modern Brigadier Gerard, a plenipoten-

The Greyhound

tiary with the open cheque-book and the licence to intrigue of an international diamond merchant, I was fully convinced that I was being offered a position it was impossible to refuse.

'Gabriele,' I said. 'Your wish is my command.'

So it was that Lieutenant Antongini, as I then was, was issued by the notorious Fiuman Forgery Office – indeed officially so called, in a splurge of wit, when it was clear that there was no other form of bureau which could hope to provide our citizens with the means to travel – with a full and properly authorised set of documents and letters of credit as the representative of the Republic of Fiume at the Conference of Versailles.

By this time the world had long ceased to expect any very dramatic or satisfying outcome of the endless deliberations which had made the conference a repetition of the famous Council of Constance in 1414. At that date it was said that a body of courtesans and loose women to the number of thirty thousand had converged on Constance for the entertainment, deception and general picking over of the vast mass of delegates. In Paris, there were fewer, but then in Paris there was always an extensive resident complement of such adjuncts to political decision-making.

The importance of the conference for the city of Fiume lay in our opportunity to secure alliances there, or at least expressions of favourable opinion, which could be brought to bear against the still recalcitrant and non-annexation-minded Signor Nitti. The streets and cafés of Paris were, indeed, jumping with a plethora of unusual connections, and I was quick to establish myself in the Rue de Madrid, a short walk from that hive of information and plotting, the Café Napolitain.

I was able to arrive relatively incognito, a valuable asset, through my decision to make my way to Paris after a trip to see some relations in Milan, one of whom, a solitary and horse-loving cousin, who rarely went farther from home than the opera and the park, was quite sufficiently like myself to attract away the attentions of the government surveillance, in the shape of a small bony man in a top-hat, who had been allocated to my pursuit and study. I journeyed on from Milan unwatched, while my poor cousin, though I think he was quite oblivious to this, enjoyed the full-time perusal and detailed reporting of a well-paid government agent.

At the frontier I had a bad experience with my most precious piece of luggage, the ceremonial sword of General Brussiloff – the famous Cossack who had invaded Galicia in 1914 – which had been presented as a souvenir to another Russian general, General Torcom, and had been left behind, in a fit of hasty departure when that worthy decided to quit Fiume in haste after the march from Ronchi. Your notable imagination and love of antique weapons inevitably seized on this lethal relic and insisted that it be carried as a present, in the way of an Arab to a bedouin tribesman, when I visited the exiled King of Montenegro, whose help you were convinced would be of enormous benefit in our affairs, whatever they might be, through the wilds of Dalmatia.

Thus it was, to cut a long and surely scarcely convincing story short, that I arrived at the Italian customs with a gold-hilted sabre, in a plush crimson scabbard, and with seemingly no very good reason for possessing it.

'I am a dealer in antique weapons,' I insisted, 'and am bearing this ancient sabre to an auction of precious militaria in the Bourse. I will willingly leave it in your charge, or the charge of the guard on my train, until such time as I arrive in Paris.'

The difficulty of exporting the sabre was finally overcome by the dispensation of most of my somewhat exiguous first quarter's funds for the Fiuman legation in Paris and in due course the weapon was, indeed, presented to the portly, bewhiskered and infinitely courteous monarch at a small tea-party in Neuilly. Alas, a lifetime of lost endeavours, and cynical liaisons, had bred a fine contempt for the romantic ventures of the young in the heart of this veteran of defeat. He accepted the sword, and listened to all I said, but offered neither verbal, nor, as

The Greyhound

would have been better, military or financial, assistance to our cause.

Indeed, this encounter was typical of many. I moved in a raffish circle of small legations, all equally deserving, querulous, drunken, lascivious, and short of means. Only the Egyptians, in fact, for some reason I never discovered, seem to have enjoyed a state of relative affluence. Under the guidance of the crafty and evidently well-heeled Zaghlu Pasha, a benign patriot with the most terrible cough that I have ever had the misfortune to stand close to, a positively herculean, wracking, disgusting expletive sort of cough that was wont to shower forth an unappetising mixture of Egyptian innards, this delegation lolled and imbibed in a cushioned atmosphere of oriental luxury. They were generous, however, and the bronchitic Pasha was prone to dispense large wallets of magnificent Ayala cigarettes, which were doubtless, over the years, a powerful contributor to the condition of his noisy and evacuating lungs.

There were others, too, who promised wealth, although it rarely materialised. A frail ascetic in a sort of fez, I would say from Armenia, or some other more exotic Russian province, announced one day over dark coffee and liqueurs at the Café Napolitain that he had access to secret funds in the shape of a priceless diamond rivière, whose black market value would still be likely to exceed two million francs.

'And where,' I remember asking, seeking to restrain my avarice, 'do you keep this great river of diamonds, Monsieur?'

'Why, but of course, Monsieur,' he replied, spreading out his hands with their seven cheap rings, 'it is hidden at Erzeroum. In a cellar.'

So as often, the vision of a shared luxury in revolution, for the possessor of the glittering flood in the cellar had promised we should all enjoy the proceeds from the sale of his wealth, receded, and then was gone, alas, for ever. The rest of us lived on in threadbare jackets, and rooms without heating, and did our own cleaning, and ate

The Lion of Pescara

frugally, and drank as well and as much as we could at the, admittedly frequent and lavish, receptions for the delegates in the major embassies.

I enjoyed the life and was, indeed, able to manage an isolated coup, for which I was duly rewarded, in months to come, by promotion to the rank of captain, the only man, I believe, in the whole of that ramshackle and democratic army at Fiume ever to achieve a rise in rank.

Through a chance remark overheard at a party for Clemenceau I gathered that a copy of a secret agreement, in the Italian embassy, involving some very damaging matters to our interests, had been drafted on paper between Nitti and President Wilson, and that this copy lay, at that very moment, upstairs in the desk of Nitti's private secretary. I thus assumed, at a blow, the mask of Raffles, and became for the first and last time in my life a successful amateur cracksman.

I managed to appear drunk, and indeed supplied much colour to the appearance by a generous quaffing of the splendid Moët et Chandon which was allowed to flow so freely, and my early retirement from the party, by way of a remote lavatory, to which I was believed to have withdrawn for rest and recuperation, was hardly bothered with. I was able to make my way unmolested, along thickly carpeted corridors, to a door most helpfully marked with the secretary's name, and even more helpfully, as it turned out, left unlocked and unoccupied.

In a comfortable swing chair, I was able to lean back and admire the paintings – a nice Bougereau, an awful Rops drawing – while I rifled the drawers and examined the trays. Incredibly enough, the file concerned was marked with a huge red seal, and stamped secret and confidential, and placed neatly and prominently in the locked central drawer of the secretary's partner's desk, with the little silver key still winking quietly in the hole.

I found clean paper, and a pen, and I leaned back and rapidly – it was mercifully, though monstrous in its implications, quite short in its phrasing – made a fair copy of the whole document. I was tempted to linger over one of

The Greyhound

the secretary's fine Havanas, exposed in a convenient box on a side table, but some wise instinct assured me that this would be tempting my angel of good fortune a little too far. I replaced the file, folded the copy into my pocket, opened the door and left the office, and began a carefully contrived stagger along the carpeted corridors back to the still bustling and oblivious reception.

Shortly after this accomplished act of burglary, or at least of illegal entry, I was recalled to Fiume, there to remain for some eight months through the exciting events of 1920 before returning, as it were, in triumph to Paris as the proper delegate of what was now, if all too briefly, an independent sovereign state.

I established our small legation this time in the more stately purlieus of the Rue Frédéric Bastiat, from whose elegant eighteenth-century windows, in due course, the inhabitants of the 8th arrondissement were able to see depending, not only the red flag of the Regency of Carnaro with its queer design of stars, but also the azure banner of Dalmatia, with its three heads of lions, since I had agreed to act also as the representative for the free island of Cherso, whose claims were identical to our own in Fiume.

Alas, these drooping, and fantastical, banners were the cause of my major brush with the French authorities during my brief stay in Paris. I was instructed to attend upon a Monsieur Vegrun, at the Quai d'Orsay, an icy and reserved scion of the *ancien régime* with a monocle, a bald head plastered with trickles of fair hair, and a nose breaking into fiery wrinkles. I took an instant dislike to him, and he to me.

Our business was soon transacted. He supposed my papers to be without visa, I knew them to have been effectively forged with the authorisation of the French consul at Trieste. My friend with the red wrinkles, acting no doubt on objections from some interfering neighbours about our flags, and their constituting some breach of local law, was entirely nonplussed by this evident authority in the shape of a properly signed sequence of official documents.

The Lion of Pescara

He fingered the papers with evident misfavour, murmured that there must be some irregularity, and dismissed me while he gave his mind to the consideration of his next move. By then, however, it was January of 1921, there had been the Christmas of Blood, and the date of my final recall was to arrive before any further objections to my tenure of office had been made. I withdrew in sadness, but with full diplomatic honours, a black Renault, flanked by two outriders on motor-bikes, escorting me through foggy streets one chill morning to the Gare du Nord, from whence a first-class carriage was to bear me, by slow but comfortable stages, into permanent exile.

I had been an ambassador. What more had life in store? Only, it soon seemed, the resumption of my perilous, but so endlessly satisfying, tenure of that lowlier, but infinitely more exacting and pleasurable role, your private secretary.

4

It was March of 1920 when I returned to Fiume. My first appointment, which had so melodramatically evolved into the role of special agent, or cat burglar, was for the moment over. My second, and more glamorous position, as ambassador extraordinary, was yet to be envisioned, and lay eight months in the future.

I had not expected, as it happened, to be away from Paris for more than a few weeks, and there was an air of urgency, as well as mystery, about the circumstances of my recall. I should like to have flown back at maximum speed, in the cockpit, or perhaps the observation compartment, of a stolen French bomber, but the opportunity to obtain such a valuable asset, alas, and to assume some tinge of the mantle of Guido Keller, eluded my grasp.

I took the Orient Express from the Gare de l'Est, and arrived at length on a slow train from Turin, via the slip-coach. It was a freezing winter's day when I reached the massive 1890s classical platforms of the central station at Fiume, and a few flakes of icy snow were falling. I was alone with my valises, but I had fortunately taken the precaution of providing myself with a fur-lined motoring-cape.

I was met at the station by Casagrande, the head of your air force. By this date, the custom of using traditional Italian ranks was largely in abeyance at Fiume, as was

The Lion of Pescara

the grading of personnel by normal uniforms, and I was shortly to be less surprised than I now was to be confronted with a senior officer in a garb of his own devising. In Casagrande's case, this was oddly appropriate, since the relatively small size and lack of fuel for the forces under his command necessarily restricted their employment in purely aerial endeavours, and their resourceful commander, a young pilot from one of your wartime squadrons, devoted his energy to exploits on land and sea as well as amidst the clouds.

'The Commandante has a mission for you,' Casagrande confided to me, as we walked along the forecourt of the station towards an official car.

I admired his cavalry boots, and the array of wings and devices parading across his tunic, and the absence of any pips on his shoulders. He had a cast in one eye, and a twisted grin, the consequence of some nerve severance in a crash over the Carso.

'A matter of the cinema,' he elaborated, as we drove through a now whirling storm of snow to the Governor's Palace. There were lights coming on in all the cafés, and, through the windows of the confectioner's shops, I could see that there were still plentiful cream cakes being hungrily devoured by the military and the civilian populace alike.

Indeed, this was a carnival city still, albeit one ravaged from time to time by an erratic shortage of ammunition or food. Whenever the Italian blockade, always rather inadequately maintained, would seem to threaten the basic stores of grain or oil, or guns, or women, your finger would beckon to the Colpi di Mano, the Office for Special Operations, and your skilful pirates, the Uscocchi, whose name recalled those medieval freebooters, the scourge of Venetian trade for centuries, would set forth in their wild variety of barques, gunned or gunless, and there would be very few hours before they returned, flags flying, and with some purloined, or surrendered, vessel towed or under full steam at their wakes. There would be Guido Keller, or one of his younger aides, knife in teeth as it were, black patch

The Greyhound

over the eye – and, indeed, this was a widespread affectation in imitation of your own perpetual patch – and the salute of victory would ring out over the quay from cannon or musket, even perhaps from one of the renovated Austrian ceremonial guns that lined the gravel to the west of the palace.

All these, like the sumptuous pastries and the fine wines ever available in the shops, were to be familiar sights again to me very shortly. At it was, I took in a swift refreshing glance at them, and was plunged, all too soon, into a more remote, and as it were artificial, picture of their significance, when I discovered at the palace exactly what the 'matter of the cinema' referred to by Casagrande was going to be.

You were standing in your office, when I was shown in, between two very obviously American gentlemen in double-breasted suits, both with sleeked-back straight hair in the modern international fashion, one with a small rough beard, and the other clean-shaven, though sporting on the end of his nose a pair of those round spectacles then made popular by the example of President Wilson. A few yards away, like a quiet visitor from another planet, stood the black metal and glass, the huge Mickey Mouse ears, of a cinema projector, leaning precariously sideways, it seemed to me, from a carefully braced tripod.

You were dressed yourself as if interrupted, as indeed you may have been, while in the middle of changing for dinner. You wore a rather perky black bow-tie over a frilled shirt, and your shoes were a polished black patent leather. But the remainder of your garb was strictly military, the jacket and breeches of a colonel in the Arditi.

'Tomaso,' you cried, as I entered. 'How very good to see you. These two gentlemen have been discoursing to me on the current state of the American cinema. They do me the honour of seeking an interview with the Director of the Fiuman National Film Office, which, of course, is why I have asked him to come over in person. May I ask you to see that they are well accommodated in Fiume during their stay with us, and while you are negotiating about the project, which I understand is dear to their hearts, of immortalising our little endeavours here, on celluloid. Tomaso, my friend, I know you will see what can be done.'

Thus it was that, at four o'clock in the afternoon of a wintry day in March 1920, the official delegate to the Peace Conference in Paris was metamorphosed, still in his fur-lined motoring-cape, into a powerful tycoon of the cinema.

The role was much to my taste. I had negotiated with men of the film world in earlier days on your behalf, and the success of *Cabiria*, even allowing for your own contemptuous dismissal of its banalities, had often made it seem that yet further forays into the magic world – as it then seemed, and indeed so does still, to me – of the silver screen, and, indeed, the Hollywood fortunes, might later be made.

So I saw to it that Mr Strottmeister and Mr Colquhoun, guaranteed as they were by the famous architect Whitney Warren, were given two of the best suites in the Hotel Europa, and in due course, while the water froze in the pipes, and the blizzard raged in the public squares, our negotiations about a documentary film on the Fiume adventure began.

As always, money was to be at the root of the matter, and I had taken the precaution of quadrupling the two hundred thousand lire that you shortly told me you thought might be suitable as a form of facility fee. Surprisingly, this exorbitant figure was at length agreed upon, provided that there should also be some brief running captions, drawn up in your own most flowing style, to be screened in between several reels.

It sounded like an excellent bargain, and I strongly advised you to agree. The work would be minimal, and the rewards, both financial and in terms of propaganda, very considerable.

Agree, in fact, you did, and for several heady days, in the wake of the serious Americans departing to draw up their contract, I had visions of all the episodes that might form the basis for their coming scenario. Alas, one clause in the

The Greyhound

contract, when it shortly arrived, insisted that your initial shooting script, involving no more admittedly than a few sides of pregnant mottoes, should be in their hands before any of the actual turning, or filming, was to begin, or indeed, worst of all, any of the money was to be transferred into an Italian bank.

It was a fatal restriction. As on so many other occasions, the pressure of a routine requirement was more than your wayward imagination would sustain. I intervened. I insisted, I made a nuisance of myself in the midst of conferences with Portuguese guerrilla fighters, at the end of intrigues with Armenian actresses, on occasions of private as of political commitment, I was thoroughly hard and unforgiving and brutal. But, alas, to no avail.

The script remained unwritten, and the money remained unpaid, and the film remained unshot. In my own mind, it was quite a tragedy. There were so many cinematic aspects of your life there in the heart of that savage winter. It might well have been an early masterpiece. For day after day I used to walk round the streets with my eye and my ear open for whatever might be strikingly realised on film.

A script, even, had evolved in my own mind, not only one that took in the daily parades, and the great occasional set-pieces, like the funeral of the aviators Aldo Bini and Giovanni Zeppegno, where you spoke in the moonlight to a kneeling crowd of thousands before the coffins in the Piazza Dante, your voice lifting like a wave as you spoke of the sign of the cross that is made by the shadow of the winged machine, no, one rather that would also sneak the camera in to your private life, where the young singer Montressor was paid five hundred lire to visit your bedroom every night for a week, and to stimulate your flagging vitality, long drained in the steady satisfaction of the jealous Luisa Baccara, who would allow no rival.

Yes, one even that would recreate the most exorbitant of those many follies of Guido Keller's, matching even his flight into a monastery in Yugoslavia, from whence he returned with a little donkey tethered as a present for you

The Lion of Pescara

to the undercarriage of his aeroplane. Keller, yes, who lived now in a haystack, and ate fruit and nuts, and was enamoured of a pet eagle you had once had stolen from him as a practical joke. Who had grown, in his way, too worried by the all-pervading influence of the cautious Baccara, supposing her to be a brake on your initiative, and to rein you back from a number of your more extravagant and dangerous ventures, anxious as she was, in too wifely a way, to keep you safe, and who had therefore persuaded you, Keller, that is, into a re-enactment of a medieval tournament, where a Queen of Beauty, Luisa herself, of course, would be assailed by all the young knights of the city, incarcerated in a castle which would, in fact, be a bathing house on the beach, and would be, from there, at the height of the festival, in cold reality, spirited away by Keller and his friend Commisso and 'put in a cage like a hen and taken to a desert island'.

It was a mad scheme, and had finally been cancelled by you, with a curious foresight of trouble, as too D'Annunzian, the sort of wild revel that your enemies would seize on as evidence of your licence and turn to adverse political account.

So it never happened, and sadly never happened a second time, as it might have done, as if an imaginary scheme that never was, in the glamorous flicker of the moving film. It would have given, as much else would, a hint of that schoolboy pranksomeness that was so common to many ventures of those hectic days in the winter of 1920.

There was, for example, The Babies Crusade. The first knights of the cradle, some two hundred and fifty in all, had been shipped from Fiume to Italy in the February before my return, ostensibly to save them from starvation, but in actual fact as a shrewd manoeuvre to publicise the Fiuman cause in the mainland press. The egregious Nitti, now regularly named in your own offensive and generic slogan simply *cagoia*, or pile of dung, was foolish enough to refuse to accept the little crusaders, and the immediate outcry against this act of barbarism was colossal. Demonstrations, largely organised by Mussolini, who was an

The Greyhound

active partner in the crusade, were shortly marshalling fur-coated battalions of middle-aged female supporters in every country town in Italy, and before the end of the summer the pressure of popular opinion, in the newspapers and elsewhere, had forced the incensed Nitti to rescind his prohibition. By the end of July several thousand widely publicised, and, I fear, very obviously well-fed, infants were enjoying a cosseted exile on the mainland.

I had visions of this wonderful propaganda gesture enshrined on film for posterity, the pathos and the irony. Alas, it was not to be. Nor, indeed, was the expedition to Zara, when you travelled with a squadron of motor-torpedo boats in a sudden descent on a little Dalmatian port, where for some hours you were entertained by, and suborned, some say, the local Italian admiral, one Enrico Millo. Nor, alas, most alas of all, the bizarre coup against the military on your borders known, later, as the adventure of the Horse of the Apocalypse, when a roaming detachment of Uscocchi made a swift raid on a depot near Abbazia, and requisitioned, or rather kidnapped, some forty-six outstanding cavalry stallions from a military stable. The arrival of these high-stepping Arab aristocrats was greeted with a special parade through Fiume, and they were duly provided with superb accommodation in the Hungarian governor's former dairy, where they fed on oats and drank iced water to their hearts' content.

However, the slight imposed on the honour of the army, already slurred and infringed upon by the earlier kidnapping of General Arturo Nigra, a vociferous opponent of the D'Annunzian regime, when his car was ambushed on the road to Trieste, and he in person detained for over a month in the city of the holocaust, this honour, I say, could hardly accept the forcible removal, under their very ostlers' noses, of nearly half a hundred noble steeds.

General Ferrario, the commander of all Italian troops in northern Italy, issued an ultimatum to the effect that, unless the horses were at once returned, the blockade of Fiume, until then somewhat relaxed, would immediately become total. You responded to this threat with a magnificent *coup de théâtre*. The knackers' yards of the city were scoured for the most spavined and exhausted nags that could be found, and, in due course, with full pomp and ceremony, forty-six of these tottering beasts, more spindly than the least favourable caricature of a mount for Don Quixote, were led to the frontier and solemnly handed over.

This act of defiance was accompanied by the publication of one of your most sarcastic ripostes, an open letter to the Italian authorities, in which you boasted, in a kind of mock abjection, of how we had had to make a meal, reduced as we all were, of the luscious flesh of fourteen of the army's horses, whose gleaming skulls you would be happy to restore as trophies. You were returning, you added, the starving skeletons of our own poor mounts in yet one further bid to underline the extremes of hunger to which all in Fiume were committed through the rigours of the cruel Italian blockade.

You ended this masterpiece, in fine style.

'We have offended Italy,' you wrote, in false contrition. 'We do not know how to think Italianly. We are not Italians. We deserve only to be starved, manacled and executed. We shall resign ourselves. But I must further confess that last night I stole the Horse of the Apocalypse to add it to the forty-six quadrupeds on the criminal barge. He has his marvellous general's harness and a divine thunderbolt in each holster. Cum timore.'

I would dearly have loved to re-run in later years the epic march of those ancient horses along the crowded and laughing streets, where men with pastry forks in their hands, and women quaffing glasses of claret, were waving from every busy café window. It would have made an arresting image, as it did at the time, of the contrast between illusion and reality, the propaganda of starvation and the feasting hundreds of actual fact.

Of course, there were indeed sometimes shortages, and the value of money, fluctuating in erratic response to unknown and incalculable forces both inside and outside

The Greyhound

the city, meant that sometimes the purchasing of goods was more a matter of barter or goodwill than of normal commercial bargaining. But for many months, and certainly over the crucial weeks during which I wined, dined and smoked with the American film-makers, crisp in the snow and eloquent amidst the icicles, we lacked for very little. The morale of the beleaguered city stood high.

At length, and I think that this must have been one morning in late April, I was buttonholed by your latest servant-in-arms, the redoubtable Italo Rossignoli, a voluble and flamboyant off-print of yourself, whose duties as valet and masseur, prolonged into other areas, had allowed him an increasing power over your private life, and were to carry him to new heights of influence later at the Vittoriale, when he would issue signed portraits of himself to adoring chambermaids, inscribed with mottoes in imitation of your own best style, and whose major flourish at the date now in question was the sporting of a green patch over his, perfectly good, right eye; it was, as I recall, at the end of April that Italo tapped me on the shoulder as I was writing in an alcove somewhere in the lower corridors of the palace.

'He would like to see you, Tomaso,' he confided, spreading his mobile hands, and with a pursing of his neat lips that recalled one of your own mannerisms. 'Good news, I fancy, mon vieux.'

So I was led by this miniature Roman creature, the puissant slave of some remote passage in Juvenal or Suetonius, the right-hand man of an emperor no longer young but eternally vain and fretful, to a place I had rarely, in all the time I had known you, been allowed to enter, your private bathroom. There you were seated on the rim of an immense alabaster tub originally scooped out for some Latin dignitary, and reserved later on for one of the Hungarian delegate's mistresses, a block of mottled green, like diseased meat, against which your tiny figure made a knubbly outline, swaddled as you were, a Caesar at his *levée*, in a mass of enormous white towels.

'Tomaso,' you said, rubbing your hair with one of these.

The Lion of Pescara

'This is one of those days when I have to be even more busy than normally. Forgive this admittedly somewhat *outré* invitation to my ablutions, or at least their less watery aftermath. Italo,' you added, 'I shall be ready in one moment.'

The tiny masseur withdrew, manipulating his fingers as if in anticipation of what sinewy prodding or gross eroticism I could only speculate. I sat down on a small mahogany commode, feeling a trifle enervated in the steam. It was excessively hot, even for one used to your standards.

'I have to apologise, Tomaso,' you said, walking over to a marble slab heavy with unguents and bottles of scent. 'This was not, as I realised, the right moment for the turning of the film. I appreciate, more than I can say, your efforts on my behalf with those grisly Americans. I should like you to accept this little gift, in remembrance.'

I have it still, cold under my fingers here in the blistering attic, a silver cigarette-case, inscribed in Latin with one of your best and most entertaining mottoes: *Fiume ignis, caetera fumus.* The city is flame, the rest is smoke.

Smoke indeed it was, your hope of gain from the film, but the city of the holocaust, the furnace of so many hopes or dreams in formal miniature, that was well enshrined, and remains here now, in the clean and gleaming lines of this little box for the instruments of fire, that burn to nothing.

I took the case, thanked you, and returned to my corridor. There in the doorway, as I passed through, stood the man you yourself had nicknamed the bottlebreaker, for some long-forgotten offence with a vial of perfume, but whose gentle massage and whose carbon-copying of your life and style were at last the heralds, and the perquisites, it seemed to me, of genius on the brink of age.

5

IN SEPTEMBER, GIOLITTI returned to power in Rome. The days of the Regency began to be numbered. Absent as I was in Paris during these heroic, and I gather very stirring, final days, I rely inevitably on your own somewhat suspect, not to say biased, account of the proceedings. There are other sources, too, of course, not least the suppressed memoirs of General Caviglia, the supreme commander of the attacking forces, and the private papers of Eugenio Coseleschi, my temporary successor as your secretary, an embezzler and an opportunist, yes, and yet, I must be fair, a man, too, who may have saved your life in those momentous seconds when the shells from the *Andrea Doria* started to fall on the Governor's Palace.

Giolitti, at any rate, requires no subtle interpreter. Your enemy since the Italo-Turkish war of 1913, when he had had occasion to censor some lines antagonistic to Austria in your *Song of Emprise Beyond the Sea*, he had had his house vandalised by your supporters during the furore over Italian intervention in 1915, and had remained a bitter, and a scornful, opponent of all your aggrandising policies. Giolitti wanted a little Italy, and a solvent one, and he saw your increasingly imperial, and some said even Bolshevist, Fiume, as a prime obstacle to this.

On December 1st, 1920, the naval blockade, which had been under the irresolute though objectionable Nitti a

The Lion of Pescara

somewhat unconvincing affair, allowing, as I have shown, much essential war material, and many civilian luxuries, to leak through the ring, this casual blockade, I say, became in one night an almost rigorous grip.

For three weeks even medical supplies became more difficult to obtain, and all efforts on the part of the Uscocchi proved largely in vain. The net was tightened. Finally, on December 21st, an ultimatum was declared. You had only two days to surrender or submit to an armed attack.

Already, this calamity had been foreseen, and on at least one day, had been resisted by a peculiarly ingenious and poetic stroke of defiance. Late in October, you had had the whole of the Piazza Dante near to the harbour cleared of its usual flurry of market stalls, and a series of gigantic whitewash letters drawn on the cobblestones. Then, at a prearranged hour, publicised throughout the city by fleets of motor-cars announcing the event with megaphones, tens of thousands of civilian men, women and children were assembled in their winter coats and ranged in lines to spell out, in literally human terms of flesh and blood, the enormous message: ITALIA O MORTE.

Seen from the air, where Casagrande in person circled in his reconnaissance biplane, the effect must have been spectacular, and, indeed, it remained so in the series of aerial photographs, later enlarged and sent throughout Italy to every organ of the press, who were delighted to print this image of the embodied voice of the people at large size on their news pages.

'Wait,' is all that the phlegmatic Giolitti seems to have said when he was greeted by this photograph over his breakfast table, and wait he did. Then, on the evening of December 24th, when the world was preparing for Christmas, and there would be no newspaper or wire service coverage of events for virtually forty-eight hours, he struck.

'Without warning,' is how you later described this assault on the part of a few battalions of Alpini and Carabinieri, who had marched along the railway line from

The Greyhound

Mattuglie, and attacked your frontier guards at Cantrida; but, in fact, the attack had been expected, and was shortly repulsed.

Further down your lines of defence, from, as you put it yourself, in your eminently flowery, and also, I think, a little touching, speech of resignation to the Fiuman Council on December 29th, 'the Case degli Emigranti, by the Viale d'Italia, the Diaz Barracks, the Cosala, the Cavalry Barracks, the Enco, to the Porto Sanso,' lines of placards, marked like the whitewash letters in the Piazza Dante, with the sounding message, Italia O Morte, and followed by orders not to cross into Fiuman territory, had been ranged for several days.

The main drive, nevertheless, now began, and by noon on December 25th, some twenty thousand Italian troops had been moved into action against a total Fiuman force of, I think, just under three thousand. Few of the invaders seem to have been deterred by the stridency of the placards, and for this the universal, or very nearly universal, opposition of the Italian press to your later endeavours, must be given the credit, or shall we say, allowed to assume the blame. The public had grown, it seemed, rather bored with the Regency of the Carnaro, and the troops were loyal, or possibly, and this was certainly true of the inveterate and smarting General Ferrario, who was put in charge of all land forces, eager for vengeance, recalling a whole series of insults and provocations which had culminated in that final humiliation of the Horse of the Apocalypse.

At sea, the *Andrea Doria*, under the command of that formerly sympathetic, and still I assume faintly uneasy, commander, Admiral Millo, steamed up the roadstead and into the harbour, from where it commenced upon a general if somewhat spasmodic bombardment of the sea-front and the coastal positions.

You slept very little that night. I see you as you must have been while you paced those echoing corridors, thronged as they were by a long succession of bizarre and conflicting advisers, rustling with papers, clattering with

The Lion of Pescara

riding boots, troubled by the occasional moaning of the wakeful Delrosa, or the more plangent music of the alert Luisa, svelte in musquash and nightgown at her Steinway, as she tried to arouse morale, or capture mood, with a selection of classical, patriotic, or military melodies.

You issued a number of propaganda statements, the best, I think, in the reverse words, rather curiously, of the English Admiral Nelson at Trafalgar, when you assured the advancing hordes from Tuscany and Calabria, many of whom had fought beside you at the Isonzo or the Timavo.

'Italy expects that this morning each man will *not* do his duty, but allow the Regency of the Carnaro, and its peaceful and peaceloving citizens, to remain in independence, and fulfil their destiny free from interference.'

It was too late, however, for these antics and divertissements. There was a martial spirit in the air, and a kind of policeman spirit in the hearts of the attacking soldiers. They saw themselves, and had indeed been instructed to see themselves, as engaged in something akin to the crowd control at a football match. A few skulls might be broken, but this was not, in effect, a military engagement so much as a matter of bringing a few hotheads to their senses.

Alas, it was more than that. All through the Christmas of 1920, Italians were killing Italians, and it seemed as if the blood of Calvary was made to run through the cradle in the stables. At dawn, you write in your memoir, you made your testament, and there was a plan in the air for a last sortie in the direction of Abbazia, where you would break through or die.

Somehow this came to nothing. Perhaps because the line in the north held, and the government troops were consistently thrown back, you became more cheerful as Christmas Day advanced, and there were jubilant throngs of Arditi in the streets with their first prisoners when you went up at seven o'clock to inspect the lines and harangue your brave defenders.

A machine-gun post had been set up in a ring of sandbags on the balcony of the palace, and you began to spend most

The Greyhound

of your time, on your return, either directing the fire from this out across the bay towards the *Andrea Doria*, which would, in my opinion, have been much too far away for any of the rounds to come anywhere near her bows, or in a calmer, and possibly more lascivious, mood inspecting the remote sailors along the decks – a few no doubt rather handsome in their close-fitting white breeches and wide collars – through an antique telescope clapped to your one good eye.

Shortly before midday, so Coseleschi tells us, Guido Keller arrived at the palace with a splendid iced Christmas cake, which he had stolen, so he claimed, from General Caviglia's mess-tent, and which there was an immediate decision to enjoy with some of your small remaining stocks of *premier cru* Bordeaux, in lieu of the more complete and formal turkey banquet which had earlier been planned, but was now delayed through the death, or desertion, of your best cook.

The Coromandel desk was cleared of its motley mixture of small Greek bronzes and unsigned letters, magazines and cartridge cases, and the carved mahogany dining chairs were brought in from other rooms. While Luisa Baccara struck up the march of Ronchi, and, so some say, the 'British Grenadiers' and 'Rule Britannia', no doubt in deference to the Nelson spirit which seems to have been a continuing thread in the morning's campaign, perhaps in the hope, very dear I suspect to your ageing heart, of a combination of death with victory, the glittering gâteau with its tiny angels and donkeys, fir trees and Virgin Mary, Christ child and visiting kings, was boldly sliced open by Keller with his bayonet, and the great hunks were being speared from plate to plate, when, lo, with a sudden thud and crash, an Italian shell from the *Andrea Doria* came right through the window, shattered the plaster of the back wall, showered everything in dust, slaughtered a sergeant at the door, whose back was broken, and flung you to the floor like a rag doll, cake in hand, with blood streaming from your bald skull.

You went, so Coseleschi says, straight to the window,

The Lion of Pescara

flung it open and stepped out on to the balcony, bareheaded, half blind from dust, and choking, as you groped your way towards the machine-gun.

'Kill me, you cowards,' you screamed. 'Kill me,' and then you had your hands on the firing-grips when they seized you bodily between them, Captain Coseleschi and a Lieutenant Tanno, and dragged you back inside and along the floor into the corridor, and out of the palace at last to a safer house in the Via Buonarroti; from where, finally recovered in time for a splendid full Christmas dinner, prepared by Mayor Gigante, giant in name as in physique, you were helped to the Town Hall located in the centre of the city, and out of range, so all thought, of the warship's guns.

It must have been quite a moment. Nobody has ever been sure whether, as you insisted yourself, the intent of the shelling was directly murderous, and on the personal orders of Giolitti, when he heard over the telephone that you were using the room alongside the balcony as your office, or whether, and I have a slight inclination to fear for this, there was an element of the suicidal in your reckless exposure of your easily recognisable figure, eye-patch and all, to the skilfully trained binoculars of the warship's gunners.

At any rate, you survived, and the battle, briefly drawing to a close, hung in mid-air, as it were, for a period of three drawn-out days, perhaps to allow the attacking troops, after all, their belated festivities, and an opportunity to blow their two-pound bonus on a local whore or a bottle of Chianti. Then, on December 28th, the bombardment recommenced, on land and on sea, and there were, I am sure, frantic and lengthy meetings to discuss the various possibilities.

It all hinged, you insisted later, on the refusal of General Ferrario to allow the women and children of the city to be evacuated, and even on his hinting that the civilian quarters would be made the specific targets of his guns. Millo, for whom you had always, and oddly in view of the shelling of your office, had a certain

The Greyhound

affection, apparently agreed to accept some hostages, or withdrawn combatants, on his ship the *Dante Alighieri*.

'There came a moment,' you told me years afterwards, on the deck of the *Puglia* in the grounds of the Vittoriale, as we gazed out across Lake Garda to an early sunset, and I watched the wrinkles quiver around the lines of your mouth, 'when I knew that there was only the decision of the gods to be sought. I took a coin, Tomaso, a golden genovese, and I spun it into the air to allow the fall, fight or surrender, to give me a sign.'

I felt the chill in the mountain air then, and saw you finger the sleeves of your jacket, and I knew that once again I was to become the receptacle of a legend.

'The coin, Tomaso,' you said, with a flash of your old smile, 'insisted that I fight on. But then I walked through the windows out on to the balcony there, and watched the sun going down into the sea, as we see it now, itself a tarnished, indomitable and still faintly precious although outmoded coin, and I stood for a while, an open target, although they had ceased firing, for the warship *Andrea Doria*. Then, as I turned and was about to re-enter my office, I looked along the harbour front.'

You paused, and I saw what seemed to be a hint of tears in your eyes, as you leaned on the tripod of the swivel machine-gun on the poop-deck.

'On every balcony, Tomaso,' you said, 'there was a woman standing with a baby in her arms. As I glanced around, as if at a signal, all began to chant in a united rhythm, "Take this one instead of him. If one must die, spare the Commandante. Take my child instead of him." I was deeply moved, I tell you, Tomaso, very deeply moved. How could I accept such a terrible sacrifice? I felt I had no choice left. I rejected the bitter decision of the genovese. I decided that the Regency of the Carnaro must come to an end.'

So indeed, albeit I feel sure in a less dramatic and visionary way than the one your own memory, and its wish to mythologise, would have recommended, the Re-

The Lion of Pescara

gency did arrive at its term, and on December 29th you offered the National Council your resignation.

Events moved fast. On December 31st a peace treaty was signed, though not, of course now, with your own signature. You had foresworn them that satisfaction. On January 2nd, in the watery sun of the New Year, there was an exchange of prisoners, and a computation of the casualties.

On the Italian side, so the joint communiqué said, there had been seventeen dead, and a hundred and twenty wounded. On the Fiuman side, eighteen dead, and thirty wounded.

Later that day, in a drear wind, spitting with occasional hail, thousands of people climbed the tall flight of steps to the little steep cemetery on the hillside, and the coffins of the dead, theirs and ours, all Italian, were consigned to the ground for which they had fought.

You were good at funerals, always, and this was one of your very best. You kissed the boards of each coffin, they say, and knelt, and made everyone kneel, while the photographers clicked their shutters, and the hail rapped on the final elm. Then you spoke in your quietest voice, and far more briefly than usual, and with a haunting cadence.

'If he who meditates beside the tomb of Lazarus,' you said, and this was your finest image, I think, 'if the Son of God were to appear now between the altar and the coffins, between the holy table and the sacred labarum, between the burning candles and the extinguished lives; if He were to appear here and if He were to evoke and resuscitate those dead soldiers, I believe that they would only rise to weep, to pardon one another, and to throw themselves into each other's arms.'

Perhaps your mind was already on further political triumphs, and this was a prophecy of reconciliation with your enemies, or a hint of compromises to come, and there were manoeuvres shortly to take place back in Italy which would have given colour to this, but I prefer to believe that for a moment you were tired only, and humble in the face of the last and most inexorable foe, and ready to see the

The Greyhound

whole gamble, the splendour and the irony, as finally no more than a pile of dust and ashes.

At any rate, you were isolated now, and felt that you were, and symbolised this in a last stroke of pageantry when the legionnaires withdrew from Fiume, colours reversed, and a slow drum playing, between weeping crowds along every street, on the morning of January 5th, 1921.

You marched alone, at the end of the line, bare-headed, wearing all your medals, and with your eyes on the ground.

So ended the great adventure of the Regency of the Carnaro, the only state in the twentieth century, I think, which was ruled, albeit only for just over a year, by a great poet who was also a warrior.

When you left Fiume, you travelled with Luisa Baccara, and the desolated Italo Rossignoli, a vulgar copy of your own grief, in a similar, though cheaper, cloak of grey serge, and with a touch of fur, too, on his motoring-cap as he drove you to San Giuliano.

There at the windswept mole, in a swirl of January mist, I was waiting for you in a motor-launch with the former commander of a Fiuman destroyer, Lieutenant Mazutto. Across the lagoon, pitted with the lights of occasional gondolas, I watched the dark low hump of Venice in the water.

It was a melancholy occasion. We shook hands and then embraced briefly under the shadow of the little house belonging to the harbour-master. Then you stepped down into the boat, helped the elegant Luisa in with her suitcases, nodded to Italo, who was to garage the car and join us later, and ordered Lieutenant Mazutto to head for the island.

There in Venice, the lease on the Casetta Rossa had run out, and was not available for renewal, and a massive apartment had been temporarily rented for you by the taciturn Dante, in a rotting warehouse of a sixteenth-century rat-haven called the Palazzo Barberigo. Choked, as it was, with the detritus of your possessions from

The Lion of Pescara

Arcachon, at length repatriated, though much damaged, and swollen further by certain fragments of your immense collections from the Capponcina, which had been bought for you by Romaine, or other friends, at that appalling auction, this grim, roasting sequence of rooms bore the air of a furniture depository, and you stood amongst the clutter in a state, so it seemed to me, of abject and final dejection.

'Tomaso,' you said. 'I give you eight days. If within that time you have failed to find me a place to live, I shall throw myself, I promise you, with all my remaining hopes and fears, and indeed with the remainder of my manuscripts and papers, head first into that abysmal and fetid canal.'

Then you took Luisa's hand, and you went to bed, amidst a corner of rubble, and will shortly, I feel sure, have done what you were still capable of doing, though not perhaps quite so often or with such fire and venom as before, and I knew that after all you had surely survived Fiume, and that a new, if a final, episode in your life would shortly commence, and that I once again was invited to be its initiator and architect.

I went to sleep, thinking about my commission.

—V—

The Tortoise

I

EVEN FROM THE first, on that foul and fair January day, with a high wind veering from the south and west, whipping the water up on the lake into tiny wavelets, and sending a mean drizzle sheering through the narrow streets of the little town, I had an idea that the villa above Gardone di Riviera, then called, with a rather too military resonance I thought now, Cargnacco, would nevertheless prove to be the simple country retreat that I knew you sought.

'A walled garden surrounded by gratings,' you had specified. 'Then two garages, Tomaso. Stables for at least three horses. A grand piano. Luisa would insist on that. Laundry, of course. Perhaps a servants' wing, or a separate cottage. Means of heating. You know my needs.'

I knew them well, and had selected the neighbourhood of Lake Garda as likely to satisfy your requirements as well as anywhere. I remembered your lyrical memory, on a flight above the lake in your biplane during the war, of how you had spent so many ecstatic days beside the water there in the arms of the equine and newly awakened Alessandra di Rudini. So to Garda I went, equipped with a briefcase full of estate agent's brochures, and government letters, and a mass of maps and guide books.

I was used to this kind of research, and I had never lost the taste, even after the fleshpots and false intrigues of

Paris, for the lonely sleuthing duties on which you had so often launched me. Indeed, there was a piquancy in the journey. I was contemplating marriage, and I knew that my days in the more intimate regions of your service might at last be numbered, or, at any rate, about to assume a new and more remote, or domesticated, form than before.

I had enjoyed the doddering local train from Venice, hunched up with my papers in the warm corner of a first-class carriage, with no companion save a faltering civil servant, or perhaps he was a private detective, ancient and unconvincing in high collar and what I would then have called a Clemenceau moustache. I got down in the rain at Gardone di Riviera, and found a porter to carry my bags, and then rode in a choking Fiat to the Hotel Fasano.

After a dubious regional dinner, and some abominable Orvieto, I managed a fair night's rest, in spite of the wind, and a groaning lecher with his quaking mistress behind the partition wall, and I rose early, confined my breakfast to a few rolls and some barren coffee, and was on my way up the slopes of the mountain well before nine o'clock.

It was green fields first of all, rolling and rinsed out, with their long grasses lying due north in the drive of the breeze, and then a ruined or shell-swept nave in a great cathedral of winter beech-trees, their grey trunks all wet with the brush of the capricious rain. I turned my collar up and trudged on through the rising wood in the direction of a long, curling wall with, and yes I could see them now, those very gratings arranged at intervals just as you had asked for.

A small stream trickled through the wood and fell into and then out of a trough beside the iron gates, over which there drooped the twining branches of what must have been in spring, I could see, a magnificent fall of honeysuckle. Above the stone arch, half concealed by ivy, I read some words carved in the coping. *Somnii explanatio.*

It seemed an excellent omen. This mysterious and crumbling motto, the slogan or crest of what earlier owner

The Tortoise

or incumbent I knew not, was bound to appeal to your enigmatic fancy, shortly, as it was, to rejoice in the devising of an equally restful legend for your own coat of arms as the Prince of Monte-Nevoso, that subtly gnomic *immotus nec iners*.

So I pushed through the gate, rusting and interestingly poised, as it seemed to me, between a piquant neglect and a creeping decay. I was in a cobbled yard, facing a small tinkling fountain in the forecourt of a very plain, unpretentious country villa, with a balcony or two, a ledge of laurel, and a splendid, solitary sentinel pine.

Very few of those who had known you in the pomposity of the Governor's Palace at Fiume would have suspected that such an ordinary little house might capture your imagination. But I knew the signs. As at the Capponcina, and the Villa Saint Dominique, there was the husk here of a poetic mansion, a magic essence to be conjured and transformed through your own will into the Aladdin's cave of a new and yet more fantastic arena for your speculations and desires.

I was sure when I rang the doorbell and huddled in a flurry of rain listening to the ponderous clang it made far off in some cavernous interior, even more sure when I confronted the dilapidated serving man in his greasy apron who offered – interrupting some obscure kitchen task that required a huge wooden spoon, which he bore as a wand of office while he walked with me – to show me round the house and grounds.

'It belonged to the widow of the German composer, Mr Richard Wagner,' this funereal acolyte whispered over his shoulder, as we shuffled, or rather he shuffled and I strove to avoid a mere imitation of his gait, through a series of quaint and involuted, though at this date rather bare and empty, corridors. 'The mansion was taken over by the government after the war.

'This room is the music-room,' he croaked, as if the great art of sound required some celebration more creaky than his usual rustling, and there over his bent shoulder I saw for the first time into one of the three largest rooms

The Lion of Pescara

amidst all those rabbit hutches of the future Vittoriale, the long sunny apartment where I would later listen to Luisa, grown crone-like in her silver dress adorned with Romanesque patterning, as her lacquered nails reached over the keys to tease out some melody by Richard Strauss.

'The original piano,' the custodian murmured. 'It belonged to a great musician, Franz Liszt.'

After that, remembering the enormous ungainly brown toad with its carved legs, under the partial covering of a white sheet, and the bare space apparently cleared all round, as if to leave gesture room for the great strokes of some brilliant sonata that the virtuoso, or his ghost, might still want to smite from the ivory, I walked through the other rooms only partly watching, counting amongst the alleged three thousand volumes in the heavy library, and noting down the views out over the garden, where there must in their day be a wealth of azaleas, freesia, and the more exotic blossoms of oleander and bougainvillaea.

The price for the lease, as I later learned, was a thousand lire a month, but the legal custodian, an old notary of Brescia, reduced it for you, since his only son had been a legionary at Fiume, to a mere six hundred. Later, of course, you bought the villa, and later still you made a present of it, in perpetuity, to the people of Italy, and were thus enabled, in the enjoyment of an unlimited sum of money for improvements, to elaborate your style of life there to your heart's desire. There are some, even, who say that Mussolini in effect had bought the house from you several times over, and that these were the bribes, or the prizes, for your agreement not to interfere in his many plans.

Be that as it may, the house became yours. You were quite as enchanted as I had expected, scorning as I had known that you would, my alternative choice, with which I had prudently supplied myself, of a classical monster whose awesome drawing-room was decorated in terracotta with a low-relief succession of the heroes of the Renaissance, the whole series, alas, only too reminiscent of the wax figures in the Musée Grevin.

The Tortoise

The Vittoriale, for so it was shortly named by you, began very rapidly to go through the usual transformations. Those who have seen it later, both in its days of triumph, which I shall describe, and in its cobwebby decline, with the great pictures fallen or lifted from their loosening fixtures, and the five hundred cushions removed or torn asunder, and the grey tarpaulins fouled with bird droppings, or the pellets of bats, and the portly guardian, who once, to begin with, gave it the impress of your most eccentric will, the out-of-work architect Maroni, reduced by circumstance to the role of resident man of all tasks, and a sombre, manic, hierophantic recaller of all that had been its glory to the handful of pilgrims, or the tax collectors, or the foreign generals, who came to gawp or spit, none of these could imagine, I suspect, or even believe, what a plain little dwelling the strange palace had once been.

More than any of your earlier houses, it became a repository of architectural jokes, of experiment and renewal, of a clustering and a literate massing of language as mortar, a summing up of a long public life that had seemed, after the Fiume episode, to have reached its zenith, albeit still perhaps with some new chapters to be written.

Indeed, there were rumours that you were about to fly to America, visiting every state by aeroplane, that you had renounced the world, and were shortly to become a monk, or a foreman, or even, perhaps in some parody of your supposed dependence on Luisa Baccara, a piano-tuner. Perhaps the religious speculation, at its most absurd, still retained the inner grain of truth, although you were never, despite an article in the *Corriere*, considering induction as a pastor of the Anglican church. One morning, after a night spent in the company of a young curate, not necessarily, in my own opinion, for the sole purpose of theological disputation, you came out at dawn, wearing only a pair of underpants and your colonel's jacket, and carved the words *ubi Gabriel, ibi ecclesia* in the bark of a tree.

You were searching for something, for a period of rest which might yield a theme, for a deep enough silence into

The Lion of Pescara

which you could sink and probe, and the monkish isolations and terminologies of your later years were already hinted at, though now less with a gravid yearning than a sort of lunatic wit and ridiculous jauntiness.

Your blasphemies became permanent, and part of your décor. One of your cheaper buddhas had a crucifix rammed through his groin to start up like a penis. There were Bibles, to all appearances retaining their original holy contents, but in actual fact encasing the more scandalous folios of Aretino.

When the Russian ambassador Tchicherin was enjoying his liqueur after a long and intensely political lunch with you, a legionnaire brought in a damascened scimitar, and you told him, the ambassador, I mean, with perfect seriousness, that you were obliged to cut off his head as a present to a French lady with whom you were then in love. The poor man was for a moment as terrified, and as taken in, as the American journalist whom you solemnly told that you had an edition of Dante printed by a firm in St Louis to read in your bath, or when seated naked under your fountain, so as not to need to take your hand out of the water when turning your page.

Water is excellent, was a motto in your bathroom, taken from Pindar. But *Woman is a pest*, was another, and printed on a golden tile.

You were anxious to shock, to seem madder than you were, and to indulge your weirdest appetites. You placed a rusted unexploded grenade between delicate amphorae from Cyrenae filled with rare perfume. You placed a skirt round the loins of Michelangelo's David. When Ida Rubinstein presented you with a magnificent tortoise from Galapagos, whose shell seemed almost large enough to form the keel for a rowing-boat, you fed her, the tortoise I mean, whose name became Caroline, with a heady mixture of lettuce and brandy, and set her to wandering, at her own slow speed, through a careful arrangement of priceless china.

You were not often so destructive. Your old friends came, and even some of your old enemies, or unpaid

The Tortoise

agents, including the lugubrious del Guzzo, with a present of a great Dane, and offers of further and even more lucrative lecture tours, and most of these visitors found you withdrawn, and melancholy, albeit a little more odd, even kinky, than they remembered.

Your wife, the Duchessina Maria Gallese, was given a suite in your guest house, and made more than one visit, although this I think was only after your elevation to the royal status, and your tendency to regard the Vittoriale as a form of principality, with its own laws, and its own powers to exist outside the normal sphere of Italian society. The Duse, too, now a very grand old lady of over sixty, was driven from the station and back for a lightning afternoon by your new chauffeur, who was christened Thunderbolt Basso, and had never been known, so you said, to allow the speedometer needle to fall below seventy-five on the open road.

I remember Eleonora stepping down from the running-board, a furled parasol in her hand, and a hint of invisible opera-glasses training on her pause from some unseen royal box in the laurel bushes, and then the haggard lines in her old face, and the trace of tears, when she left, alone, and still erect, and yes, it seemed obvious even then, for the last time.

There were telegrams from the Marchesa Casati, enclosing photographs of herself in the role of Scheherazade at St Moritz, or as Salammbo at Nice, and invitations, as often before, to sleazy balls. You were tired of conforming to the style of others, though, and were already beginning to establish the ritual of your private parties, in which the only participants were those willing to submit entirely to the demands of your own fantasy.

Romaine came once, I know, and was given lunch with her girl-friend Nathalie Barney, in the red dining-room on the second floor, where the curtains were always kept drawn, and the lights burned very low.

'Why do you keep the room so dark?' I remember the American Miss Barney asking.

She had proved already somewhat insensible to your

The Lion of Pescara

famous charm, and had no doubt over the years formed a stock of disreputable tales of your squalid and largely heterosexual adventures, and you were angry, I think, to see your former lover so much in her toils.

'Miss Barney,' you said, as I poured more wine. 'You see those two funeral urns on the mantelpiece.'

I followed your eyes over Persian carpet and Florentine leather dado, over paunchy Venus on marble pedestal, across a hanging-shelf of Chinese snuff bottles, and a what-not with a pile of machine-gun cartridges and a woman's brassière, all in the flickering light from the few candles and the chinks of sun through the drawn damask appearing subtly unreal, and as if shimmering, in a haze, as in part they were, from a series of hidden joss-sticks that exuded a wispy smoke at the room's four corners, and, yes, I picked out, as at length I think Miss Barney did, the two fluted vessels of porphyry amidst a clutter of other bric-a-brac on the shelf above the unlit fire.

'I see them,' I heard her say.

'In those urns,' you said, rising and walking slowly round the table, lifting one finger as if for silence as you did so, and stooping over Nathalie Barney's shoulder with a tall glass of orange juice in your hand, 'I have encapsulated the ashes of the soldiers who fell in the Christmas of Blood at Fiume. The lights in this room are always kept low in remembrance of their sacrifice, and to honour their memory.'

It may have been true. Like so many of your more preposterous claims, it was entirely consistent with what could so often be proved, and yet so rarely was. Your air of authority, in those days, already precluded any demand for corroboration.

After lunch, the two ladies, tweedy now, and rather thickset in their comfortable, rich middle age, were led through the various chambers of the enchanted mansion.

'Here I keep photographs of all the women who have shared my bed,' you said, as you paraded the manuscripts, the plaster casts, and the low, head-cracking lintel of your study.

The Tortoise

'Dear Gabriele,' Romaine said, with a certain sweetness, I thought, and an urge to be friendly, even in the presence of her ferocious paramour. 'Show me mine.'

But you were the equal of this. You had, I fancy, been savouring this climax to your tour.

'My dear Romaine,' you murmured, with hands outstretched in surprise, and with a frankly suggestive glance at the massive Miss Barney. 'You are scarcely a woman.'

It was all done, of course, as in other cases, with such an inveterate and schoolboy kind of naughtiness that even the most ill disposed of visitors found it hard to take umbrage at your insulting, or inept, or atrocious, behaviour. Even Miss Barney, I noticed, was able to swallow her irritation, and avoid any overt remark.

So the visit ended, and we watched them whirl away towards their hotel, and you took out of your pocket a small folder for holding photographs, and passed it over for me to see. There was a clear snapshot taken I should suppose about the turn of the century, judging from the hat and the pile of clothes in one corner of the frame. It showed a completely naked girl of about twenty lying on a bed of moss.

'Nathalie Barney,' you murmured. 'At the age when she seduced the most sought-after French whore of her day, Liane de Pougy. She was queer even then, Tomaso. But she was pretty.'

'Yes,' I agreed. 'She was very attractive.'

You smiled, very sadly.

'They all change,' you said. 'Even I shall change one day. Even I, Tomaso.'

'Never,' I swore, and indeed at this date, in the prime of your joking vigour, and with Fiume only a year behind you, it seemed a not eccentric assertion.

But I was wrong, of course. The years had been waiting to take their toll. You were fifty-eight years old, and you went in alone for what you called a rest that evening after your visitors had gone. It was an omen, albeit a small one, of what was to come.

2

IT WAS IN the late April of 1921 that Mussolini first came to the Vittoriale. All the doors and windows of the house were open, and it was filled with the scent of roses and the humming of bees. It was a lyrical, expressive day for your encounter with someone all too soon to become the evil genius, or perhaps the inner benefactor, of your later days.

I had been summoned for one o'clock to keep notes on the conversation, which you were expecting to be political. The future Duce was at this time thirty-eight years of age, and already showing signals of his coming plumpness, no less than his, to you of course fairly flattering, baldness of skull. He wore, however, as often later, a solemn rather formal bowler hat, and a raincoat, and was loath, I noticed, to be separated from either. He had the air of a man still needing to keep his hands in his pockets for fear of showing signs of nervousness.

There were aides, of course, though far more on your side than his, and I have a recollection of only two rather niggardly bodyguards, and a frail chauffeur in a dusty black limousine. Lunch was taken on the terrace, now a more florid affair, with busts of Roman senators, and a floor of majolica tiles.

Mussolini had spoken of his plans to stand for election the next month, and, indeed, his campaign, I believe, had already begun, and he was perhaps not altogether unhope-

The Tortoise

ful of some booster, in the form of speech or letter, that would aid his cause. For my own part I was very sceptical still of his chances, and much surprised, within the month of May, to read that he and thirty-seven of his Fascists, as they were now being called, had been returned to power.

'Benito,' you said, 'the important thing is goodness. The goodness of action, the internal flowering of the will.'

You were slicing an apple, moving the blade with care in the rind. It was very hot, and I saw Mussolini wipe his brow as he gestured to the shorter of his aides to note down on paper this evident word of wisdom.

'Exactly,' he murmured. 'Exactly, Commandante. The armed seizure of power. The force of the living stem driving through granite, if need be. Through all opposition.'

You smiled, then. You knew what he, as how many others, was after. Some poetically charged, though suitably committal, view of what was to be done in the military or political arena to set the country to rights. You were less keen now, though. The experience of Fiume had chastened, if not exhausted, your eagerness to see something done.

'You are young, Benito,' you said. 'I wish you luck.'

He was clever, though. More ingenious than a bagful of monkeys in some ways was the fattening young Mussolini, and he saw the route, through a quick shift of key, to extort your interest.

'You know, Commandante,' he said, veering as he did still between this form of address and Colonel, but never allowing himself a presumptuous Gabriele, 'your villa is already a monument, a splendid extrapolation of your whole career. Your brilliant sense of design. Your feel for history.'

He had risen and was walking slowly to and fro, pointing up at the once plain brick of the walls which had already been plastered over with heavy pilasters and hollowed out into niches for busts and plaques.

'Only one element,' he added softly, 'only one is missing.'

The Lion of Pescara

You were frowning then, laying aside your half-eaten apple, a bridling Eve in the sudden presence of the tempting serpent. For several years you had been little used, except by your most intimate and witty friends, to this kind of criticism of your taste in decoration. It was what you prided yourself on most.

'You are our greatest writer,' Mussolini was continuing. 'And your sense of the culture of Italy, from which you spring, is everywhere in this wonderful house. Yes,' he said with a laugh, and I began to realise that he was quite an actor in his portly way, 'even in your architectural jokes. There is Belli, Colonel, as well as Dante in your external spirit here.'

A wasp had settled on the bowl of fruit and was crawling over a pomegranate. I saw that the aide with the pencil was fascinated by it, as he might have been by a leopard, or a military aeroplane.

'But you are also,' Mussolini went on, 'as well as our greatest poet our greatest soldier. One gold medal, two silver medals and two bronze. Who else can show so many? And yet where, in all this marvellous decoration, do we see the visible emblems of your career on the Isonzo, above the skies of Vienna, on the waters of the Adriatic?'

You were leaning back then, and pretending to clap. You rose and put an arm around Mussolini's shoulder.

'Splendid, my dear Benito,' you said. 'You have caught my style even better than my own valet. I shall have to get you, and not Italo Rossignoli, eh Tomaso, to prepare my next public speech.'

It was not exactly an insult, although it bore a trace of contempt, I thought, and I saw a shadow of some kind of rage, almost a vow of vengeance it seemed, go over the face of Mussolini's aides. They were not men with much sense of humour. But their master was an angler far too shrewd for any throwing off. He had his hook in.

'Seriously, Colonel,' he said. 'If I ever come to power, you shall have a warship and a squadron of aeroplanes as a present. And I shall hope to see an artillery shell, and not a

The Tortoise

sitting hare, on top of your two gateposts. And a pistol stuck in the belt of St Francis's robe.'

You had much in common, after all, both of you, and the idea of military elements in your décor, had already crossed your mind, I know, and yet it was finally Mussolini, on that boiling day in April, amidst the May blossom and the jars of honey, who crystallised your later plans for the Vittoriale. Perhaps, when he spoke, it was in riddles then, and by way of symbolism, expecting less your passive acceptance of this idea than your immediate translation of its meaning into the language of action, a willingness to march with him, or to stand at his side on balcony or in piazza, even, perhaps, to share the ultimate burden of ruling.

The following year, on August 3rd, when Mussolini's Fascists had seized the city hall in Milan, and hung the balcony with the red flags of the Regency as well as their own black ones, you were persuaded to stand alongside them there and harangue the crowd, albeit with one of your most sibylline orations, far indeed from the explicit urging towards the overthrow of democracy that they had sought.

Nevertheless, you spoke, and you must, I think, afterwards, have realised that you had made a mistake. Your time for action was over. You no longer wanted the cut and thrust of everyday political life, least of all in the chancy venturings of the *fasci di combattimento*.

Ten days later you were lying on the ground underneath the window of the music-room at the Vittoriale, blood flowing from your head. I was there then, as I was not in Milan, and I see still the grouping within the long salon, hung with the portraits of Liszt and Wagner, and thronged in the hot summer night with the twenty or thirty friends who had waited after a party to hear Luisa at the grand piano, she herself with her back stiff and her hands poised like the claws of an owl, a trio of visiting Fascists, among them the sinister Aldo Finzi, who was later to murder Matteotti, and die, yes, I remember this too, fighting against Mussolini at the end in the Ardennes, a half-dozen

The Lion of Pescara

or so of your legionnaires, a few servants, the maid Aelis, who had returned still slim and lascivious to your service, long after Arcachon, and was now dividing the empire of the bedroom, some said, with the jealous Luisa, the quaintly stooping professor, Alceste de Ambris, who had never ceased to approach you on anarchistic schemes, and was disillusioned with your alliance, as he believed it to be, with Mussolini, and I, there amongst them, in a seat near to the grand piano, and with a view from the corner of my eye of you in the window, legs crossed, as you leaned against the lower iron bars.

Very much has been written, and said, about that sultry evening above Lake Garda. There were many mosquitoes in the room, I know, and I was badly bitten. The music was Beethoven, I think, and a great symphony was drawing to its massive close when I heard a crash and a cry. I was weary of the piano, I know, and my eyes were drooping, if not closed. How many others must have been in the same position?

I was out and on to the terrace through the window – the drop was no more than a dozen feet – and I bent over your prostrate, and indeed very defunct-seeming, body, within twenty seconds, but I was hardly the first. Aldo Finzi was there, with your head in his arms, and Aelis, kneeling, as if to pray, and then everyone else, military and civilian, and then the doctors, and then the police, and then, it seemed, the newspapers, and then there was no end to it.

ACCIDENT AT THE VITTORIALE was the usual tone of the commentary, but more than one observer was sure that there was no accident. Murder, I suppose, was the usual secret interpretation, and there were many to believe that the resident mistresses were the prime cause, with the flighty Luisa organising the vicious push.

It could have been so. But hardly, I think, with her own hand, in the midst of the last movement of the seventh symphony. Accomplices there might have been, but this kind of deliberate scheming was hardly the way of a jealous mistress with ample opportunity to wield a knife

The Tortoise

or a bottle of pills in private. Political assassination seems much more likely, and I have had my doubts, over the years, about the role of Aldo Finzi.

The Fascists, though, and I think certainly Mussolini himself, were still not absolutely convinced that you were unwilling to co-operate with their plans, and I hardly believe that the Duce, sentimental as he always was over your career, would have countenanced such a mediocre closing of it.

The legionnaires, then, I have heard some say, may have had a hand in the business, but it scarcely seems a possibility. You commanded still such mystic loyalty that it would have been hard to imagine the most irate or disillusioned of your former soldiers raising a hand against his leader.

At any rate, you survived, and recovered, indeed, with an astonishing speed. The doctors had diagnosed a fracture of the skull, and an effusion of the cerebro-spinal fluid. You lay for two days in a coma, on the immense damask-spread mahogany bed in your own room, with the curtains drawn against the sun, and the shutters against the insects, and the whole house feared that you would recover, if at all, with some permanent damage to your brain.

On the evening of the second day, though, you asked for Aelis to bring in your supper, and there were sounds, behind the door, of giggling and bumping, and she emerged, after half an hour, flushed and rumpled, and then Italo Rossignoli was called in to give you a full massage, and then I was asked for, and went in, and found you sitting up in bed in a maroon kimono, with a folio of obscene engravings on your knees.

'You look much better,' I said. 'How do you feel?'

'Tomaso,' you said, waving to me to sit down on the edge of the bed. 'You know as well as I do how I feel. I feel very old. And the wing of death is never far away. For the moment the shadow has passed, and I feel the better for it. But the wing will cover me again.'

So we talked of other matters, and I let the circumstances rest. I knew, though, and I think for the first time, that your life had assumed a new form. You were waiting now. For however long it might be, and it was at this date to be over seventeen years you would have to wait, you were dedicated to a new service, the contemplation of your own slow decline, and the ever-present chances of a sudden, violent, or contrived interruption of it.

You had seen the face of death, and the face of corruption, in the body of Giuseppe Miraglia, in the corpses along the Timavo, in the coffins of your fallen heroes after the battle for Fiume. It was your own face now, clamped down like a mask of clay, the one you saw when you shaved in the rococo bathroom mirror, the one you pressed with your manicured hands after the volatile kisses of every pressing or tentative mistress. You knew it well, and you were going to give up your final years to cherishing its most intimate outlines.

Within a week, however, you were on your feet, and the bustling Renata, summoned as once before to Venice, and now evidently the regular matron and acolyte of your indispositions, was urged to pack her bags and withdraw again to the seclusion, I think in Naples, from which she had come. She did so, in some dudgeon, and with dark warnings, I fear unheeded, about the malevolent Luisa, at whose door she most emphatically placed the responsibility for your accident.

'I loathe her, Father,' she confessed, and left, as I say, unlistened to. This was hardly so of Mussolini, though, who returned, and this time with a fleet of small dark cars, and a hint of entourage, on a misty night in October, unheralded, and unrecorded. I knew of the visit, and yet there was no invitation to be present, or to keep my own notes of the talk.

From midnight until nearly dawn, the two of you were closeted alone in the *officina*, and then seen to walk, if I am to believe Aelis, beneath the umbrella pines in the Arengo, where you would hold, later, by torchlight, so many of your final rituals, murmuring in a cracked voice the slogans or mottoes of former days to a captive audience of aged legionnaires.

The Tortoise

What words were spoken or plans made, or promises extended, or broken, in those fog-ridden hours before the dawn, perhaps history will never know. But the march on Rome, begun on October 28th, was only fifteen days away, and when it came, you were quietly seated at home, writing and reading, and not for your sins or to your undying glory at the head of the column, or somewhere, cowed or exuberant, in the jostling wings.

The ninth wave had come, and the new Italy been born, but not entirely, after all, in your own image, albeit undoubtedly with some lineaments of your features, and some traces of your style.

Mussolini, though, had got, I think, what he wanted. I remember well the last time I saw him at the Vittoriale, shortly before I moved away to live in Rome, and our paths began to cross at longer, and more complicated, intervals.

It was the autumn of 1925, and I see still the motorbike outriders winding up the hill, the steady flow of the black limousines, like a mafia funeral, and the stout, florid man in the uniform, stepping like Al Capone from his rear seat, and shaking hands with one thumb in his belt, and a wide grin, the grin of condescension and victory, split right across his puffy cheeks.

It was more, though, than a courtesy call. He stayed for three nights, and in those nights, the culminating honours were bestowed, and the last touches, I think, moulded on the noble statue that Mussolini felt he was building, the living monument to Gabriele D'Annunzio, the greatest, after himself of course, of all Italians since Cola de Rienzo.

Already the plans were in motion for the enormous morocco edition of all your collected works, to be produced with no expense spared, and with many photographs and samples of your flowing hand in facsimile, already the famous title, the Prince of Monte-Nevoso, was being offered in recognition of your services to Italy in preserving, as they said, her eastern frontier. Already, the great cruiser on which your legionnaire had been assassinated at Spalato, had been dragged up from the bay, and built, with what colossal labour, directly into the hillside

The Lion of Pescara

at the bottom of your land, and there, to the tunes of a string quartet, and perched on little X-shaped folding chairs, the two of you conferred, and were seen to drink wine together, and were photographed for posterity, and for propaganda.

I still have one of those photographs here in my desk, a little stained and rumpled now, but what a bizarre memorial of that odd misalliance! You stand, the two of you, on the deck of the *Puglia*, Mussolini with his hands on the firing-grip of a machine-gun, fixed on a tripod and facing backwards over his shoulder, as if to threaten some unseen enemy in the rear, or perhaps, who knows, in his own depleted ranks. You lean beside him there, a grim dwarf, unsmiling, one hand on your hip, the other out as if to support your weight on the leg of the tripod. You wear a fur cap, and a leather jacket belted at the waist, and a pair of pointed cavalry boots with puttees tucked in at the top. You look exhausted, as Mussolini looks bored.

So it must have been perhaps, then as later. The busy statesman taking time off to exalt his old comrade-in-arms. The fossil hero knuckling down at last to the praise, preoccupied, and with his mind on ulterior things, the lubricious privacies of his own besotted mind, the concluding rites of a life once more given over to poetry, debauchery, and the palace intrigue of a household isolated out of time, and as horrible, as bickering, and as lurid as anything ever imagined for the worst of the Roman emperors by Suetonius or Martial.

3

YES, THINGS CHANGED after your accident, or your suicide, or your murder, whatever it was, and the steady steps of your withdrawal began to assume more and more the outlines of a monastic, even a kind of Franciscan, seclusion. A statue, indeed, of St Francis, elegant in sandstone, with outstretched arms as if to receive you into the bosom of eternity, or at least the chastity of the Church, was rapidly erected, to the smart and modern designs of a young sculptor, thought to be sleeping with Maroni, on the very spot underneath the music-room window where you had fallen amidst the rose bushes on that sinister afternoon in the August of 1922.

Like a hermit, you began to withdraw. Like a snail into its shell, or as the mad Ludwig into his several castles in Bavaria, where a table would be sent up on stilts from the kitchen, so that he might dine absolutely alone, without even the sight of a serving maid, even perhaps as a brother in some meretricious and yet rather intensive order whose fixed instructions were solitude and lasciviousness, you commenced on the slow cultivation of your final period.

It began, perhaps, with the funeral of the Duse, one of the last more public events to which you felt it essential to go in person, after her absurd and rather squalorful demise in a suburb of Pittsburgh, and your insistence to Mussolini that she should have a state funeral, and the arrangement

The Lion of Pescara

of this in the church of St Mary of the Angels in Rome, where you were seen, though only as a tiny bowing figure in the back row, incognito in dark glasses, by the still young and rather more observant Marquis de Casa-Fuerte, with whom you exchanged neither word nor nod, nor even, I have heard him say, and that this surprised him more, a squeeze of the knee or arm.

As on other occasions, you arrived in your great yellow limousine, the product of some rare inspiration or special order to the Fiat factory, and with so much space in the rear that you could eat there, if need be, and sleep, and not necessarily alone either, if guests were invited, and some have claimed, though I never saw this myself, that a group of three, not all women, have been observed locked in a claustrophobic knot there behind the tinted, albeit not entirely opaque, glass of the windows.

You drove away alone, then, though, according to Illan Alvarez de Casa-Fuerte, and with tears in your eyes, or at least the lines of them down your cheeks below those eye-reserving shades, and with your cautious, vigilant chauffeur, conspicuous by his neckerchief and his lumpy inside pocket, holding the door open like a bodyguard, or a colour sergeant in your Praetorian elite. Then the door snapped, and the four huge exhausts roared, and the wheels ground in the gravel, and the Prince of Monte-Nevoso, soon to be, was whirled away again to his mountain retreat in the north.

There were moments when you received some news from the outside world with a smile. As, for example, when Mussolini sent you a letter consisting only of the stage directions from your long-derided and, alas, quite unsuccessful drama, *La Gloria*:

A large, bare room, its powerful stone vertebrae visible to the eye. A heavy table stands in the middle, cluttered with maps like the table of a strategist, still animated by recent deliberations, by the meditations and then the unanimous agreement of the men who

The Tortoise

had been gathered round it only a short time ago: a motionless support from which is radiated and propagated a central thought, a regulating energy. On each architrave of the four doors, two to the right and two to the left, is carved the emblem of a flame that is revived by the breath of a contrary wind, with the motto VIM EX VI. At the back of the room a balcony opens onto the vast city.

and below the Duce had added the single phrase, 'this is me.'

But more and more the events that mattered most were those enacted within the cloistered confines of your own walls, where even the death of a greyhound, or a fox terrier, could assume the massive proportions of a tragedy. There once, at some indeterminate epoch and yet one, I think, when I was still in my cottage out in the gardens, the Galapagos tortoise, that enormous present from Ida Rubinstein, herself now still an occasional visitor, and one who had taken up flying, and had formed her own film company, and made, as I have said elsewhere, a fair shot at your better drama, *La Nave*, this wondrous tortoise, I say, that might have lived, in the normal course of her race's destiny, for a hundred and fifty years, expired, and alas, indeed, in a most unusual, and yet rather imitative and flattering manner, groping her slow way, one moonlit night, through the terrace gardens, and nipping off in her sharp little teeth no less than three thousand tuberoses, which, in spite of a famous digestion, long tested on other less perfumed delicacies, proved rapt a little too far beyond her all-absorptive capacity, and led to a sudden decline, a fever, and shortly afterwards, a final collapse.

This was, indeed, in the style of the household, a most D'Annunzian death, recalling, as it did, the fate of your heroine in *La Pisanella*, who died suffocated by roses, herself a follower in the footsteps, adverse critics have hinted, of the sixteen-year-old blonde girl in *The Fate of the Abbé Mouret*, who committed suicide on her Louis-Quinze bed, as the English artist the Hon. John Collier has aptly and poignantly shown us, immersed in a great sea of heavy-scented blossoms.

'Her mouth was our nose,' you were heard to murmur enigmatically, as you stood looking down a trifle lugubriously at the bulky corpse on the Persian tiles. 'We must gild her for posterity.'

And thus the skilful Maroni was employed, or rather another of his boy-friends was, this time a metalsmith, one Brozzi, to refashion the poor beast's physiognomy in bronze, and to incarcerate this reproduction under the canopy of the living shell, and to have it set, shrouded in grey velvet, as under a palanquin, at the very centre of the red dining-room, to one side of the great refectory table itself, there to form an awful and lasting warning, as I always thought it, against the dangers of over-eating, or at least of experimenting with too strange a diet.

For you, however, the element of the skull beneath the skin was already what held you to this macabre re-enactment, and led to your placing, on a small plaque, in the middle of the pedestal, the Latin motto: *intra me maneo*, I stay inside myself.

You lived in your own dream, one furnished with the paraphernalia of a monastery and a whorehouse, presided over by the twin deities of Luisa Baccara, the music-box, and the servant-wench, Aelis, the big-eyed procuress, as all knew, of so many titillating young mistresses from the surrounding villages. It was a decadent, and a bizarre, ménage, and yet one, in its day, where the tenderness of old age could mingle at times with the vacillating coarseness of a fleeting antique lust.

The years went by, and I left with my wife and young daughter, Nerina, and made a career in the cinema for a while, though still there, I confess, when you needed me, albeit at far less frequent intervals, and by way, more, of an agent on special missions than a regular body-servant. That role, as I have hinted, had been long taken over by your wee jockey of a valet and masseur, Italo Rossignoli, whose penchant for being a copy-cat had extended now to an assumption of your own polished riding-boots, and a

The Tortoise

permanent patch, which he never needed, since his sight I believe was perfect, incongruously placed over the right eye, and thus providing a book end, or balance, to your own.

I came to visit, sometimes, *en famille*, and as my daughter grew, and assumed a little of the gawky sensuousness of a young adult, I could see your ancient, roué eyes half linger on her thighs, or stoop to the hidden places under her childish frocks.

I asked Nerina once, after you had shown her over the house, what you had spoken of, and how she had liked you. She must have been about eleven years old then, an advanced girl for her age, and we sat in the back, open seat of your car, a sort of grandiose landaulette, like an older man, and his mistress, waiting to be driven to the station. Alas, no longer however, by Thunderbolt Basso, who had taken up motor-bike racing and flung his bullet shoulders and his nearly impenetrable skull clean over the handle bars at a hundred and twenty miles an hour, striving to pass a Bugatti on some obscure corniche in the Riviera, and was now long mourned, and buried, and replaced by a calmer, and a more secure and taciturn, chauffeur.

'Tell me about it all, Nerina,' I suggested, as the new chauffeur arrived and the car began to move.

She was thin and blonde, sweet and cool that day in a lemon dress, and the wind blew her hair in the winding drive, and I loved her very much, more even, I thought, than our friendship of thirty years.

'He was wonderful,' she murmured, staring across the drive through a gap in the oleander towards the far prow of the *Puglia*. 'He was very kind to me, and he said such amazing things.'

'Tell me,' I said.

So she told me. Of how you had met her in the masking room, as it was called, the room for shedding outdoor clothes, and for assuming the masque of circumstance, and of how you had bowed, and kissed her hand, and had then looked up, with a mischievous grin and said,

'Isn't this fun?'

The Lion of Pescara

Then he had led you, as I knew he would, through the short corridor, lined with books and shadowy prints, into what was then still called The Room of The Leper, although it was later to be known as The Room of Death.

It was a small room, though it sounded rather bigger and more cavernous, in my daughter's awe-inspired recollection. I knew it well. In the middle stood a bier, with a cavalry sword across it, and an open coffin at the foot, on the floor. The walls were of ash-coloured leather, and the light, vague and misty, as in some great cathedral, of which this might have been a small chapel, used to filter in through large panels of coloured glass, engraved with the images of soldiers and angels.

'The sword is lying here,' you had said to Nerina, with a sepulchral, mock-awesome tone in your voice, modified, it seems, with a conniving wink, 'so that when I am dead, one of my legionnaires, already chosen, may sever my left ear, and place it there, on the bier.'

And you had stepped forward, and tapped a space on the velvet marked with a tiny scar.

'Later,' you had gone on, 'I shall be placed in this fine coffin of cedar-wood, and allowed to rest in state, visited, I have no doubt, by a long assemblage of great bores, whom I shall have spent most of my life striving never to see again. You are very pretty, do you know that, my little Nerina?'

The mixture, familiar to me from so many accounts, and such frequent observation, of a macabre fantasy, a touch of sweetness and poignancy, and a sudden swoop, as if by force of extreme feeling, into flattery and attention, yes, I knew it well. Few women, my daughter no more than most, were proof against these tactics.

'Let me tell my story myself, Daddy,' Nerina said at one point, when I had been interrupting more than I should have done. And I let her speak.

I wanted to kneel, she said, and perhaps pray, beside the bier. But he turned away, and opened a drawer in a tiny cabinet, and pulled out a heap of strange clothes, things like veils and sashes, and long stockings, and a tray of

The Tortoise

cosmetics, kohl and lipstick and a lot of creams and powders.

'Religion,' he said, suddenly treating me like a grown-up, 'is all a form of superstition, my dear. We have to enjoy its mystery, and then return to everyday life. So let's dress up.'

Then he held out a sort of nun's robe, a long grey thing that reached all the way down to my feet, and I took it from him, and then it was over my head and I was inside it, and he was fastening the rope around my waist.

'Little sister of the sorrows,' he was saying, 'wherefore do you look so sadly now? We two are acolytes of a cult. The cult of ice cream.'

And then he was laughing and pulling out an ice box from under a table, and there inside it, were two glass tripod bowls with cassata in them, and two spoons to eat it with. I expected the Mad Hatter and the March Hare to appear at any moment.

So we sat down, or rather sort of lay down, on a pile of cushions someone had helpfully left in a corner, and he was feeding the ice cream to me as if I was a baby, and then I did the same for him, and O it was quite amazingly good fun, Daddy, and not at all what you think, I know.

Then he said, 'You know, Nerina, I bring wicked women in here sometimes, and they put on their nun's habits, and I make love to them, down here on the cushions, or even up on the bier.' 'You are joking, Commandante,' I said. And he laughed and said, 'Well of course, I'm joking.'

'You're a naughty old man,' I said, and he laughed, and agreed, and we got up and he took me down a corridor where there was the most disgusting picture I've ever seen in my life, and I blushed, and he saw I did, and he said, 'Why you wicked young woman, you really shouldn't know what that's all about. I have it there, you know, because this is the way to my bedroom, and, as I said once to a visiting delegate from the Pope, a lewd and sultry representation suffices to sate the appetite and thus keep one's thoughts away from the base means of delight on the way to bed. He was not amused, my dear, he was not amused.'

'And neither am I,' I said, Daddy, I promise you, 'neither am I.' He saw that I really was put out, so he took me through a little door in the wall and there we were, coming out of what had seemed to be a bookcase, into his main library, and he was plucking down a huge book like a brass-bound Bible, and, when I looked over his shoulder, it was actually a sort of dictionary of swear-words.

'Well, Commandante,' I said, laughing, in spite of myself, 'you never let up, now do you? It's just as my father says, I must never do anything you tell me to.'

Then he was quite serious, Daddy, he was, I tell you, and he walked over to the window, and stood with his hand on a bust of Napoleon, and said, in his most moving voice, that you were the most loyal and the most devoted friend that he'd ever had.

Then we sat down, and he held my hand, and I asked him about, O about a hundred things, Fiume, and how well he knew the Duce, and what it was like to be old and famous, and what writers he most admired and the woman, of all he'd known, that he loved most. That was the one thing he never told me. He just looked in my eyes and said there were none to equal me.

He's quite worried about how bald he is, you know, though he doesn't tell people, because his head gets cold at night. So I told him he ought to rub it with a woollen cloth before he goes to bed, and he said he'd never thought of that, and I told him it made the blood run faster, and he'd have no trouble if he stuck to this piece of advice.

We were walking then in the gardens, along a series of pergolas – are they called that? – sort of wooden trellises with roses across the top, and then under the bow of that ship stuck out in the hill, and all the sailors on the deck stood to attention and saluted, and then we met a neat little man in a black uniform, and the Commandante said, 'O Nerina, this is my jailer, allow me to introduce, the Chief of the Gardone Police, Giovanni Rizzi, he is paid by the Duce to be my protector, and to stop me from doing

The Tortoise

anything unpatriotic or stupid.' And then the neat little man kissed my hand, and they hugged each other, and laughed, and yet there was an odd feeling about it all, and he seemed, the Commandante, as we walked on, a little preoccupied, and he said suddenly, 'Rome, you know, my dear, has become the Cloaca Maxima. I hate what it smells of.'

I knew he was really serious, but I didn't like the change in his mood, and I made a joke about it and said, 'Well, I think I need to go to the Cloaca Minima. Will you excuse me?'

But he came in with me, and showed me the guest lavatory, and there inside the door was a sign in bronze reading, The Little Dung Library, and I was very glad he couldn't see me blushing again while I felt that I was providing him with a set of new volumes for what must already, so my imagination was declaring, be a quite extensive collection. Yes, Daddy, I'm going too far, I know, so let me tell you that when I came out he showed me The Room of The Stump, and there in a glass hand was a bunch of letters bound in yellow ribbon, and he said that they were the ones written to him by his mother, and that all the drawers in the room were filled with his archives of correspondence, the answered files to the left of the door and the ones unanswered to the right.

And yes, I know that you've seen it all a hundred times before, and the drawing of the hand writing itself by that strange Dutchman, and the etching of Dürer's hand, and all the others, but he told me, and did you know this, that when he was once in Turin, he took a taxi cab and the driver, with the reins in his fingers, offered to draw his hand, and asked him what his profession was, and when he said, 'writer,' rummaged under his seat and produced a drawing of what he said was the hand of Benedetto Croce.

'I wonder,' he said, 'whose hand he might have produced if I'd said I was an engineer? Marconi's? Or maybe the hand of Giolitti, if I'd said I was a prostitute.' And then he saw I was bored with his politics, and he kissed my hand again and I came away. And I think he's marvellous, Daddy, I really do. I'd never have thought that a man so old could seem so young, or make me feel so much that I was his equal in age.

Twelve years had to go by, though, and Nerina to be married herself, and grown to a less innocent, and more bitchy, twenty-three, before I was to learn the real culmination of that so jaunty episode of the early 1930s. For it was not to the Little Dung Library that you had led my eleven-year-old daughter, I then learned, as we sat in anger, hearing the news of the Italian surrender at Sidi Barani, and the turn of the tide, no, it was into your own somewhat Levantine and louchely blue bathroom, where you had locked the door on the inside, and lain down with your head in the basin of the bidet, and pleaded, yes, Nerina claimed then, pleaded that she would squat above your face and empty her bowels into your mouth, and how she, in her excitement, and the urgency of her need to evacuate, had lifted her robe and her skirt and pulled her child's briefs off, and done what she had to do there exactly as you asked, and you had gulped and swallowed, and she had seen the lumpy place in your breeches decline, and a wet stain spread over your groin.

Such were the practices, and the squalors, to which your ancient lechery was driven, and how, in my heart, I wonder, could I feel horror, or she disgust, at what was desired so much, and so simply, and proved soon over, and scoured away, and replaced, in only a moment, by the mint tea and the witty conversation of the great man she had walked with a few minutes earlier in the sunny garden? *Sic transit gloria mundi.* And afterwards, the *cagoia*. Only the *cagoia*.

4

IT WAS ALL so claustrophobic. There were women, like the beautiful young actress, Elena Sangro, who spent weeks on end in darkness with you, and the shutters were often drawn, as in the house of Miss Havisham, that analogue perhaps for the lamenting Queen Victoria, with whom you in fact had so little in common, the very moment the rising sun broke above the horizon, and often, too, only folded back, like seaside postcards, into their vaulted recesses, when the shades of night had finally fallen over the cypresses, and brought the bats out of the outhouses to cry and swoop around the eaves.

Very often then, during those final years, the household would be gathered into the music-room, by the light of the moon, and forced to sit in silence around a particular rickety pedestal-table, which was believed, according to the increasingly mesmerised Maroni, to possess the power of attracting spirits. I was present myself on one of these occasions, together with Nerina and my wife, and I well remember the awed hush of the several servants, the creaking of the immense, numerous pieces of unseen furniture in the shadows, and the occasional pale glow from the arm of a Chiparus dancer, or an Aphrodite bending her bow, where these recent concessions to the flourishing cult of the Art Deco were poised in the beams of the celestial Diana.

The Lion of Pescara

I had always regarded your many forays into the occult as dictated by some latent sexual motive, and spiritualism, in particular, with its essential concomitant of darkness, appeared to offer you ample opportunities for a covert sampling of rounded bosom or fleshy thigh. You had placed yourself, on the night I was there myself, between the elegant Elena, whom you were doubtless by then entitled to finger in public or private to your heart's content, or so the watchful presiding deities of your lechery, the big-eyed matronly Aelis, and the boxy Luisa, were evidently supposing, to judge from their tight lips, and their bitchy commentaries, and, yes, I must yield the news, a suave groom's boy, to whom you were keen, you insisted at length, to impart some details of how these pretty seances were conducted.

Little happened, of course. There were far-off shrieks, and howls, and these might have been either the dead summoning us to their benisons, or more likely, birds of prey, hunting your woods above the lake. Only once did anything manifest itself that might have been construed as a human voice, and this, in my view, though throaty and distorted, was rather obviously some ejaculation, conscious or no, from the complicit vocal machinery of the devoted Maroni.

'La Duse,' he whispered, afterwards. 'She wishes to speak with you, Commandante. She has a message about your theatre.'

But the message was not repeated, either through some reluctance on the part of the absent Eleonora, or perhaps, as I believed, some lack of security in his impersonation on the part of our temporary medium, who, indeed, architect of your improvements as he was, had a special interest in all that might pertain to the at that date halted construction of the Greek amphitheatre on the slopes of a rock garden. It was finished later, and indeed served, at the height of the Ethiopian War, for a midnight recital, to which I was bidden, of the major part of a new diatribe, or poem, which you had composed on the machinations and infirmities of the black races, a universal peril, you then

The Tortoise

thought, no less than the more widely scouted and canvased yellow one.

You had written enthusiastically to Mussolini, when the troops were advancing through Abyssinia, and that little bearded Emperor, across the distance between whose palace gateposts two tethered lions had been chained to spring, and whose luxury and decadence were, indeed, a match in many ways for your own, was a frequent stalking-horse for some of your more vitriolic invective.

I remember thinking, as I sat alongside my wife in the moonlight, and felt the airless heat of that so well known room, topped now, as I knew it was by the gathered sheets of silk that gave it, you felt, the quality of a medieval warrior's tent, and thus pleased your fantasy, but which, in fact, offered an awful repository in all their fetid nooks for the breeding of perverse insects, whose broods and rubbish would shower down, at times, on the heads of unsuspecting visitors, yes, I remember thinking, even as I cringed and flinched against some anticipated onslaught of moth or mosquito, of how I had once attended another of your encounters with the unknowable, at the sinister rite of *involtura*, performed in Rome in 1915, when you had assisted the satanic Marchesa Casati in the baptism of a wax figure, pricking its groin with a sequence of devilish pins, and calling upon the powers of darkness to afflict the one it represented with impotence and desolation.

'Of course the ceremony was entirely successful,' you insisted later, at some tea party in Fiume. 'The man has never, as you know, Tomaso, been able to achieve a proper erection from that day to this.'

But the fearsome victim, against whom the sorcery of *envoûtement* was thus invoked, and with all the correct amulets in your pockets, and the proper jewel placed in a certain required cranny of the Marchesa's anatomy, and on the stroke of midnight, and in front of the tomb of Horace in the Via Appia, alas, the despised and inveterate one, your enemy, Giolitti, was at least able later to boast of a family of three fine daughters, and was often seen, into the bargain, to smile like a Cheshire cat in public, and to eat his dinners with every appearance of a vast and unaffected enjoyment.

No, it was play for you, I think, this toying with the games and rituals of the other world. The groom's boy was thought to rise, at least in my own eyes, with his face a little flushed, and a small disarrangement, even, of his rather close-fitting trousers, but, after all, there was more than just a weird excuse for some exotic fumbling there, when this could so easily, at any rate, have taken place by sunlight and amidst the warm straw of the hay-loft.

We stood in the light of sudden, flickering candles, after the seance was over, and a few plates of dry cake were handed round by Aelis, and a gloomy note or two was struck on the organ – a new acquisition, and one more in key with a votary of St Francis, one might have thought, than the original Steinway – by the still deft and virtuoso Luisa, whose hands were then, though, I would suppose, more often employed on the stops and keys than around the interstices of what Maria Gravina had once called your nether bassoon.

The game was over, and yet it was not over, nor indeed entirely a game, at least so long as the shutters remained unopened, and the doors of the house locked – as they always were, as soon as a visitor entered – and the electric light switched off at the mains until you required it.

'Excuse me, friends,' you murmured, raising one gnarled hand above a candelabra. 'I must leave you soon, although I am with you now, in body and in spirit. Eat what I have given. Drink of my blood and wine. Be wise and merry. Tomaso.'

Then you beckoned me aside, and stood under a fluted chandelier, with a green ball at the top, the very epitome of the odeon style that had begun to afflict the restless genius of Maroni, and I smelt for a second the dank odour of your breath, a sudden analogue for what you had once claimed so playfully about Renata, and which was now in reality, as then, one fears, too, for so many of your women, the grim result of neglect amidst those eloquent and decaying tombstones, your teeth.

The Tortoise

'Tomorrow,' you murmured, laying a hand on my arm. 'At the hour of seven. Attend me in The Room of The Oratory.'

Then you were gone, limping a little, I thought, through the door into one of Maroni's Gothic atria, with all their monastic sofas, and little chests for imaginary chasubles and real contraceptives, and I knew that you were still what you had once been, for all the dressing of meditative seclusion and a sort of Benedictine religiosity, a writer on the way to his cave of making.

'He writes at night now, I gather,' I had said to Aelis, while she was shredding peaches into a bowl for one of the sweet salads you had come to adore, and she had confirmed this shift in emphasis.

'Always at night,' she agreed. 'I switch off the lights every morning when I rise for work.'

I knew already, for there had been articles in many of the papers, about your methods of composition. You would sit at a huge walnut refectory table, with a box of steel pens at your hand, and a roller blotter to mop up the ink flashed aside as your hand struck fire, almost across the vellum. So they said.

Sitting, then, as you had stood once in your great days at the Capponcina, and with a pen of steel instead of the quill from a chosen goose, and with, too, as I knew from my visits to the *officina*, where it all took place, a series of shell-shaped lights throwing upwards a glow like the brightness of a dull day on to the ceiling, an even, cold light instead of the warm, golden glimmer of burning oil in your several clepsydra at Florence, you would let your eyes travel along the moving horses in the Parthenon frieze, or the plaster version of it that you had ranged above your bookcases, and the Muse, or her elderly and raddled equivalent, the granddaughter in high heels and lipstick, I suppose, of the *fin de siècle* lady who had once cultivated your numbers, would step aside from her slow riding and whisper some message from the stews of eternity into your willing and receptive ear.

The Secret Book, your last masterpiece, has many of

The Lion of Pescara

these. You wrote about the war, of course, remembering some of your first and most vivid feelings as you honed out, or simply selected from a mass of notes made at the time, your recollections of that visit up the line when you saw the French troops in 1914 withdrawing towards Paris.

Haystacks have sometimes the perfect form of Saracen cupolas. Hills of leaden blue. Great grey horses with knotted tails. Red Cross everywhere. Yellow lights. Green trees. Dead leaves blowing about. Sensation of how easy it is to lose hold on life.

At Neufchelles: a cat eating the flesh from the bones of a horse. Piles of ammunition. Laughing sunshine on the hills. A statue of Racine near the canal. In the canal, an overturned boat. Shell-shattered houses. A red butcher shop. Red apples. Willows and poplars. White clouds. Damp sky. Roses. Apple-trees laden with ripe fruit.

At Faverolles: a shadowy square, a little tower, a rooster.

At Touty: the road is encumbered with artillery. Long trains. A lame horse shot at a cross-roads. He falls in his own blood. Soldiers with bayonets. One with a helmet, the head of Achilles. A pick over his shoulder.

At Corcy: a dead horse. A calm green river with swans. A garden of dahlias. Ambulances. An automobile full of women in mourning. Floating black veils. Tragic faces.

At Longpoint: a cathedral in ruins. Soldiers everywhere. Wagons. Ambulances. Red breeches.

At Courmelles: from the heights of the belfry of the Soissons Cathedral in the valley. All the hills slope down toward the city. One of the spires is broken.

You wrote then, as often in *Notturno*, with a kind of directness they say you never had, and which your enemy, the American Hemingway, to judge from his book *A Farewell to Arms*, would appear to have learnt from, and which you yourself – I wonder – may have picked up from

The Tortoise

that nineteenth-century war correspondent, the English writer for *The Times* in the Crimea.

You wrote about sex, or what was left of that excellence, veiling thinly your warped reachings after satisfaction in what you could find to say about other matters:

> I had not seen a forge in action for a long time. A virgin stupor was born within me, like a primitive spirit. The iron became red and twisted, resisting and giving off sparks. I watched the one who seized it with the tongs, holding it firmly and taming it. It was a young boy with long hair and covered with soot. The coloured sweat stuck to his body like blood. The whites of the eyes drew me. Like those of a wild beast in a menagerie.

Perhaps, though, the best passages are those about vanity, or your own approaching death, where a sort of abstract elegance, and a noble, brooding restraint has taken over:

> I am like a shadow across the bronze door, neither living nor dead, incapable of destiny, neither earthly nor subterranean, between the days which are to come and those which have been. Everything lives and everything perishes through form.

So I pictured you, as my wife and I lay in our ordinary bed, in the guest-house at the end of the garden, where statesmen and legionnaires, discarded mistresses and lovers as yet to be, old men who had taught you as a boy, and young hopefuls who thought you might look at their sonnets, composers and whoremongers, agents and Bolshevists, Armenians, Egyptologists and amazing contortionists, the whole boiling of strange and unwanted, or sometimes, far more rarely now, much sought after, visitors, had slept and waited and eaten and dreamed before us, and I turned over and lost myself in my own dreams, and in due course, wakened by Aelis at six o'clock, for she knew what would be required of me, I rose, washed, and walked bleary-eyed through the dew to the encrusted frontage of the Vittoriale

The Lion of Pescara

itself, to which I was shortly admitted, as if by some unseen signal, by Italo Rossignoli in shorts and plimsolls, who had just been fencing, or so it would appear, to keep himself fit, in the gymnasium.

'Alas,' he murmured, as he showed me in, 'the Colonel is more rarely able to try himself in the ways of the foils nowadays. I fence alone, comrade.'

I found you then, where I knew you would be, not yet, as you had promised in the close confines of the oratory, at your blasphemous prayers, with bell, book and possibly Elena Sangro and her dildo, but no, still half asleep, and in your coffin, at the foot of the bier in The Room of The Leper.

'Tomaso,' you said, starting up in your dressing-gown, whose cords hung down below your knees like the tassels of a bell, 'you have caught me out, as I guessed you might, in my most enjoyable weekly pleasure. I spend each Monday night accustoming my creaky bones to their future mattress of cedarwood.'

'As John Donne three centuries before you,' I answered, seeing you lively and very sprightly, it would seem, and happy for this lucid interval, and eager to make the most of it.

'You know, Tomaso,' you said, reaching out a hand for me to help you over the side and on to the floor, 'you should try this occupation yourself. You're getting on, you know. The years will take their toll.'

The light was coloured like the scatter of gleams within a kaleidoscope, and the stale scent of dyed incense and candlewax hung heavy in my nostrils. I did, indeed, I remember, feel a trifle decayed as I loomed there at six-thirty on a winter's morning, and I realised, also, with a sudden shock, what else was unusual, that the room was freezing, icy cold, and I found that I was right to be shivering.

'I allow myself only this one time of the week,' you said, anticipating my comment, 'when I adjust my frame to the final chill. However, there was yet another motive, my dear Tomaso, in the withdrawal from my accustomed

The Tortoise

sleeping-place. A nude statue, which you may recall as the Aphrodite of Naxos, collapsed on my feet from a pedestal by the head of the bed, and it seemed an omen of which I ought to take heed. There is always danger in sleeping too near to a naked woman. Flesh or stone, it makes little difference.'

By this time, you had sloughed aside your heavy dressing-gown, revealing a pair of your more familiar powder-blue pyjamas, but of a more warming and furry material than your earlier pairs. You had soon, however, managed to exclude all sight of these compromising night-things below a swashbuckling kimono, cut, it seemed to me, in the style of a friar's robe, and we were standing, and then oddly squatting, I on the rim of a Victorian prie-dieu, and you, knees clasped on the step of a lectern, under the hammered ironwork, and, rather incongruously, the crumbling giant-hogweed, of The Room of The Oratory.

The skeletal flowers, and there were friable and rustling stems of honesty, of all things, and of a sort of fossilised cow parsley, the victims of Luisa's winter urge to substitute something for the blossoms of gaudy summer, made an added aura of the charnel house in a room already thick with such grave and salutary associations.

'Tomaso,' you said, 'I have only one thing to discuss with you. I want your opinion, which I shall greatly value, on the site for my tomb.'

So, after a moment or two to prepare ourselves, you with your eyes closed, and a mumble of Latin, I with a mere amen and a turmoil of thoughts, we strolled through the house and out into the garden, where, beyond the *Puglia*, grey and warlike again in this frosty dawn, you led me along a lane of yews to an extensive clearing in a glade of conifers. There, already, a variety of your officers from Fiume had found their final resting-place, and the stones held a solemn granitic glitter in the rising sun.

You stopped in the very middle of the clearing, where a small bronze plaque had been inlaid on a rock. The words

The Lion of Pescara

incised on the bronze had a striking and rather typical urgency,

> hinc resurrecturus pro patria, Gabriele D'Annunzio,
> Prince of Montevenoso.

But it was not, of course – appropriate as my carnal error in vision might seem – the Prince of the Mons Veneris, the mount of Venus, but only your more wintry and familiar Monte-Nevoso, the Prince of the Snowy Mountain, which your hired craftsmen had engraved in the metal.

'The first rays of the sun,' you said simply, 'will strike the word "resurrecturus" in the morning. I like the idea.'

So there it was that in time, though not until three years after your death, Maroni supervised the construction of the enormous rotunda, a thing like a barrel of biscuits made in concrete for a giant, which now houses, albeit still, I believe, unfinished in all its motley details, your mortal remains. And the morning sun, unless provided with the penetrating power of a flame-thrower at close range, would scarcely be able to shed any light, or cast the slightest hint of a refreshing beam, on to the deeply buried and entirely invisible and, alas, largely forgotten, plaque with its bronze words and its extinguished flame in the mouldering substance under the block of Parian marble.

5

IT WAS ONLY a few months before you died that I saw you last. The Anschluss was over, and the Spanish Civil War had begun. I would like to have asked your opinion about the future of the falangists, and the chances of the little Austrian house-painter going to war with the world, but you were no longer interested in the present, or its possible exfoliations.

We met in the dining-room, under the veiled oil by Alessandro de Medici, which no one, so far as I knew, had ever seen uncovered, and which was always believed to portray a particularly humiliating representation of a choirboy, with a striking resemblance to Mussolini. The shutters were drawn, as always now, and there were candles burning, although it was the middle of the day.

I was shown in by the faithful Aelis, who had warned me to expect a change.

'He is not as he was,' she murmured, and shrugged her shoulders.

You were in a chair carved like a throne, hunched as if shrunken by some diminishing spell, and with a blanket around your knees. I had seen you so before, I thought as I came in, but that was when you were convalescing in Venice. Your face was in shadow now, bowed as if in thought, and your hands were grasped like walnuts on the lion masks which made up the ends of the chair-arms.

The Lion of Pescara

'Commandante,' Aelis called, rather louder than I would have expected, as we approached across the wooden floor. 'Tomaso is here to see you.'

But you made no sound, nor any movement, until the woman had reached your chair, and put her hand on your shoulder, and seemed, as I watched from a little distance away, to give you a rather violent shake, as a nurse might do to a somewhat unsatisfactory thermometer.

You roused yourself then, and signalled, with a lift of one hand, so that Aelis moved away, and I stepped forward into the aura of light from the candelabra at your elbow. Your face turned, and lifted, and I bent, scarcely able to restrain a start of shock, as I looked from a few feet away at what you had become.

You were a mass of wrinkles now, a twitching petulant mouth, and a pair of eyes of which the whites, as if under the influence of a powerful drug, seemed to enlarge and force the pupils upwards.

'Tomaso,' you whispered, and it was the old voice I remembered, albeit ravaged and echoing as though from some submerged recess in your being, where it was being preserved, as best you could, against the perpetual onslaughts of age. 'I am like a tortoise without its shell. Forgive me.'

You nodded then, over towards the gilded remains of Caroline, gleaming in the candlelight, and indeed, no more saurian and fluted, it seemed, than this new and evidently final face of your own.

'Help me, Tomaso,' you said, struggling in the wooden bonds of the chair. 'I need an arm.'

So I gave you, as I had never done before, the means to lift yourself on to your feet, and stand alone for a moment, and then lead me, shuffling in worn slippers, across the floor to the gleaming dome of the shell, where you paused, and murmured again.

'I am dying of not dying.'

Then, seeming to revive a little, perhaps in the sense that you were able to play the part of your decline still with a certain style, you slapped the tortoise with the flat

The Tortoise

of your hand, and shook loose from my arm, and limped through the doorway into the first of the circling atria, round which for the next half hour we were to progress by fits and starts, halting for a rest on some X-formed stool, or lofty heap of cushions.

'I heard from the Marchesa Casati the other day,' I said, anxious to test your interest in the several conquests of your past. 'It seems that she held a magician's ball at the Villa Rose, and was dressed herself as Cagliostro, but there was a fearful storm, and the guests, and even, she says, the Marchesa herself, were forced to flee for shelter to a nearby hotel.'

But you were uninterested in the current machinations and gaieties of your first Luisa.

'I saw Barbara Leoni the other day,' you whispered. 'I failed utterly to recognise her. She was just a pathetic old woman. I felt so sorry. She stopped on the threshold when she saw me, Tomaso, exactly as you did. I think she was frightened.'

I remembered the articles in the *Corriere* and how they spoke of interviews with a man who seemed still to carry himself like a boy in his late teens, and whose face was as bright and mobile as that of a young girl. You seemed, though, in my obviously embarrassed silence, to have gained a second wind.

'I have better days than this,' you said, reaching over to pat my arm. 'You must excuse me, Tomaso. I even ride a little, when I feel well.'

Indeed, I was later to verify this claim from the jockey-sized Italo Rossignoli, who was given the unpalatable job of hoisting your incontinent rectum into the saddle, and riding alongside the impuissant legs, which no longer retained the power to control or guide your docile mount.

Your body, yes, was a closer model of your old self than your raddled face, and your mind, or should I say your heart, on its eager days, had the need still, and even a little of the energy, to elaborate extravagant projects, the majority of which were sexual, and largely perverse, and fortunately, I suppose, not capable, at least on your own part, of any execution.

The Room of The Stump, in which I was able to browse later, under the pretext of researching an article for you, contained the drafts of many letters penned in a quavering and unstable hand to a girl I later learned was a Princess from Roumania, whom you had immortalised as Maya, and sometimes Tormentilla, and once or twice, Sthenele. The suggestions which they contained were couched in a tone audacious even by your own earlier standards, and formed a chastening contrast, for one like myself already sensing the passage of the years, with the obvious incapacity of the writer.

So that you were alive inside still, with a burning flame, like a candle locked in a vault, and yet, on your bad days, as I had now seen, the will to allow the flame to blaze forth blew inwards, instead, like a cold wind seeking only extinction.

At your funeral, only nine months later, the darkling child, as it seemed, whose conception I had already witnessed amidst the spring daffodils, I walked in the rear alongside Luisa Baccara, and was quick to note the very hand that reached out to catch her arm, when she tripped and seemed in danger of falling, the hand of Guido Keller, his red hair now tipped with grey, who had planned, those years ago in Fiume, to spirit her away from the castle of love on the beach, and lock her up like a hen. She was only one of many on that majestic day, and not amongst the senior mourners, up there in front ahead of the generals, and the admirals, and the air force officers with their chains of medals, not there with Donna Maria, erect and magnificent in her black train, the wife brought by death again to her legal position, a yard or so behind your draped coffin, and only a foot or two from the senior mourner himself, the Duce in his pork-pie hat with the dipping feathers on top, and his pout arranged somewhere between a scowl and a tear, as he marched like a comic-opera field-marshal to do honour to his great, if latterly somewhat neglected, hero.

The Tortoise

You had gone, one last time, to meet his train at Verona when he returned from his famous visit to Hitler, and you had walked with him along a red carpet, your hands moving in gesticulation as you maintained a constant monologue, of which the Duce, amidst the cheering crowds, heard not a single word. He was rumoured, also, to have cried out, 'At last,' when the news of your death reached the Palazzo Venezia, and you had no doubt long since become an asset likely to seem greater in retrospect, or in effigy, than in gloomy physical presence, like a trivial and ailing relation who brings a shadow of corruption and vulgarity to the rich company.

Nevertheless, he was truly your heir in his grasp of the propaganda value of seeming sorry. It was quite a funeral, surpassing by far, I would say, the final journey of the recently defunct Marconi, whose yacht had visited you long ago in Fiume, and whom you had succeeded, alas all too briefly, as president of the Italian Academy.

The details of the frequently macabre and always grandiloquent ceremony were, inevitably, all your own. The parchment on which you had inscribed, with a more invigorating flourish than usual in your last days, the very complex and ritual elements which were to compose your final journey, incorporating, as they did, a riot of luxury in carriages, difficult, roundabout routes for the procession, and invitations to a positive province of undesirable and freakish guests, this parchment, I say, was nevertheless most exactingly studied and its provisos meticulously enacted, and under severe penalty of displeasure from on high, one gathered, in the event of any minor feature being omitted, by the emissaries and the celebrants of Mussolini himself.

The news had reached the Duce quickly, and he drove all night to the Vittoriale, and had the building closed, and remained alone with you in meditation, and then alone, more practically, with your archives, and then in public, the whole of the next night, while flaming torches held by his own sailors guarded your catafalque at the vigil on the windy deck of the *Puglia*.

The Lion of Pescara

I was far away on a film set, in Naples, but I saw the pictures in all the papers, and heard the readings from *Alcione*, and *La Gloria*, and some of your best war speeches, on the state radio, and I realised that the era which seemed to have ended with your death was in fact only just beginning.

The apocalypse was already into its first act, and you, who had been its Casanova, were now to become its martyr, and the first of its many heroes and villains. I threw my roses down on the coffin, as many others did, and they seemed almost immediately lost there, amidst so many, and I walked away, comforting friends and enemies, recalling moments that both had shared, and sure in my mind of many secrets that this was hardly the time to disclose.

I heard from the friendly, and I think very truly grieving, Aelis, of how you had come to die. She told me about your fear of March, and your certainty that this month would bring your death, as it had once brought the death of Julius Caesar, and of how you had listened one night to Luisa Baccara playing Rachmaninov and had said suddenly, 'This is it,' and no one had known until later, from a note on your desk, and in your will, that you had been choosing the music for your funeral.

'Signor Antongini,' she said, as we strolled alone together across the Piazza Navona, and the rain began to fall, and I sheltered us both under my umbrella, 'he was waiting to go into dinner. I was there, as I often was towards the end, to lend him the comfort of my arm. I was walking towards him, in the library, when he stumbled, and nearly fell. He looked up at the picture of one of the Doges, and he asked for a glass of water.

'"Mineral water?" I asked.

'"No," he said, screwing up his eyes. "Pure water. A goblet of pure water."'

So that you, of all men I had known the most original and extraordinary, a paragon of all the vices, and a follower of whatever grotesque or bizarre pursuit your decadence could imagine, nevertheless could find no more subtle or

The Tortoise

memorable last word, or final request, as you stood, obol in mouth as it were, on the very brink of the Styx, with the ferryman at your ear, than this ordinary, and so commonplace and scarcely believable, 'glass of water'. It struck me like a stab of purity, an icicle to the heart, as though you had died of a wound made by a dagger of clear air, that would float away, and leave no mark or trace behind. Only the corpse, and the dull words.

'Then he stumbled again,' Aelis continued, 'and we called the doctor, and he gave him an injection, but it was too late. He had a stroke, and he died within hours. They sent for the priest, of course, but I doubt if he heard the words of extreme unction.'

It seemed very doubtful to me, as I raised my hat, and said farewell to Aelis, if you would have made the sign of contrition, but then, you were often cautious, and always respectful to the Church, and your last act, I suppose, might after all have been cast in the same prudential and courteous mode.

At any rate, Maroni, who became the curator of the great museum that he had helped you to create, and who in the process was able to bundle off the spiteful and so poorly treated Luisa, and several of the lesser servants, too, although never the helpful Aelis, and only after many months, and the outbreak of hostilities in Greece, the now warlike Italo Rossignoli, who performed a most creditable service to the state in the Western Desert, and left his boots, and then his body, outside Tobruk, Maroni, yes, who would spend his evenings playing the organ, with a somewhat Teutonic sonority, and to the accompaniment of a special Indian incense, believed that you had died a believer, though not, he would say, or not necessarily, a Christian.

'He returns, of course, Tomaso,' Maroni assured me once, when I visited the Vittoriale on the anniversary of your death in 1941. 'I keep a record of all he says in this leather book.'

I leafed through it with much of my usual scepticism. It appeared, I saw, that you had begun your messages with an

The Lion of Pescara

initial appearance to Signor Maroni on the night of your death, when you had murmured only,

'There is nothing. There was nothing.'

But then this appropriate notion was all too unbelievably similar to so much you had already written, I thought, and sometimes in better phrasing, for the publication of the *Libro Segreto*.

Such nihilistic ideas, of course, were interspersed in the leather book with a good mass of material more relevant, and more inspiring, to a nation now in the throes of a massive, and unexpectedly rigorous, war. You were often, it seemed, still able to announce a hopeful outcome in some venture likely to be dear to the heart of the Duce, and certainly liable to ensure a proper continuance of your medium's tenure of office in the undoubtedly comfortable and spacious shrine he was being allowed to preserve.

It ended, though. The invasion of Sicily, and the capture and rescue of the Duce, and finally, the dire turn in our affairs when the Republic of Salo was formed in the autumn of 1943, and the Fascists regrouped, albeit very briefly, around Lake Garda, initiated a new role for the cosseted Vittoriale, and the permanent withdrawal of the spiritualist Maroni, who was replaced, and in summary fashion, when the German High Command assigned the villa as, and one might sense in this an improbable access of Teutonic humour, a love nest, or private mansion, for the Duce's mistress, Clara Petacci.

I wonder. Did you appear, and this seems a more likely occasion than many others, when Mussolini visited his lecherous Clara, hovering, perhaps, like your own charioteer from Delphi, with empty eyes, and the reins of a forgotten passion in your hands, as you watched their grosser human embraces amidst the exotic cushions on which you had yourself laboured so often for the pleasure, or the subjugation, of a likely lady?

I imagine you reaching out an incisive finger, priapic from behind some fallen column, as the imprisoned victim would pace amidst your relics, and eager too, to

The Tortoise

cuckold your younger rival, now so far fallen from his high estate as to rule a principality not very much larger than your own state of Fiume, and shortly, indeed, with his blonde Clara for company, to be hanged upside down, and reviled by the partisans, outside the cathedral in the great square at Milan.

So ended the twenty years of Mussolini's rule, with your own monument still present, and with a role to play, so near to the end. I was in Bologna then, and already under the rule of the allied troops, and the news was hardly a surprise, or indeed very shocking amidst those other, inevitably closer, horrors of one's own war.

But that would form another story. I would still go back, if I could, though, stepping out again on the station platform at Gardone, and climb the hill beyond the town through the open fields, perhaps pitted with shell holes now, and then up through the wood of beeches, if some are still standing, and in through the dilapidated ruins of the gate, and across the broken cobblestones, and towards the brass-bound entrance, under the shattered flurry of pillar and motto, slogan and pilaster, that the front of that simple former villa has long since become.

I would ring the bell, and listen for some sound within those cloistered, stifling rooms, perhaps the shuffle of feet, or a monastic clanging, or even a burst of giggling female laughter, even, if there was nothing else, the raucous crowing of a rook, or the cry of a bat or an owl.

But there would be nothing, I fear. I would have to turn away, and make my journey down through the gardens, and under the keel of the *Puglia*, with the plaster flaking from the figurehead, and the metalwork rusting, and walk along the avenue of overgrown yews, and find that enormous drum of concrete in the west, and pass up the stairs into the vestibule, and cross to the well, and look down on to the tomb, and read, not those words you caused to be written across the porphyry, but that earlier, and longer, inscription which you had written for chiselling in the piece of porcelain that stood in The

Greater Dung Library, the secret room that no one used except yourself:

> The whole of life is unchanging. Melancholy has but one face. The summit of all thought is folly. And love is inseparable from treachery.

Chronology

Gabriele D'Annunzio

1863 Born in Pescara.
1872 To school in Florence with the Jesuits. Early sexual exploits.
1881 To Rome to study law. Becomes gossip columnist and dandy.
1883 Marries a Roman aristocrat, Donna Maria Gallese. A volume of scandalous poems is published during their honeymoon.
1886 Fights two duels. Acid is poured on his scalp to staunch a wound. He goes bald.
1887 Meets his first countess, a girl of middle-class origins, Barbara Leoni.
1888 Publishes a voluptuous and squalid novel, *The Triumph of Death*, which details their passionate affair.
1889 Compulsory military service for one year.
1890 Wife attempts suicide. Legal separation.
1891 Meets his second countess, Maria Gravina, in Naples. She bears him a daughter, Renata.
1894 Elected to Parliament as the member for Pescara.
1895 Makes love, for the first time, to Eleonora Duse, the great actress and singer. Appoints Tomaso Antongini as his confidant, procurer and secretary.
1898 Première of *The Dead City*, written for Eleonora Duse, starred in by Sarah Bernhardt, in Paris. Travels in

Egypt and Greece. Settles at the Villa Capponcina, north-east of Florence. Eleonora Duse near by.

1900 Moves from the extreme right to the extreme left in the Chamber of Deputies. Defeated as candidate for a district of Florence. The great odes of *Alcione* are begun.

1904 Final severance with Eleonora Duse, after she tries to burn down the Capponcina. Makes love to his first marchioness, Alessandra Rudini. Extravagance becomes unlimited.

1905 Remains devoted to Alessandra Rudini during her operation for cancer and gradual convalescence. Travels to Switzerland with Antongini to arrange a divorce. Returns to Italy, undivorced.

1906 First meeting with the Marchesa Casati, described as 'the Medusa of the great hotels', the original vamp of the silent films.

1907 Passionate affair with his fourth countess, the wife of a local wine-grower, the Contessa Mancini. She goes mad, and is incarcerated in a mental hospital.

1908 Première of *The Ship*, attended by the King and Queen of Italy. A triumph. Alessandra Rudini, who inspired the play, does not attend. An affair begins with the Russian, Nathalie de Goloubeff, whose bust has been sculpted by Rodin.

1910 *Annus mirabilis*. Meeting with Blériot, after the flight across the channel. Absorbed by the idea of Icarus. Flees from Florence to Paris, to escape bankruptcy. Publishes his greatest novel, *It May Be So, It May Be Not*. Settles in the Villa Saint-Dominique at Arcachon, with the American millionaire painter, Romaine Brooks. The furniture at the Capponcina is sold by auction to pay his debts. Meets the decadent poet and entrepreneur, the Comte de Montesquieu. At Montesquieu's suggestion, he composes, in French, the libretto for *The Martyrdom of Saint Sebastian*. An affair begins with Ida Rubinstein, the slender Jewish star, then married to the brewer, Walter Guinness.

1911 Twelve performances of *The Martyrdom*, with

Chronology

music by Debussy, sets by Bakst, succeed without triumph.
1914 The war begins. Withdrawal to Paris. Visits the front, inspired and fascinated.
1915 The return to Italy. Speeches up and down the country, starting in Genoa, which reveal an astounding gift for political rhetoric and bring Italy into the war. Volunteers, at the age of fifty-two, as a combatant and is commissioned in a cavalry regiment.
1916 Begins his affair, only to be ended by his death, with the young pianist, Luisa Baccara. Crashes in a seaplane and is temporarily blinded. Recuperates in the Casetta Rossa, in Venice, on the Grand Canal, nursed by his daughter, Renata. Composes his great prose memoir, *Notturno*, writing on ten thousand cards, many still illegible, on a board across his knee. Loses, permanently, the sight of his right eye. Returns to the front.
1917 His mother dies. Exploits on land, on sea, and in the air. Storms the Veliki, and is awarded a soldier's crown, carved by a bayonet from a shell-case. Bombs Vienna with leaflets. Conducts a daring motor-torpedo raid into an Austrian harbour. Wins many medals, including the gold.
1919 Intrigues over the Dalmatian question. Marches at the head of a disaffected army to Fiume, and receives the surrender of the city without bloodshed. Is elected governor, and begins his reign as the only poet-monarch of modern times.
1920 Presides over the city of the holocaust, a cauldron of social and sexual change. Involves himself with anarchists, Fascists and revolutionaries in the formation of a political charter decades ahead of its time. Sleeps with boys. Organises piracy. Invents mottoes, rituals and slogans. Corresponds with Mussolini and Lenin. Is attacked by superior Italian forces and wounded in his palace by a shell fired from a warship.
1921 Resigns as governor. Withdraws from Fiume walking bareheaded at the rear of his troops. Returns to Venice. Rents – later buys – a small property on the

The Lion of Pescara

shores of Lake Garda, the Vittoriale, formerly the home of Wagner's daughter.

1922 Is courted by Mussolini. Refuses to play. Falls from a window at the Vittoriale during a concert by Luisa Baccara and nearly dies. Both suicide and murder are mooted as possibilities. Is offered a position of leadership on the Fascist march to Rome, but turns it down.

1924 Is created, by Mussolini, the Prince of the Snowy Mountain, a peak in the Carso around which much of his war had been fought. Attends the funeral, in Rome, of Eleonora Duse. The elaboration of the simple Vittoriale into a monstrous and spectacular shrine begins.

1925 Is already a prey to senile erotomania, soliciting mistresses with the carnal aid of his housekeeper and friends. The blasphemous orgies of a sumptuous old age begin.

1935 Publishes *The Secret Book*, his greatest work in prose.

1938 Becomes interested in spiritualism. Foresees his own death and plans the music for his funeral. Dies on the way to dinner, asking for a glass of water. Mussolini drives from Rome to inspect his papers. A state funeral, legionnaires and mistresses walking side by side. Burial at the Vittoriale. He begins to appear to his architect and curator, Maroni, announcing messages from the Beyond. But none surprises.